Christy® Juvenile Fiction Series

VOLUME TWO

Christy® Juvenile Fiction Series

Christy® Juvenile Fiction Series
VOLUME TWO

Midnight Rescue
The Proposal
Christy's Choice

Catherine Marshall
adapted by C. Archer

Tommy Nelson™

A Division of Thomas Nelson Publishers
Since 1798

www.thomasnelson.com

VOLUME TWO
Midnight Rescue
The Proposal
Christy's Choice
in the *Christy*® Juvenile Fiction Series

Copyright © 1995, 1996
by the Estate of Catherine Marshall LeSourd

The *Christy*® Juvenile Fiction Series is based on
Christy® by Catherine Marshall LeSourd © 1967
by Catherine Marshall LeSourd © renewed
1995, 1996 by Marshall-LeSourd, L.L.C.

The *Christy*® name and logo are officially registered
trademarks of Marshall-LeSourd, L.L.C.

Published in Nashville, Tennessee, by Tommy Nelson®,
a Division of Thomas Nelson, Inc.

ISBN 1-4003-0773-2

Printed in the United States of America
05 06 07 08 09 BANTA 9 8 7 6 5 4 3 2 1

Midnight Rescue

The Characters

CHRISTY RUDD HUDDLESTON, a nineteen-year-old girl.

CHRISTY'S STUDENTS:
    ROB ALLEN, age fourteen.
    CREED ALLEN, age nine.
    LITTLE BURL ALLEN, age six.
    BESSIE COBURN, age twelve.
    LIZETTE HOLCOMBE, age fifteen.
    WRAIGHT HOLT, age seventeen.
    MOUNTIE O'TEALE, age ten.
    RUBY MAE MORRISON, age thirteen.
    JOHN SPENCER, age fifteen.
    LUNDY TAYLOR, age seventeen.

DAVID GRANTLAND, the young minister.
IDA GRANTLAND, David's sister.

ALICE HENDERSON, a Quaker mission worker from Ardmore, Pennsylvania.

DR. NEIL MACNEILL, the physician of the Cove.

JEB SPENCER, a mountain man.
FAIRLIGHT SPENCER, his wife.
    (Parents of Christy's student John.)

DUGGIN MORRISON, stepfather of Ruby Mae Morrison.

MRS. MORRISON, Ruby Mae's mother.

TOM MCHONE, a mountain man.

BIRD'S-EYE TAYLOR, feuder and moonshiner.
(Father of Christy's student Lundy.)

BEN PENTLAND, the mailman.

JAKE PENTLAND, Ben's nephew.

ELIAS TUTTLE, owner of the El Pano general store.

BOB ALLEN, keeper of the mill by Blackberry Creek.
(Father of Christy's students Rob, Creed, and Little Burl.)

GRANNY O'TEALE, great-grandmother of Christy's student Mountie.

JUBAL MCSWEEN, a moonshiner.

JANEY COOK, a pregnant mountain woman.

PRINCE, black stallion donated to the mission.

GOLDIE, mare belonging to Miss Alice Henderson.

LIGHTNING, dapple gray stallion belonging to Lundy Taylor.

ROBERT E. LEE, chesnut mare belonging to Ben Pentland.

POSSUM, bay gelding belonging to Elias Tuttle.

PEGASUS (PEG), piebald mare belonging to Rob Allen's father, Bob.

OLD THEO, crippled mule owned by the mission.

BILL, Dr. MacNeill's horse.

MABEL, one of the schoolhouse hogs.

SCALAWAG, raccoon belonging to Creed Allen.

❧ One ❧

May I have this dance, Miss Huddleston?"

Christy Huddleston grinned. "I have to warn you, David. I'm not a very good dancer."

"Then we'll make the perfect couple."

Christy joined David Grantland on the wide lawn in front of the mission house where she lived. David, the young mission minister, looked especially charming today. He was wearing his best suit, and his dark hair was slicked back neatly. Christy was wearing her favorite dress, made of bright yellow linen with crisp white lace down the bodice. In her braided, sun-streaked hair she wore a matching yellow bow.

Today, Saturday, April 6, 1912, everyone in Cutter Gap was wearing their Sunday-best clothes, which for most people here in this community were not much more than rags.

Christy's dress was by far the nicest. It was Miss Alice Henderson's birthday, and Christy and David had arranged a party in her honor.

Miss Alice had been a pillar in the community ever since she helped establish the mission school where Christy taught. She cared for the sick and ministered to the needy. And Miss Alice had often been a wise voice in times of trouble. Everyone from this mountain cove knew and respected her. People had even come from as far away as El Pano and Cataleechie, over rugged mountain trails, to attend her birthday party.

It was turning out to be quite a celebration, too. On this early April afternoon, the air was warm and sweetly scented. The Great Smoky Mountains in this remote corner of Tennessee had finally begun to cast off the winter gloom. Children danced and twirled to the music of dulcimer and fiddle. The mountain women wore sprigs of flowers in their hair. Even Cutter Gap's gruff Doctor Neil MacNeill wore a daffodil in his lapel.

It was all so different from the fancy afternoon teas Christy used to attend back home in Asheville, North Carolina. She'd left her well-to-do family to come teach in Cutter Gap just four months ago. When she'd first arrived, these mountain people had seemed backward, poor, and uneducated. Sometimes Christy had even found them frightening.

But many things had changed—herself included—in those few short months. And now when she looked around the lawn, she saw past the shabby clothes and the bare feet. Instead, among the crowd she saw some of her students and her friends. And the memories of Asheville seemed a little dull by comparison.

David had just put his arm around Christy's waist when, suddenly, three large hogs came racing across the lawn, squealing loudly. They were being chased by Creed Allen, an energetic nine-year-old. Two of the hogs, which lived under the school, had bright pink bows tied around their necks. Creed was carrying a third bow.

Christy and David had to jump back to avoid being trampled. "'Scuse us, Miz Christy and Preacher," Creed yelled as he ran.

"Looks like Creed is dressing the school pigs for Miss Alice's party," David said.

"I'm certain that Miss Alice will feel honored," Christy said with a laugh. "Now, where were we?"

Again David put his arm around Christy's waist. Awkwardly, Christy placed her hand on David's shoulder. He was taller than she was by several inches, with a lean build and wide-set brown eyes.

"You look quite lovely this afternoon," David said, a little nervously. "Like . . . like the prettiest flower in these mountains." He looked at the ground and shrugged. "Sorry. Awfully corny, I know. I guess I speak a better sermon than I do a compliment."

"It was a wonderful compliment," Christy said. "Not that I deserve it, mind you."

And the truth was, she didn't. She knew that her face was a little too plain, her blue eyes a little too big, for her to ever be considered truly beautiful. Still, she almost *felt* beautiful, seeing the way David was looking at her with a mixture of hope and nervousness.

On the front porch of the mission house, several of the mountain men were playing a sprightly tune. Jeb Spencer, the father of several of Christy's students, was strumming his dulcimer, a box-like stringed instrument with a sweet tone. Duggin Morrison was tapping a pair of spoons on his knee, while Tom McHone sawed away on a worn-looking fiddle.

The doors and the windows of the white, three-story mission house were wide open. From the living room came the sounds of the mission's new grand piano, as Wraight Holt, one of Christy's older students, played along.

Before Christy and David could begin dancing, the song came to an end. "All right, then," David said with a rueful laugh, "we'll dance this next tune."

"How come you're not playing your ukelele, David?" Christy asked.

"There's plenty of time for that," David said. "I wanted to dance with you first. And as soon as Tom gets done tuning that fiddle of his . . ."

Christy laughed. "You may regret it."

"I could never regret it," David said, suddenly sounding very sincere. Then he laughed again. "Besides, you're the one being brave, risking your feet this way."

"Not so brave," came a male voice from nearby. "After all, she danced with me at the mission open house a while back. I doubt you can be any worse a dancer than I, David."

Christy grinned as Doctor MacNeill strode over. He was a big, ruggedly-handsome man. His tousled, red hair gave him a boyish look. He had a way of smiling at Christy with his hazel eyes that made her feel like he could read her mind.

"Oh, you weren't so bad," Christy teased. The truth was, the doctor had turned out to be a surprisingly good dancer, but there was no point in telling David that. She had noticed there were times when the two men seemed to aggravate each other. Christy wasn't sure if it was because they disagreed on many things, like religion. Or if it was—as some had told her—that they both had a romantic interest in Christy.

"I was going to ask you for this dance," the doctor said to Christy. He cast a wry grin at David. "But I can see I'm too late."

"Maybe the next dance," Christy said, feeling her cheeks heat up, "that is—if I survive this one!"

"Well, we'd better make it soon. I hear talk of a horse race starting soon over in the field," the doctor cautioned.

"Once that gets started, we'll lose our musicians, I wager. They'll all be wanting to watch."

"Sorry, Doc," David said, with a tiny hint of a smug smile, "better luck next time."

"The lady's got a mind of her own," the doctor warned. "Watch yourself or she'll try to lead!"

The music started up again, a jaunty tune led by Tom McHone's fiddle. David swung Christy around and they started across the yard. It was still a bit muddy, but fresh bright green grass was making an appearance, cushioning the mostly bare feet of the dancers.

They had only gone just a few steps when a hand tapped on David's right shoulder. He stopped and spun around. "Don't tell me you're trying to cut in, Doctor—" he began.

But it wasn't the doctor. Ruby Mae Morrison, a red-haired, freckled thirteen-year-old, was standing behind him. "Miz Christy," she said breathlessly, "you just got to help me!"

"What's wrong, Ruby Mae?" Christy asked, speaking loudly to be heard over the music.

"And can't it wait?" David asked impatiently. "The dance is already half over. And I was finally getting the hang of that step—"

Ruby Mae shook her head regretfully. "Truth to tell, Preacher," she said, "you weren't even close. When the good Lord was passin' out feet, he musta given you two left ones."

"Don't listen to her, David," Christy said. "I still have all the feeling in most of my toes. Now, what is it, Ruby Mae?"

"I was wantin' to ask you private-like first," Ruby Mae hesitated.

"Whatever you have to say, you can say to Mr. Grantland, too."

Ruby Mae twirled a finger around a long lock of hair. "Actually, it do sort of involve Preacher. It's just that I was a-hopin' you could . . . well, my mama always says you can get a man to take the bitterest medicine, if'n you sweeten it first with honey."

David crossed his arms over his chest. "Come on, Ruby Mae. Miss Christy's not going to sweeten me up. I can't be sweetened."

"Oh, is that right?" Christy asked, fluttering her eyelashes at David.

David ignored her. "Out with it," he said to Ruby Mae.

Ruby Mae took a deep breath, then let the words tumble out. "I want to race Prince

13

'cause I just know I can beat the pants off'n the rest of the men 'cause you know he's plumb faster than the wind when I'm a-ridin' him. But I can't less'n you say so 'cause he belongs to the mission and please, please, please say it's all right, Preacher."

She took another deep breath, smiled wide and batted her eyes. "So I reckon the answer's yes?"

David shook his head. "Assuming I understood you correctly, I'm afraid the answer's no." He patted her on the shoulder. "Too bad they're not having a talking race. You'd be sure to win, Ruby Mae."

Ruby Mae groaned. "But, Preacher—"

"No buts, Ruby Mae."

"But wouldn't you just burst with pride if'n Prince won? Everybody in Cutter Gap would be a-sayin, 'That preacher owns the finest horse in these here mountains!'"

"To begin with, I don't own Prince. He belongs to the mission."

"You may as well own him," Ruby Mae said. "Everybody thinks of him as your horse. You're always ridin' Prince here and there when you minister to folks, sittin' proud and lookin' all fine and fancy."

"The answer is still no, Ruby Mae."

"But why?" she persisted, turning her pleading gaze on Christy.

"Are you sure she can't, David?" Christy

asked. "After all, Ruby Mae's been riding Prince every day since he was donated to the mission. And she is a wonderful rider."

Ruby Mae tugged on David's arm. "Miz Christy's right," she said.

David gave Christy a skeptical look. "What Miss Christy doesn't realize is that when the mountain people throw a race, the prize is usually a bottle of illegal liquor."

"Moonshine?" Christy cried.

Just then, the music came to a stop and the dancers parted, panting and laughing.

"Now look," David pouted. "We missed our dance."

"Next time," Christy promised. "Now, Ruby Mae, tell me the truth—is David right? Is this a race for moonshine?"

"I don't care none about the prize," Ruby Mae said. "It ain't about that."

"I think maybe David's right, Ruby Mae. Besides, it might be dangerous."

"Ain't dangerous," Ruby Mae said. "Just flat-out racin' in the field over yonder. No jumpin' or turnin', Miz Christy. Easy as pie."

"Still, it's Mr. Grantland's decision. He's the one who takes care of Prince."

"But like you say, Prince is the mission's horse," Ruby Mae argued. "And besides, I'm the one what's been muckin' out his stall and givin' him baths and kissin' him goodnight."

David grinned. "She has a point. I never kiss Prince goodnight."

"And it is true she's been spending a lot of time with Prince," Christy added. She rolled her eyes. "Some might even say too much time, judging from the way she's been shirking some of her chores and schoolwork."

"I promise I'll do better on my chores and homework, Miz Christy," Ruby Mae said. "But you just gotta let me race. For all us gal-women in the Cove."

"What do you mean?" Christy asked.

"I mean none of them smarty-pants men thinks a girl can win."

One of the musicians nearby laughed loudly. Christy looked over to see Duggin Morrison, Ruby Mae's stepfather, spit out a brown stream of tobacco. He looked old enough to be her grandfather, with his long white beard and wrinkled skin. Ruby Mae and her stepfather had been having trouble getting along, so she was staying at the mission house with Christy and David's sister, Miss Ida.

"No gal-woman can beat the Taylors' horse, Lightning," Duggin said. "'Specially no spoiled-rotten, trouble-makin', no-good stepdaughter o' mine."

"Hush up, Daddy," Ruby Mae said. "I can *so* ride better than any man in Cutter Gap."

"You hear how she sasses me?" Duggin cried. "Talkin' like that to her own step-pa!"

Christy pulled Ruby Mae away from Duggin. There was no point in starting up a family feud, right in the middle of Miss Alice's party.

Christy and David led Ruby Mae over to the schoolhouse, which also served as the church on Sundays. Miss Alice was sitting on the porch steps, calmly watching the festivities with her deep gray, gentle gaze. She was wearing a long, green dress, and her slightly graying hair was swept up in a bun. Her right arm was in a sling. She'd sprained her wrist last week when she'd slipped on a muddy incline on her way to help deliver a baby in a remote cabin.

"What do you think about Ruby Mae riding in the race?" Christy asked.

"Well, she's a fine rider, no doubt about that," Miss Alice said. "And Prince has incredible speed. Not like my Goldie," she said fondly. Miss Alice's sturdy palomino was getting on in years.

"Oh, Prince do have speed, Miss Alice, he do," Ruby Mae cried. "One day last week I ran him straight over Big Spoon Creek, and he jumped so high I thought I'd touch heaven—" She glanced over at David, who was frowning. "Oops. Don't get me wrong. It were just a little jump, Preacher, I promise—"

Doctor MacNeill joined them. He was eating one of the gingerbread cookies that Fairlight Spencer had brought for the celebration. "I watched you two dancing," said the doctor with a grin. "That was some fancy footwork, David. All ten seconds' worth."

"We were interrupted," David grumbled.

"Probably a good thing," the doctor joked. "How's that wrist of yours, Miss Alice?"

"Still swollen," Miss Alice said. "But I'll be fine soon. Wish it had been my left hand. I can't even write my name. And it makes my nursing duties difficult."

Ruby Mae tugged on David's sleeve. "You heard Miss Alice, Preacher. Can I ride Prince?"

"Not if there's moonshine involved," David said firmly.

"I hate to think there's illegal liquor here at your birthday party," Christy said to Miss Alice.

"Oh, it's here, whether we like it or not," said the doctor. "Moonshine's a part of mountain life."

"I'm afraid the doctor's right," Miss Alice said. "Bird's-Eye Taylor appears to have consumed quite a bit already." She nodded over toward the lattice-covered springhouse where Bird's-Eye was dozing, snoring loudly. His dirty felt hat covered one eye.

Christy shook her head. Bird's-Eye was the father of her most difficult and troublesome student, seventeen-year-old Lundy. Lundy was big and mean, a constant bully with a chip on his shoulder. From what Christy had seen of his father, it was easy to see why Lundy was so difficult.

"So is the answer no?" Ruby Mae pressed again. "Or yes?"

"I can't let you ride in a race for moonshine," David said. "As a matter of fact, I won't let a race like that take place here at all."

"I've already taken care of that," Miss Alice said with a grin. "I put up two of Miss Ida's apple pies as a prize for the winner of the race, instead of liquor. As much as liquor is prized in this Cove, Miss Ida's pies are even more coveted."

David laughed. "My sister does make a fine pie."

"For my part, David, I think you should let Ruby Mae enter the race," Miss Alice said. "She has as good a chance as any of the men."

"And it would teach them a lesson," Christy added. "Sometimes I'm amazed at the way men treat women here in Cutter Gap."

"Miz Christy is right," Ruby Mae said. "These men got no respect for womenfolks."

"I don't know," David said, rubbing his chin.

Just then, Ruby Mae's stepfather sauntered by. He was weaving a little, as if he might have been drinking, too. "Don't you bother racin', gal," he yelled. "You ain't got a chance, Ruby Mae."

Christy spun around. "Mr. Morrison, I think you're going to have to eat your words. Ruby Mae on Prince can beat any man."

David rolled his eyes. "I didn't give permission yet," he reminded her.

"But you were going to, weren't you?" Christy asked, giving him a nudge.

David shook his head and sighed. "I can tell when I'm outnumbered. Come on, Ruby Mae. I'll help you get Prince saddled up."

✺ TWO ✺

Ruby Mae stood next to Prince, stroking his glossy neck. They were waiting by the starting line for all the other riders and their horses. "You and me, boy," she whispered to the beautiful black stallion. "We're a-goin' to show them others."

"Don't count on it." Lundy Taylor strode up on Lightning. The big gray stallion gave a hard nudge on Prince's shoulder.

Ruby Mae rolled her eyes. It figured. Even the Taylors' horse was mean. Meanness just plain ran in the family. Maybe it was because Bird's-Eye, Lundy's pa, was a moonshiner. Of course, Ruby Mae's own step-pa had done his share of moonshinin', too.

"You ain't got a chance, Ruby Mae Morrison," Lundy said with a sneer. "Womenfolk is good for two things—cookin' and jabberin'. Lord knows you know how to talk. I don't know what kind of cook you is, but one way or t'other, you ain't got a chance, you and that preacher-horse."

"Just you wait and see, Lundy," Ruby Mae shot back. She ran her hand through Prince's mane, soft and long as the silk in an ear of corn. "Prince is faster'n a fox on fire. You'll see."

She gazed around at the other entrants. Jake Pentland—nephew of Ben Pentland, the local mailman—was there with a stocky little chestnut mare. Elias Tuttle—the owner of the general store in El Pano, a town about seven miles from Cutter Gap—was riding up on a fancy bay gelding with a wonderful leather saddle, all shiny and tooled. Elias often donated food and supplies to Miz Alice for the mission.

Just then, someone rode up on the other side of her. It was Rob Allen, a tall, slender fourteen-year-old who was one of the best students at school. Miz Christy had even appointed him a Junior Teacher who got to help the other students. Rob was riding a piebald mare named Pegasus, a name Rob had gotten from one of the books he liked to read. Of course, *Pegasus* was such a mouthful that most folks just called the horse "Peg."

Rob wanted to be a writer when he grew

up. Ruby Mae thought that was a grand idea. She wished she wanted to be something, too, but she hadn't quite figured out what it was. She knew she wished her hair wouldn't act like it had a mind of its own on humid summer afternoons. She knew she wished her freckles weren't so darn . . . well, *freckle-y*. And she knew she wished she had two whole pairs of leather shoes as fine and fancy as Miz Christy's.

But those things didn't nearly seem as good as wanting to be something bigger than all outdoors, like a writer. Ruby Mae thought Rob was very special for wanting something so huge and impossible and fine. She also thought he had the cutest little bitty dimple in his cheek when he smiled just so, but of course she'd never told him *that*. And he looked mighty tall, sitting astride his horse and gazing down at her.

"You going to race Peg?" Ruby Mae asked Rob.

"Why, Pegasus is plumb fast, when she puts her mind to it." Rob smiled shyly. "Course, she's got a mind of her own. Never do know when she's in the mood to run."

"I s'pose you're goin' to tell me how I ain't got a chance of winnin'," Ruby Mae said.

"Nope. I seen you ridin' Prince. For a girl, you handle a horse fine. Even for a man, I reckon." He gave a cockeyed grin, then shrugged. "Truth is, you ride like you was part horse yourself, Ruby Mae."

Ruby Mae could hardly keep from hollering, she was so thrilled at Rob's words. No man or boy had ever admitted to her she was a good rider before. But all she said was, "Well, then, may the best man . . . or gal . . . win."

By now, quite a crowd had formed to watch the race. Everywhere Ruby Mae looked, it seemed like she saw happy couples. It must be because spring was in the air. Lizette Holcombe was holding hands with Wraight Holt, who'd stopped playing the piano to come watch the fun. Bessie Coburn, Ruby Mae's best friend, was whispering to John Spencer, a boy Bessie had a crush on for what seemed like forever and a day. And as for Miz Christy—well, she seemed to have two fellows sweet on her—the doctor and the preacher. Miz Christy said Ruby Mae was imagining things, but Ruby Mae had an eye for romance. She could tell the doctor and the preacher both liked Miz Christy, all right. Question was, which one was Miz Christy hankering after?

Of course, Ruby Mae was in love, too—but not with any fellow. She was in love with a horse. Since Prince had come to the mission, it was all she could do to think about anything else. Before school, after school, sometimes during school, if she could find an excuse—Ruby Mae spent every waking moment thinking about Prince. She'd always loved animals, from the little three-footed squirrel she'd nursed back to health after he'd been attacked by an animal, to the old owl who lived in the sycamore near her cabin. But Prince was different. When she was riding him, she felt like anything was possible.

"Ruby Mae, you be careful, now, ya' hear?" Ruby Mae looked over to see her mother approaching. Her graying hair was tied with a piece of frayed rope. In the bright sunshine, the harsh lines in her face made her look even more worn and tired than usual.

"I will, Ma," Ruby Mae promised. She toyed with her reins. "I . . . I miss you and Pa."

"You can come visit any time. Ain't like you don't know the way." Mrs. Morrison nodded at Prince. "Looks like you're gettin' spoiled, livin' here with that teacher in the mission house. Your own horse to ride, plenty of food." She clucked her tongue at Ruby Mae's braids, the ones Miz Christy had taught her to make. "Why, I'll just bet you take a bath in that metal tub of theirs every single day."

Ruby Mae hesitated. She didn't know what to say. The truth was, she did like living at the mission house. She missed her parents, but they were always yelling at each other and at her. It was a relief to get away from all the fussing. When Miss Alice had first suggested that Ruby Mae stay at the mission house for a while, Ruby Mae had wondered if it were a good idea. But now she knew that it was.

"Maybe I can come back home soon, Ma," Ruby Mae said softly. She wondered if Rob was listening. She glanced over at him, but he was fiddling with his stirrups. Ruby Mae lowered her voice. "But it just seems like whenever we're all together, we start in on fightin' like wildcats in a flour sack."

"If you weren't so ornery," Mrs. Morrison began, "that mouth of yours runnin' on like a waterfall—" She stopped. "Well, no point in startin' that again. I just wanted to say be careful, is all."

From behind them came a drunken whoop. It was Bird's-Eye, Lundy's father, with Ruby Mae's stepfather. Bird's-Eye was walking lopsidedly, leaning on Duggin for support.

"Looky here!" Bird's-Eye cried. "That your stepdaughter, Duggin? She think she's a boy, do she?"

"Told her she ain't got a prayer of winnin', but you know that Ruby Mae," Duggin said, propping up Bird's-Eye as he nearly tripped. "That gal gets a notion in her head, it's stuck there like honey in a hive."

Mrs. Morrison scowled. "Don't pay him no never-mind, girl," she whispered. "I seen you ride before. You can beat 'em all, if'n you put that stubborn will of your'n to it."

"Yes, ma'am," Ruby Mae said. She smiled gratefully at her mother, then put her left foot in the stirrup and swung herself up onto Prince's sleek back. She nudged him gently toward the starting line. She was proud of the way he stood there, ready to run, but calm. Not fidgeting and fussing, like some of the other horses.

Miss Alice appeared in front of the line of riders. She winked at Ruby Mae, and Ruby Mae gave her thumbs-up, to show she was confident.

Ruby Mae loved Miss Alice. Miss Alice had a way of talking about God that made Him seem not so fearsome and far away, but kind and loving and close as your own heartbeat.

"All right, I see we have our riders assembled," Miss Alice said. "Lundy Taylor on Lightning. Jake Pentland on Robert E. Lee. Elias Tuttle on Possum. Ruby Mae Morrison on Prince—"

At the sound of Ruby Mae's name, Duggin and Bird's-Eye, along with some of the other men, began to hoot and whistle.

Rob looked over at her and winked. "Don't pay 'em no never-mind," he said.

"And last but not least," Miss Alice continued, "Rob Allen on Pegasus. Now, as this is my birthday, I will officiate over the race, to be sure it's run fair and square. On the count of three, you will race to the edge of the field to that big oak, turn, and come back to this spot. Be careful on that turn, by the way. It's a tight one. Winner receives two of Miss Ida's finest apple pies."

"Woulda liked a jug o' likker better," Lundy grumbled.

Miss Alice ignored him. "Are there any questions?"

"Can't rightly start a race without a gun," said Ruby Mae's stepfather. He waved his shotgun in the air. "Ain't proper."

"There'll be no shooting at my birthday party, Duggin Morrison," Miss Alice warned. She spoke so quietly and firmly that he put down his gun. Miss Alice had a way about her, Ruby Mae thought, smiling to herself. She could put the fear of God into any man, even Ruby Mae's stepfather.

"But on second thought, Duggin," Miss Alice continued with a smile, "since my own hand is temporarily out of order, I'll allow you to start the riders off, on the count of three. One shot straight up, Duggin, and that's all, understood?"

Ruby Mae's stepfather grinned. He pointed his old hunting rifle toward the sky.

"Riders, are you ready?" Miss Alice called.

Everyone nodded. "Ready to beat the pants off'n the rest o' these losers!" Lundy cried.

Ruby Mae cast a quick smile at Rob. She bent down and whispered to Prince, "We can beat 'em all, boy. You just show 'em what you're made of, and so will I." She looked back and saw Miz Christy watching her. Miz Christy held up her fingers, to show they were crossed for good luck.

"On your marks," Miss Alice called. A hush fell over the crowd.

"Get set," she said.

Ruby crouched low, tightening her grip on the reins. She could feel Prince tense beneath her. His ears were pricked. He pounded a foot on the ground.

He was ready, and so was Ruby Mae.

Duggin Morrison fired his gun. The powerful blast shook the air.

"Hah, boy!" Ruby Mae pressed her bare heels into Prince's sides and gave him plenty of rein as he thrust into a full gallop. To her left, Lundy's horse, Lightning, and Elias' horse, Possum, were neck and neck, just a few yards ahead of her. To her right, Peg and Robert E. Lee had fallen back.

"Atta boy!" she screamed. Prince's hooves slashed the grass, filling the air with a noise like slow thunder. He was flying, that was all there was to it. If she didn't know better, she'd swear the mighty horse had wings.

Ruby Mae kept her eyes focused on the great oak at the end of the field. It would be a tricky turn. She'd have to slow Prince down enough to take it sharply and avoid running into the other riders. But she didn't want to slow down too much. Especially not when Prince was starting to overtake Lightning and Possum.

Down the field they flew. She could hear the whooping and hollering of the crowd behind her. But this was no time to think about them. She needed to think about Prince.

By the time she reached the tree, Ruby Mae and Lundy were in the lead as their two stallions, Lightning and Prince, struggled to win. She eased to the right of the tree, while Lundy and his horse went to the left. It was all she could do to rein in Prince. The leather straps burned in her hands as she slowed him down to a fast trot. "Whoa, boy, whoa," she cried. "We're only halfway home."

At the sound of her voice, Prince responded instantly. Pulling hard on the left rein, Ruby Mae turned him in a tight veer. She nearly lost her balance, the turn was so sharp, but she grabbed a hunk of Prince's mane and held on for dear life.

She was still trying to regain her seat as she signaled him back into an all-out gallop. Possum, Robert E. Lee, and Peg were just approaching the tree. The field ahead of her was clear. She didn't want to look around for Lundy and lose a precious second.

"Go, Prince!" Ruby Mae cried, giving him a hard kick with her heels.

Just then, she heard the sound of thundering hooves coming from her right. It was Lightning, closing in fast. He was going to ram right into her!

"I'll get you yet, preacher-horse!" Lundy screamed.

Frantically, Ruby Mae yanked back on the reins. Prince hesitated, then pulled back to a trot. Lundy and Lightning zoomed past, just inches from Prince's head.

What if I hadn't slowed? Ruby Mae wondered for a split second. Was Lundy such a bully that he would have risked his own horse? Or was he just sure that, because she was a girl, she would stop to save Prince . . . and herself?

Well, she thought fiercely, *there's no point in being too sure, Lundy Taylor.*

"Get him, Prince!" Ruby Mae screamed. She pushed him into a full gallop, and Prince was glad for the chance.

Twenty yards ahead of them—an impossible distance to make up—Lundy and Lightning were flying across the field to the cheers of the crowd. *We don't have a chance*, Ruby Mae thought. She knew there was no way Prince could catch Lightning now.

Fortunately, Prince did not know any such thing. Driven by the sight of another horse so

31

close at hand, he dug his hooves deeper into the soft soil. His neck lunged. His mouth foamed. His feet flew so fast it seemed to Ruby Mae that she and Prince were no longer touching ground at all.

Faster and faster. He hurled himself on. Lundy glanced back. Ruby Mae could see both surprise and panic on his face. He whipped Lightning's shoulder with his reins. "Git on, you old nag!" he screamed.

But it was too late. Prince was not about to let Lightning win. In a final, wild surge, he flung himself forward, past Lundy and the crowd, past Miss Alice, and over the finish line. He didn't want to stop running, didn't seem to care where he was going, as long as he and Ruby Mae could fly through the air together.

Ruby Mae let him circle the crowd, still galloping. Finally she reined him into a fine trot. He pranced across the field toward the cheers, proud and haughty. His head was high, and so was Ruby Mae's. She caught sight of Miz Christy, waving and cheering. Ruby Mae's mother was smiling, nodding her head. Rob Allen gave her a wink. Lundy was scowling, of course, shooting daggers at Ruby Mae with his eyes.

Then she noticed her stepfather. His gun was cradled in his arms. He wasn't exactly smiling, you couldn't say that. But he was looking at her like he'd never quite seen her before.

Ruby Mae took one more circle around the field. In spite of Miss Alice's warning, someone shot off a gun in celebration. More shots followed. The cheers and shouts were music in the air. She slowed Prince down to a walk, leaning down long enough to stroke his damp, hot coat.

"Hear those shouts and them guns a-firin', boy?" she crooned. "That's for you. All for you."

Suddenly the shouts and shots silenced. Someone screamed, and then the field grew still.

It wasn't until Ruby Mae rode closer that she saw the fallen figure of Doctor MacNeill, lying on the ground in a pool of blood. And nearby stood her stepfather, smoke still spiraling from the barrel of his gun.

❧ Three ❧

Even before she knew who'd been shot, Christy saw the bright red pool of blood.

Then she heard a child scream. "The doc! The doc's been shot!"

Frantically, Christy pushed her way through the crowd. Doctor MacNeill lay on the ground. He was bleeding badly from his left shoulder. Miss Alice was kneeling next to him. The crowd, murmuring, formed a tight circle around them.

"Neil!" Christy cried. She knelt on the other side of him. He tried to sit up, but Miss Alice eased him back down. "It's nothing," the doctor said, but his face was pale.

"Why don't you let me be the judge of that?" Miss Alice said, as she pressed a handkerchief against the wound with her left hand.

Christy watched, horrified, as the white handkerchief turned deep red. "You're going to be fine," she assured the doctor, but her voice was shaking.

Miss Alice stood up. She seemed to be trying to remove her own sprained right arm from the sling that held it. Christy saw her wince in pain from the attempt. Her eyes, always so calm, were worried. "Let's get you over to the mission house."

Ruby Mae rushed over on Prince. "I'll ride him over, Miss Alice," she said. "If'n he can get a leg up."

"I can walk, thank you all very much," the doctor said. Using Christy for support, he managed to stand with his arm around her shoulder. David rushed to his other side.

"I want to make this perfectly clear," Miss Alice said to the crowd sternly. "I'm going to assume that shot was an accident." She leveled her gaze at Duggin Morrison, who stared down at the ground. "But it was an accident born of mixing moonshine and guns. And those are two things I will not tolerate here at the mission. Next gun I hear go off, next jug of illegal liquor I see poured, I'll be getting my own gun. And you know I'm a better shot than most of you men. Even without the use of my good hand."

Christy and David helped Doctor MacNeill walk a few feet. The doctor's face was white, and his forehead was dotted with sweat. Ruby Mae followed closely on Prince.

"Ruby Mae," the doctor said, "I think I may just take you up on that offer, after all. By the way," he added with a wink and a weak smile, "that was a fine race."

Ruby Mae slid from the saddle, and with David's help, the doctor climbed onto Prince. "I feel so bad about this, Doctor," Ruby Mae muttered as she led Prince toward the mission house, with Christy, David and Miss Alice close at hand. "It were my step-pa what shot you, I 'spect," she muttered. "Dang drunk that he is."

"It could have been anyone, Ruby Mae," the doctor assured her. "Everyone was shooting off their guns."

"No, it was him," Ruby Mae muttered. "I heard him tell Ma that he was shooting toward the clouds, but he lost his balance and the gun went off."

"I'll tell you what to blame," David muttered angrily. "Blame the liquor in those jugs. Blame the moonshine these mountain people insist on making and drinking and selling."

"That's something you can't hope to change, David," said the doctor wearily. "Take it from me. I've lived in these mountains a long time. You're new here."

"It's something I'm *going* to change, you just wait and see," David said firmly.

"There's plenty of time for this talk later," Miss Alice interrupted as they approached the steps of the mission house. "Let's get the doctor inside."

David helped Doctor MacNeill climb down off of Prince. The doctor groaned on landing, then reluctantly leaned on David for support.

"Ruby Mae," Miss Alice directed, "run on over to my cabin and fetch my medical bag, will you?"

In the upstairs hallway, Miss Alice pulled Christy aside while David helped the doctor into bed.

"I'm going to need you to help get that bullet out of the doctor," Miss Alice whispered. "Without my right hand, I'm not much of a surgeon."

"Me?" Christy cried in horror. "Help with . . . But I don't know the first thing about surgery—"

"How about during your journey here, when the doctor had to do that operation on Bob Allen? You helped him then, didn't you?" Miss Alice patted her on the arm. "That makes you more experienced than either David or Ruby Mae. And they're the only other two possibilities."

"But I can't—"

"Don't worry, dear. I'll help you through it. And the Lord will guide your hands."

Reluctantly, Christy followed Miss Alice into the bedroom. At the sight of the broadening stain across the doctor's shirt, her stomach did a sharp somersault. Somewhere beneath that shirt was a bullet—a bullet that Miss Alice expected her to remove. She felt her knees buckle under her, and she reached for a chair.

"Better keep an eye on that girl," the doctor joked. "She's turning the nicest shade of green you ever did see."

"I'm fine," Christy said through clenched teeth.

"What would you call that, Preacher?" the doctor continued, determined to seem unconcerned. "Spring green? Or maybe it's more of an emerald green—"

"I'm *fine*," Christy repeated more firmly.

Miss Alice helped the doctor remove his shirt. His broad chest was smeared with blood. Carefully she felt the area of the wound.

"Watch your poking," the doctor muttered, wincing.

He felt the wound himself, grimacing as his fingers ran over the bullet. "Not so deep at all," he pronounced. "No fractures. A little messy, but no problem to remove."

Ruby Mae clumped up the stairs and rushed into the bedroom, carrying Miss Alice's bag. Following close behind was Miss Ida, David's prudish and fussy older sister.

"Oh my goodness!" Ida cried. "I was just putting the finishing touches on Miss Alice's cake when I heard the ruckus up here. What on earth happened? Look at this mess!"

"Moonshine and guns," David said darkly. "They don't mix."

"You can just bring that bag to me, Ruby Mae," the doctor instructed. She set it next to him and he began digging through its contents.

"Miss Ida, we could use some boiling water and fresh towels," Miss Alice said.

"Of course," Miss Ida said. "Will he be all right?"

"I expect so. The doctor's pretty tough," Miss Alice said with a forced smile.

The doctor removed a scalpel and a pair of forceps from Miss Alice's bag. "Just what exactly is it you're preparing to do, Neil?" Miss Alice asked.

"I'm going to remove the bullet, of course," he said.

"Lordamercy!" Ruby Mae cried. "He's the bravest man what ever lived, I reckon!"

"There's a fine line between bravery and foolishness, Ruby Mae," said Miss Alice. Turning to the doctor, she said curtly, "As I recall, you're left-handed, are you not, Neil?"

"That I am." He dug through her bag, muttering to himself. "Where do you keep your needles and suturing thread, anyway?"

"And," Miss Alice continued, pulling the

bag away from him, "isn't that bullet in your *left* shoulder?"

Doctor MacNeill looked up at Miss Alice. His expression was a mixture of pain, amusement, and annoyance. "I see what you're getting at, Miss Alice. But you and I are the only medical practitioners for a hundred miles or more, and, nothing personal, but I'd rather go at this bullet myself than have you try to remove it with that sprained hand of yours." He gave her a wry look and retorted, "As I recall, you're right-handed, are you not? And isn't that your right hand in a sling?" He sat up a little straighter, wincing at the pain. "So it looks like I'm elected."

Miss Alice shook her head. "Christy will do the surgery."

"Christy!" the doctor cried. "Not likely! Just look at her! She's the color of a green apple! And you expect me to let her pull a bullet out of my own flesh?"

"We have no choice," Miss Alice said.

"Believe me, I would rather *not* have to play doctor," Christy said. "But—"

"You! *You'd* rather not? How do you think *I* feel about it?" the doctor cried. "You're a teacher, not a doctor."

"Lordamercy," Ruby Mae said in a loud whisper, "this is even more excitin' than the race!"

"Behave, Neil," Miss Alice chided. "You're acting like a child. You and I both know

40

there's often not much more to surgery than being a good tailor."

The doctor grabbed Miss Alice's hand. "Please," he said. "Have mercy. I beg of you. I've heard about Christy's seamstress efforts. Granny O'Teale said her quilting skills leave a lot to be desired."

"I'm a fine seamstress!" Christy cried indignantly.

"Actually, Miz Christy," Ruby Mae interjected, "those buttons you done sewed on Mountie O'Teale's coat a while back fell off. Remember how you had to stitch 'em all on again?"

"Oh, wonderful." The doctor covered his eyes with his right hand, groaning.

Miss Ida reappeared with a pile of towels. She had torn them into strips to use for bandages. "The water's boiling," she announced.

"Good," Christy said, taking the towels. "Let's get these instruments sterilized so we can get this over with." She looked at Miss Alice. "Right?"

"Exactly," Miss Alice said.

Miss Ida gasped. She gazed at Miss Alice's arm in its sling, then at the doctor's wound. "Oh, my," she whispered. "What is the world coming to when Christy Huddleston is our only medical hope?"

"Thank you for that vote of confidence, Miss Ida," Christy said with a sigh.

Miss Ida patted the doctor's forearm gently.

When everything was ready at last, Christy washed her hands thoroughly in a basin, then positioned herself in a chair beside the doctor's bed. Miss Alice stood behind her, observing and instructing. David and Ruby Mae watched from a distance.

"First, you'll need to cleanse the area of the wound," Miss Alice instructed.

Christy bit her lip. Her stomach felt queasy. Her hands were shaking.

She met the doctor's eyes. He was smiling at her weakly, looking at her with that way he had when she was certain he was reading her mind.

"You'll do fine," the doctor said gently.

Christy took a deep, steadying breath. "I hope so."

"You did fine when you helped me with Bob Allen," the doctor reminded her. "You're stronger than you think, Christy Huddleston. I only hope I am, too."

Christy cast him a grateful smile. "I'll do my best."

When Christy had cleaned the wound, Miss Alice leaned close to examine it. "You're going to need to make a small incision to reach the slug," she said. "Pick up the scalpel."

Christy picked up the sharp blade. She forced her hand to stop trembling.

"Hold the scalpel firmly in your right hand

while you feel the position of the bullet with your left," Miss Alice instructed. "Then draw a small line, maybe a half an inch from the point of entry, with the scalpel. Press firmly."

"But not *too* firmly," the doctor added with a reassuring smile.

Christy closed her eyes. *Please, Lord,* she prayed silently, *give me the strength to meet this challenge.*

"It helps," the doctor suggested, "if you open your eyes."

"I was praying for assistance," Christy explained.

"Wonderful," the doctor moaned.

Steadying her shaking hands, Christy did as Miss Alice instructed. Suddenly the joking mood vanished. Everyone was silent. She could feel the doctor go rigid as she pressed the scalpel down.

"Fine, fine," Miss Alice said.

Christy lifted the scalpel and looked over at the doctor. His eyes were closed, the muscles of his handsome face tight as he grimaced against the pain.

"This ain't turnin' out nearly like I thought," Ruby Mae whispered, rushing from the room.

"I'll go see if Ruby Mae's all right," David offered quickly.

As David darted toward the door, Christy noticed that he looked a little green himself.

"Now, wipe away that blood," Miss Alice said.

Christy did as she was instructed. To her relief, the queasiness had passed. Now she just wanted to finish the operation as quickly as possible to spare the doctor any more pain.

"Take that small pair of forceps and, using your other hand, locate the bullet. You may need to poke around a little." Miss Alice placed a cool cloth over the doctor's forehead. "You doing all right, Neil? I would offer you some ether, but I know you'd never take it."

"Oh, no," he said through gritted teeth. "Go to sleep while Christy is carving me like a Thanksgiving turkey? Not likely."

Carefully, Christy eased the forceps closer to the bullet. With each fraction of an inch, she could feel the doctor's pain as if it were her own. Once, he groaned out loud.

"I'm hurting you," Christy wailed desperately.

"No," the doctor said. "Keep going. You're almost there. You're doing fine."

Christy searched Miss Alice's face. "I can't do this, Miss Alice."

"Of course you can," she encouraged.

Again Christy struggled to find the bullet. Once she managed to get the ends around the slug, but when she tried to pull, the forceps came free. She did not let herself look at the doctor's face. She couldn't bear it. But she could see his chest rising and falling quickly, and she could see his fists, balled tightly.

"I can't seem to reach it," Christy said after another unsuccessful try.

"Yes, you can," the doctor said. She could hear the pain in his voice. "You can do anything you set your mind to, Christy."

Again Christy tried. This time, when she reached the bullet, she tightened her grip on the forceps. She held tight to the bullet. It came free at last.

She stared at the big, twisted piece of bloody lead. Her fingers were trembling again. Just a few inches more and it might have struck the doctor's heart. This bullet was a symbol of all that was wrong and dangerous and evil in these beautiful mountains.

She let the slug drop into a basin.

"Fine job," Miss Alice said, squeezing Christy's shoulders.

"Not bad for a first-timer," the doctor said weakly.

Christy let herself meet his eyes. She saw terrible pain there, but a half-smile was still waiting for her. He touched her arm with his hand. "I knew you you could do it."

"Now, let's get that incision sutured up," Miss Alice said.

The doctor sighed. "Was that really true, about Mountie's buttons?"

Christy smiled. "Yes," she admitted. "But I've been taking quilting lessons from some local women since then. I've improved, really I have."

"Oh, well," the doctor said with another sigh. "At least it will make an interesting scar."

❧ Four ❧

How are you feeling?" Christy asked the next morning as she carried a breakfast tray into the doctor's room.

"Like someone shot me in the shoulder." The doctor sat up slowly, groaning. His hair was mussed, and there were dark circles under his eyes. A fresh white bandage covered much of his shoulder. His arm was in a sling.

"You look terrible," Christy said, placing the tray on his lap. She plumped his pillows.

"Talk to my surgeon. She's the one responsible," the doctor said as he took a sip of coffee.

"Actually, Miss Alice told me she already examined your stitches this morning, and she said they looked beautiful."

"Well, they're holding so far, which is more than we can say for Mountie O'Teale's

47

buttons," the doctor teased. He lifted the napkin covering a bowl of oatmeal and frowned.

"What exactly is this?" he demanded.

"Miss Ida made you oatmeal. Ruby Mae helped. She put a little molasses and cinnamon in it for flavor."

The doctor took one bite, then rolled his eyes. He set the tray aside. "I think it's time for me to be heading on home, where I can make my own breakfast. Something that doesn't involve Ruby Mae's special flavor."

"You'll do no such thing," Christy said firmly, pushing him back against the pillow.

He winced. "Watch it. Your bedside manner needs a little work."

"Sorry," Christy apologized. "But Miss Alice said you've got a low fever. You need to stay here until we're sure you're healing properly."

"Yes, Doctor," he chided Christy.

"I'm just quoting Miss Alice," Christy said defensively. She handed him the tray, and he took it reluctantly. "She also told me that doctors make terrible patients."

"She's right about that, I'll wager."

Christy put her hand on the doctor's forehead. "You do feel a little warm."

He reached up and held her hand. His own was large and strong and warm to the touch.

"I want to thank you for what you did yesterday," he said. "I know how hard it was for you. And despite my teasing, I knew you would do a first-rate job. And that you did." Then he added with a chuckle, "Far better than I would have done, trying to stand in as a teacher to that huge class of rambunctious children you teach."

"Thank you for saying that," Christy said, suddenly feeling shy under his intense gaze.

Just then, David knocked on the door and peered inside. At the sight of Christy and the doctor holding hands, he stammered, "Maybe . . . should I come back?"

"No, come on in, David," Christy said quickly, withdrawing her hand.

David cleared his throat. "So how's the patient?" he asked. He was dressed in his proper ministerial clothes—striped pants, a white shirt, and a dark tie. His hair was carefully combed. Christy always thought he looked older and more dignified on Sundays.

"The patient is already complaining," Christy said. "I'm not sure if that's a good sign or not."

"I happen to be suffering in silence." The doctor held up his coffee cup. "You know, Christy, as much pain as you put me through, I could really use something stronger. A little of that moonshine would come in handy right around now."

"How can you joke about that?" Christy cried. "It's moonshine that nearly got you killed! What if that bullet had been a few inches nearer your heart? What if Duggin had hit your head?" She rolled her eyes. "Come to think of it, if he'd hit your head, the bullet would probably just have ricocheted off."

David nodded. "I agree with Christy, Doctor. As a matter of fact, my sermon this morning is going to be on the evils of moonshine. I'm hoping it will have some effect."

"Take my advice, David." The doctor poked at his oatmeal with a spoon. "Don't go meddling where you don't belong."

"Meddling?" David demanded. "You're sitting there with a hole in you, talking about meddling? Maybe you think these mountain men can guzzle all the homemade liquor they please, but when they endanger others. . . . Suppose that bullet had hit a child, Doctor? What then?"

The doctor leveled his gaze at David. "No one knows more than I do about the pain and death these mountains have seen. But I've been here a lot longer than you. And I'm telling you, if you climb up in that pulpit today and preach against the evils of illegal liquor, you won't accomplish what you're hoping for."

"How can you be so sure?" Christy asked. "You've never set foot in that church. You've never heard David preach, either. But I have. And he is a very persuasive speaker."

"I'm no theologian," the doctor said. He pushed his tray aside once again, dropping the napkin over his now-cold oatmeal. "But I know that when you accuse people, a wall goes up. The last thing they're interested in then is changing their views. All they do is crouch behind that wall to defend themselves."

"Sometimes that's true," David said, "but just the same, I have to try."

The doctor ran his hand through his messy hair. "There's something you two need to understand. Back in these mountains, there's only one real source of money, and that's the sale of good whiskey to outsiders. These people need food and clothes and medicine. How else are they going to get it?"

"But that's not the only way!" Christy cried in frustration. "They could come to us—to the mission—for help."

The doctor shook his head. "Too proud. That's not the way of these folks. They don't want charity."

Silence fell. Christy looked over at David. He seemed as frustrated by the doctor's words as she was.

"Well, I need to get over to the church. I'll see you there, Christy," David said curtly. "Glad you're doing better, Doctor."

"David?" the doctor said.

"Yes?"

"Be careful what you say. Or you may live to regret it." He paused. "As a friend, I'm warning you."

David's eyes flashed. He opened his mouth to speak, then seemed to think the better of it. He left briskly, slamming the door behind him.

A moment later, there was a knock on the door. Ruby Mae poked her head inside. "Miz Christy?" she asked. "You about ready to head on to church?"

"In a minute, Ruby Mae."

Ruby Mae gave a little wave to the doctor. "How'd you like the oatmeal, Doctor? I helped Miss Ida do it up for you. Put my own special fixin's in."

"It had a . . . unique . . . flavor," said Doctor MacNeill.

Ruby Mae grinned at Christy. "Knew he'd like it," she said.

"Ruby Mae, did you wash up the breakfast dishes, like Miss Ida reminded you to?" Christy asked.

Ruby Mae pursed her lips. "No'm, I can't rightly say that I did. I had to give this nice bran mash I made to Prince, on account of him winning the race and all. By the way, Doctor, your horse is doin' fine, too, though I 'spect he misses you. I gave him a little bran mash, too."

Christy sighed. "Those dishes—"

"Won't wash themselves, yes'm, I know. Miss Ida tells me that all the time. I'll do 'em as soon as church is over."

"All right, then. Wait for me in the parlor. I'll be right down."

As the door closed behind Ruby Mae, Christy stared at the doctor's white bandage. It brought back vivid memories of the dark blood, the gaping hole, and the look of pain in the doctor's eyes as she'd removed the bullet. A feeling of anger seared through her. "I don't understand you," she muttered.

"Many women have tried," the doctor joked, but Christy was not amused.

"It's only by the grace of God that you're alive, Neil," Christy said in a hushed voice, barely controlling her anger. "How can you see the enemy and not want to fight back?"

"The enemy?"

"Moonshine, of course. Illegal liquor and the drunkenness and the feuding that come with it."

The doctor gave her a weary smile. "I wish it were that simple, Christy. But the enemy is much bigger. It's ignorance. And poverty." He closed his eyes. "And that," he added, "is an enemy you are not going to defeat with one sermon."

The service was well under way, and as far as Ruby Mae was concerned, the fun part—the singing and foot-tapping and clapping—was done. Now the preacher was speaking.

Ruby Mae sat in one of the front pews. Miz Ida sat on one side, her hands folded primly in her lap. Miz Christy sat on the other. She had a far-off look in her eyes, as if she were figuring something complicated, like one of those math problems Rob Allen liked to work on so much.

Of course, Miz Christy was big on thinking. Ruby Mae knew, because she'd taken a peek at Miz Christy's diary a while back. It was full of big thoughts, deep as the well in the mission yard. Miz Christy had been mad as a plucked hen when she'd caught Ruby Mae reading it, but she'd forgiven her eventually.

She'd even given Ruby Mae a diary of her own to write in. What she wrote, though, wasn't what you'd call deep. Mostly, Ruby Mae just wrote about how wonderful Prince was. Once or twice she'd even written about Rob Allen's dimples.

Ruby Mae craned her neck, scanning the rows behind her. The preacher was just getting to speechifying, and she didn't want to be rude. But still, she was curious about whether Rob was here today.

She saw her ma and nodded. Ruby Mae was surprised to see her step-pa there, too. He hardly ever came to church. He always said, "I don't take no stock in a brought-on city fellow comin' here, a-telling us how to live." Maybe her ma had dragged him here today to show he was sorry for shooting the doctor and all.

Just then, Ruby Mae caught sight of Rob sitting at a desk in the back corner. She gave a little wave, and he waved back.

Miz Ida elbowed her hard in the ribs. "Behave, Ruby Mae," she scolded.

Ruby Mae sighed. Between Miz Alice, Miz Christy, and Miz Ida, you couldn't take a breath without one of them telling you how and when and why.

She focused her gaze on the preacher. His face was red, and his eyes were burning. He pounded his fist on the pulpit.

Maybe she was missing something. He always talked mighty pretty, about God and love and such things, but she wasn't much on listening to preaching.

Still, there was a strange kind of silence in the church today. The usual coughing and shifting and baby-crying had stopped. The only sound was the shuffling of the pigs who often slept under the floorboards in a crawl space. The room was as still and waiting as the moment before a storm comes.

"Some of you," the preacher was saying, "feel that after a minister has finished his Sunday service, he should shut his eyes to everything going on outside the church. 'Mind your own business,' I have been told."

The preacher paused, gazing out at the

crowded room. "Now, in the last twenty-four hours, I've done a lot of thinking about what Jesus' attitude would be toward us here in Cutter Gap, right now in 1912. You'll recall that Jesus said, 'Everyone that doeth evil hateth the light lest his deeds should be reproved. But he that doeth truth cometh to the light.'" The preacher took a deep breath. "He also said, 'No man can serve two masters.' In other words, you can't serve Christ on Sunday, and then serve evil on Monday. That just is not possible."

A long silence followed. Suddenly, the preacher pounded the pulpit with his fist again, and Ruby Mae jumped.

"Men and women," he cried, "in this Cove there are those who are working at night—in the darkness—and they are serving evil!"

His voice rang out, climbing into the high rafters. People shifted and murmured. *What did he mean,* Ruby Mae wondered. *What evil?* She looked over at Miz Christy for an answer, but her teacher's eyes were glued on the preacher.

"Yesterday, we saw the truth of what I'm saying," the preacher continued, his voice lowered to a near-whisper. "We had a celebration, a celebration for a woman, Miss Alice Henderson, who has devoted her life to doing God's work. There was a race, you may recall."

56

The preacher fixed his gaze on Ruby Mae, and she felt prickles travel the length of her spine. Was he mad at her? Was she somehow doing evil? Sure, she'd been shirking her chores, but was that enough of a sin to get the preacher so all-fired angry?

"Ruby Mae Morrison surprised us all by winning," the preacher continued. He smiled right at her, and she relaxed a little.

"And then—" his voice boomed, "a shot rang out, and a man . . . an innocent man . . . nearly lost his life."

The preacher moved away from the pulpit. He walked down the aisle separating the two halves of the room. Ruby Mae had never seen him so angry. It scared her. Judging from the looks of others in the room, it scared them, too. Some people even looked a little angry.

"The liquor being brewed hereabouts is the devil's own brew," the preacher said. "You know and I know that it leads to fights and killings. Christ meant for our actions on Sunday and every other day to be alike. Don't make the mistake, men and women, of underestimating Him. Our God cannot lose. He will not lose the fight against evil in this Cove, or anywhere in our world!"

Suddenly there was a scraping sound, as a pew was pushed back across the wooden floor. Ruby Mae turned to see Jubal McSween jump to his feet. Jubal, she knew, was one of the Cove men who made moonshine. His face was twitching angrily. He looked as if he might say something, but instead he just slammed his hat down on his head and stormed out through the door.

The preacher's face was flushed, his eyes glowing as he watched Jubal depart. "How many of you want to be on the Lord's side?" he demanded. "Do you?" He pointed his finger out into the crowd. "And you? How about you?"

No one moved. His voice echoed in the silent room. A baby sobbed softly. Ruby Mae felt someone move beside her. She looked up to see Miz Christy, standing proud and tall.

"I do," she said.

On the other side of her, Ruby Mae felt Miz Ida stand.

"And so do I," she called out.

Ruby Mae hesitated. No one else was standing. The whole room seemed to be holding its breath.

Her knees trembling, Ruby Mae slowly stood. Miz Christy smiled down at her. "I do," Ruby Mae called out in a voice that seemed thin and puny in the huge room.

She glanced back. Her ma was staring at her with a face that showed no emotion.

Just then, her step-pa climbed to his feet. He sent a cold look toward the preacher. Ruby Mae knew that angry stare far too well.

"Best stay out of other folks' affairs, Preacher," Mr. Morrison warned. "Next time I fire off my rifle, it may not be no accident."

One by one, several other men stood and followed Ruby Mae's stepfather out the door.

⫷ Five ⫸

That evening, Christy retrieved her diary before crawling into bed. It was late and she was tired, but she wanted to sort out her complicated feelings about the past day.

And it had been a very long day. The doctor, feverish and grumpy, was proving to be a difficult patient. Nothing was ever right. His sheets were tangled. His tea was cold. His dinner was bland. He was bored. He wanted to go home to his own cabin. He had work to do.

But that was just a minor concern. Ida and Miss Alice could handle Doctor MacNeill.

It was David's sermon that had Christy so worried. She was afraid that his stern words had just served to drive away the people he'd hoped to win over. After the service, she'd sensed them staying far away, just as the doctor had warned. Even among those who had stayed through the service, the usual happy chatter had been replaced with terse goodbyes and sullen stares. Obviously, feelings ran very deep on the subject of illegal liquor.

Christy uncapped her pen and began to write:

April 7, 1912

I'm so worried. Miss Alice and David have often warned me that these beautiful mountains are full of danger, and that these wonderful people are capable of dark and dangerous acts. But these past couple of days, I've begun to see it for myself.

During David's sermon today about the evils of moonshine, several men stormed out. And afterward there was a tension in the air I've never felt before. The doctor says David and I are too new to Cutter Gap to understand these people. He says we shouldn't interfere.

But yesterday I was the one who had to remove a bullet from that man's shoulder—a bullet that wouldn't have been there without the help of liquor. Doesn't that give me a right to an opinion? How can it be wrong to try to change a hurtful thing?

And the illegal liquor that is everywhere here is a hurtful thing. I have only to remember the sound of that gunfire, or the sight of Doctor MacNeill's blood-stained shirt, to know that much.

Still, I feel uneasy. I can't say why, exactly. But something about the look in the faces of those mountain people, even more than Duggin Morrison's outright threat, makes me feel like we haven't seen the last of the trouble over moonshine.

Christy set her pen down on the bedside stand. The light from her kerosene lamp flickered. Writing down her thoughts wasn't making her feel any better.

Maybe she should take a walk. Besides, it wouldn't hurt to check on the doctor. His fever had been higher tonight. That wasn't unusual, Miss Alice had said. But she wanted to keep a close eye on him. She'd refused his many demands to let him go back to his own cabin.

Christy put on her robe and slippers and stepped into the hallway, carrying her lamp. She walked down to the doctor's room. The door was ajar. She peered in. His eyes were closed. Asleep, he almost looked sweet and boyish—nothing like the stubborn, annoying man he could be when wide awake.

She tiptoed inside and set the lamp on the dresser. The doctor's forehead was bathed in sweat. She wondered if his fever had gone up. Quietly, she soaked a cloth in the basin of water near his bed.

As she reached over to place the cloth on his forehead, he opened his eyes. "I was having this wonderful dream," he murmured. "This beautiful angel tiptoed into my room to take care of me. Now I see it wasn't a dream."

Christy smiled. "You're still running a fever. Perhaps you're delirious. Is there anything I can get you?"

"My own bed to sleep in."

"Sorry. Miss Alice says you're stuck here for a while longer." Christy retrieved the lamp, then hesitated near the door. "Neil?" she asked softly. "Do you really think David made a mistake, giving that sermon today?"

"From the way you described it to me, yes, I do," the doctor answered gravely.

"Well, I think you're wrong."

"Why did you ask me, then?"

Christy sighed. There was no point in having this conversation. "Goodnight, Doctor."

"Christy?"

"Yes?"

"Don't let Ruby Mae help with breakfast tomorrow, promise?"

Back in the hallway, Christy noticed that Ruby Mae's door was open. She peeked inside. The bed was empty.

Where could that girl be, in the middle of the night? Grabbing a midnight snack, perhaps?

There were still a few pieces of Miss Alice's birthday cake left. No doubt Ruby Mae had taken it upon herself to finish them off.

Christy headed downstairs. The kitchen was empty. So was the parlor. Strange. Where on earth could Ruby Mae have gone, unless . . . Christy smiled. Of course.

She put the lamp aside and stepped outside. It was still very cold at night. The mountains took their sweet time warming up to spring, Fairlight Spencer liked to say.

Christy walked across the wet lawn quickly, shivering in her thin robe. Miss Alice's cabin was dark. David's bunkhouse wasn't visible from here. Christy wondered if he were having trouble sleeping, too. He'd seemed as surprised as she'd been by the hot rage and the icy silence that had greeted his sermon.

The little shed that housed Prince, Miss Alice's horse, Goldie, and the mission's crippled mule, Old Theo, was just past the schoolhouse. Christy was almost there when she heard an odd shuffling noise. It seemed to be coming from the crawl space under the schoolhouse.

She paused, listening. Nothing. Probably just the hogs who lived under there. It had taken her a while to get used to the notion of teaching in a one-room schoolhouse with hogs as downstairs neighbors. Once they had even gotten loose in her classroom, causing quite a commotion.

When she reached the shed, Christy swung open the wooden door. It let out a tired creak.

"Who's there?" came a frightened voice.

"Don't worry, Ruby Mae, it's just me, Miss Christy."

Ruby was sitting in Prince's stall. He was lying down in the sweet-smelling hay. A patch of moonlight, coming from the only window, streaked his velvet side. Ruby Mae sat next to him, a horse blanket over her legs. Her diary was nearby.

"Miz Christy!" she exclaimed. "You nearly scared me to death!"

"I'm sorry." Christy joined her in the stall. The hay was prickly and warm. Prince gazed at her sleepily, clearly wondering why he was getting so many late-night visitors. "I couldn't sleep, and then I saw you were gone and got worried."

"Well, I'm glad it's just you. I thought I was hearin' noises before," Ruby Mae said.

"Probably just the hogs. Or the wind," Christy said.

She stroked Prince's soft muzzle. "Do you sneak out here often?"

"Some," Ruby Mae said guardedly.

"You love Prince a lot, don't you?"

"More'n anything in the whole wide world, I reckon." Ruby Mae pulled a piece of straw out of her curly hair. "More'n my ma and step-pa, even, I sometimes think. Is that wrong, Miz Christy, to feel like that?"

"You're just going through a rough time with your parents right now, Ruby Mae. It'll pass."

Ruby Mae sighed. "I hope you're right. But my step-pa looked right mad at me today, after that sermon by the preacher. After church he told me I was getting carried away, living here at the mission. Said he might even make me come back home to live." She sighed. "My step-pa thinks people like you and the preacher are pokin' in where you don't belong. He said there'd be trouble, if'n you didn't tend to your own business."

"Do you think a lot of people feel that way?" Christy asked.

"Reckon so. It's just the way folks is, Miz Christy. They get set in their ways, and they don't like gettin' un-set, if you follow my meanin'. Preacher, he's maybe goin' too fast . . . not that I got any right to say."

Christy leaned back against the rough, cool wood of the wall. She pointed to Ruby Mae's diary and smiled. "I was writing in my diary, too."

"What did you say?" Ruby Mae asked. Her hand flew to her mouth. "Oops. I forgot how they're private-like. You don't have to tell me. But I'll tell you mine. I was writin' how when I'm here with Prince, it seems like the whole rest of the world can just float away, for all I care. I was writin' about this place we go to, over past Blackberry Creek. There's a spot—a cave, like—where we just sit and watch the world a-spinnin', and I think actual thoughts sometimes."

Christy smiled. "Actual thoughts? I'm very impressed."

"I mean, I know I ain't no John Spencer or Rob Allen or nothin'." She laughed. "My step-pa says I have chicken feathers for brains. But still, I think sometimes." She hesitated. "You think someone as all-fired smart as Rob could ever hanker after someone with feathers for brains?"

"Of course he could. But don't you ever say that about yourself, Ruby Mae. I've probably learned as much about the Cove from you as I have from Miss Alice."

"Truly?"

"Truly. Of course, I wouldn't mind if you paid a little more attention to your studies and chores and a little less attention to Prince."

"But can't you see why?" Ruby Mae asked. She hugged Prince's neck. "Isn't bein' here just the plumb best place in the whole world?

Christy nodded. "You're right. It just may be."

Using Prince's broad back for a pillow, Ruby Mae stretched out in the hay. Christy joined her, and together they covered themselves with the scratchy, horse-smelling blanket. The little window on the far wall gave them a tiny square of sky to look at.

"Peaceful-like, ain't it?" Ruby Mae whispered.

Staring up at the little patch of star-studded sky, it did seem peaceful. Guns and moonshine and anger seemed very, very far away indeed. Christy rested her cheek on Prince's warm, soft back, and let herself drift into a restless sleep.

⁓ ⁓ ⁓

"Ruby Mae, could you come over here, please?" Christy called the next afternoon. Recess was over, and the children were reluctantly heading back into the classroom.

They all had a bad case of spring fever, Christy had decided. She'd had a hard time getting anyone to pay attention to her lesson on the American Revolution that morning. There had been a lot of daydreaming going on. Still, no one seemed to be shirking schoolwork more than Ruby Mae. And Christy had a feeling it wasn't the fine early spring weather that was the culprit. It was a certain black stallion by the name of Prince.

"Yes, Miz Christy?" Ruby Mae called. She and Rob Allen were sauntering toward the school. Ruby Mae's cheeks were flushed, and she was grinning from ear to ear.

Well, Christy thought, *maybe Prince isn't the only distraction in Ruby Mae's life.*

"I need to talk to you for a minute, Ruby Mae," Christy said. "Privately."

Rob cleared his throat. "I'll head on inside," he said quickly, giving Ruby Mae a shy smile.

Christy led Ruby Mae away from the school into the cool shade of a large oak.

"Don't he just have the cutest little dimples you ever did see?" Ruby Mae asked.

"Ruby Mae," Christy said, "we need to talk. I graded your history test during recess. And it was not a pretty sight. Did you even read the assignment I gave the class?"

Ruby Mae gulped. "I sort of . . . shinnied over it, quick-like. Truth to tell, it was dull as dishwater."

Christy leaned against the oak, her arms crossed over her chest. "Speaking of dishwater, Miss Ida told me you shinnied over the breakfast dishes this morning, too."

"I was groomin' Prince. He ain't had a proper hoof-pickin' in days. Stones get caught in there, and it hurts somethin' fierce if'n—"

"Ruby Mae, I'm afraid I'm going to have to take away your riding privileges for a while. For the next few weeks, David will take care of Prince, until your grades improve and you start paying attention to your chores."

"But—but you just can't take away Prince,

Miz Christy!" Ruby Mae cried, so loudly that some of the students peered out the windows to see what all the commotion was about. "He's the most important thing in the world to me! I promise I'll work on my grades and read my history, even if it is borin'. And I'll do my chores proper-like. Only you just can't take Prince away from me! I'll like to die if'n you do."

Christy touched Ruby Mae's shoulder, but the girl yanked away angrily. "It's not forever, Ruby Mae. Just for a little while. It's for your own good. Miss Alice and David and I discussed it this morning."

"What do you-all know about my own good?" Ruby Mae screamed. Tears streamed down her freckled cheeks. "Prince needs me. And I need him! You . . . you saw how it was, last night. I thought you understood."

"I do understand," Christy said gently. "It isn't like he's going away, Ruby Mae. He'll be right here at the mission, if you want to say hello." She sighed. "I'm sorry to have to do this, Ruby Mae, but the sooner you get back on track, the sooner you can spend time with Prince again."

Ruby Mae stared at her in disbelief, her eyes glistening with tears. She opened her mouth, as if to argue, then gave up, spun on her heel and dashed into the school.

"What's with Ruby Mae?"

Christy turned to see David, crossing the lawn with his usual long, determined stride. He was carrying the textbook he used for the math class he taught in the afternoon.

"She's furious about our decision. Poor thing. I feel so badly for her. But she's got to keep up with her schoolwork." Christy shook her head. "It's hard, being the disciplinarian. Just a few months ago, my parents were telling me what to do—trying, anyway. I'm not used to being the bad guy."

"Then you can imagine how I felt yesterday, telling my whole congregation to stop doing something that they insist is their God-given right." David gazed back at the mission house. "The doctor and I had another argument this morning. He insisted I shouldn't have given that sermon. And that the reception it got shouldn't have surprised me."

"And what did you say?" Christy asked.

"I told him to mind his own business—"

"To which he said, you should be minding yours," Christy finished his explanation.

David gave a grim smile. "You do know how the doctor's mind works, don't you?"

"Yes." Christy laughed.

Just then, she heard a low grunt coming from the rear of the school. One of the hogs who resided under the building sauntered out into the sunshine, making its way along the side of the school.

"Looks like Mabel's up from her nap," Christy said, pointing to the big hog.

"Mabel?"

"Creed Allen named her. Says she looks like his Great-aunt Mabel over in Big Gap—except for the tail, of course."

"I'll wager that Mabel's the only one who heard my sermon yesterday and didn't mind it."

"*I* thought it was a very fine sermon," Christy said.

"Thanks—" David began, then paused. "Am I crazy, or is that hog walking a bit oddly?"

They watched as Mabel took a few faltering steps. She was walking on a slant, as if she were fighting a stiff wind.

"Very strange," Christy murmured. "Maybe she's sick. Let's go check it out."

As they approached the side of the school, Christy noticed an intense, almost sickeningly sweet, medicine-like odor. Toward the back of the building, she stumbled over a broken jug. Nearby were several hogs, stretched out asleep—*very* asleep. As Christy and David approached, they did not stir. They were breathing heavily.

David stared at the pigs. He gently poked first one and then another with his foot, but they just kept snoring.

"This is very odd," Christy said. The hogs never slept this soundly. Usually, she could hear them snuffling and rooting around under the building while she taught.

"I don't get it." David stooped to look under the floor. "It's almost too dark to see anything. I'll have to go in under there."

He crouched over, slowly making his way under the building. Christy could hear his fingers groping, then some boards being moved.

Suddenly he gave a loud whistle. "Christy, you should see this!" David cried, his voice filled with amazement and anger.

❧ Six ❧

Christy knelt down. "What is it, David?"

"Jugs, lots of them! Moonshine whiskey! I should have recognized the smell."

"But . . . right here, underneath the school?" Christy cried in disbelief.

She heard voices and turned to see several of her students. Ruby Mae hung back from the group. Her face was red and blotchy from crying.

"Miz Christy," asked Creed Allen. "What in tarnation is wrong with all these hogs? Mabel's walkin' like she's got her legs screwed on backwards. And the rest of 'em—well, I ain't never heard this much hog-snorin' in all my days!"

"Christy," David called from under the school, "can you take these jugs from me? I'll hand them to you, one at a time."

"Just a minute, David. Some of the children are here—"

"Let them see!" David called angrily. "Let them see the evil hidden under their own schoolhouse."

"What's hidden?" asked Little Burl Allen, Creed's sweet six-year-old brother. "Is the preacher a-playin' hide-and-seek, Teacher?"

"Not exactly, Little Burl," Christy said, just as David passed her a thick brown jug. She set it on the ground. The children stared at it curiously.

"Moonshine?" whispered John Spencer, one of the older students.

"There's moonshine under the school?" Creed cried. "No wonder them hogs is snorin' so loud! They's drunk on homemade whiskey!"

Most of the children began to laugh, although a few of the older boys, like Lundy Taylor, kept watching Christy guardedly.

"I know it seems funny," Christy said as she accepted more jugs from David. "But this is no laughing matter, children."

"I'll say it ain't," Lundy muttered darkly. "My pa says you-all are messin' where you don't belong. This ain't the business of a teacher or a preacher-person."

David crawled out from under the floor space. His face was smudged with dirt. His eyes were hot with anger.

"I heard that, Lundy," he said as he stood.

"And let me tell you something you can pass on to your pa. When I find illegal liquor on mission property, it becomes my business, whether your pa and his friends like it or not."

David stooped down and grabbed one of the jugs. He uncorked it and sniffed the contents with a look of disgust. Then he turned the jug upside down. The amber liquid gurgled and spattered as it poured onto the ground. The air filled with a sharp, sweet smell.

"You ain't got no right to throw away good moonshine like that!" Lundy cried.

"There's nothing good about moonshine, Lundy Taylor," Christy said with feeling. "Didn't you see what happened to Doctor MacNeill?"

"But ain't that worth a lot of money, Teacher?" Creed asked innocently. "Pa says moonshine fetches a big price, 'specially over the state lines where it's hard to get."

"It's also worth a lot of pain, Creed," Christy said.

David uncorked another bottle. His hands were trembling. Christy had never seen him so furious.

"Children, I want you all to go back inside now," she instructed.

"But what about them hogs?" Little Burl asked, worried.

"They'll sleep it off, Little Burl," Christy assured him, patting his tangled hair. "Don't you worry."

"When my grandpa gets to drinkin', he'll sleep for two days straight," said Bessie Coburn.

"Yes, well, we can talk about that more inside," Christy said, shooing the children away. Slowly they returned to class, until only Lundy was left. He was a big boy, almost as tall as David. And with the threatening look in his eyes right now, he seemed even bigger.

"Do you know anything about who put these jugs here, Lundy?" Christy asked, her voice quivering.

Lundy glared at her. "I ain't a-tellin' you nothin' except this—you mission folks is makin' a big mistake."

"Don't you go threatening us, Lundy Taylor," David warned.

"We have to get rid of the moonshine, Lundy," Christy said gently, yet firmly. "Can't you see that?"

Lundy backed away slowly. "All I see is a heap more trouble than the sorry likes of you can handle."

Without another word, he raced off into the thick woods.

"I still don't understand why they put the moonshine there," Christy said at dinner that night. "Right under the church! It's such a crazy place to store illegal liquor."

Silence fell over the table. It had been a tense meal. David was still fuming about the moonshine. Ruby Mae was still pouting about Prince. Doctor MacNeill, who'd insisted on coming downstairs to join them for dinner, was still running a fever. Miss Alice was gathering up supplies. She was on her way to help a woman in Big Gap deliver a baby. And Miss Ida was annoyed that no one was eating the meal she'd prepared.

"I wonder how long those jugs have been down there," Christy continued.

"They may have put them there long ago," David suggested, "thinking it would be the last place anyone would look. Or it could have been a defiant gesture—an answer, if you can call it that, to my sermon last Sunday."

"Come to think of it, I did hear noises out by the school late last night," Christy said.

"You were outside last night?" David asked in surprise.

Christy glanced over at Ruby Mae. "Oh, just for a few minutes. A little walk, to clear my head."

David looked over at the doctor. "I suppose, with this latest development, you're dying to say I told you so?"

Doctor MacNeill shifted positions in his chair. He'd barely touched his food. "No, David," he said after a moment of reflection. "I'm not about to gloat. What would be the point?"

"Since when do you keep your opinions to yourself?" David demanded.

The doctor sighed heavily. "I will tell you this. I am worried about this situation. It was one thing to preach a sermon about moonshine. It was quite another to dump out jug after jug. That was someone's property, like it or not—"

"Property!" David cried. "That was illegal liquor, on *my* property!" He paused. "On *our* property, I should say."

"That's not the point," the doctor said. "The point is that you've just added fuel to a very dangerous fire. I'm worried that whoever put that moonshine there will try to retaliate now."

"Retaliate?" Miss Ida echoed. "Against whom?"

"Against the mission. Against David, or maybe Christy. After all, the children witnessed them dumping the moonshine together."

David looked at Christy and frowned. "*I'm* the one who did the dumping and gave the sermon. Why would they act against Christy?"

"Because she represents the mission, too," the doctor answered. "In a way, she has more contact with these people than you do. You see them every Sunday for an hour, if you're lucky. She's the one teaching the children of these moonshiners, every single day."

The doctor winced as he tried to reach for a glass of water. Ruby Mae moved it closer for him. "Thanks, Ruby Mae. Say, you've been awfully quiet this evening."

Ruby Mae stared at her plate, her lower lip jutting.

"She's pouting," Christy explained.

"And why is that?" asked Doctor MacNeill.

"They won't let me take care of Prince anymore and he's just gonna plain starve out there without me!" Ruby Mae cried.

"Ruby Mae," David said gently, "I fed Prince an hour ago. He ate like . . . well, like a horse. Trust me. He is not going to starve."

"Without me, he's a-goin' to starve for love!" Ruby Mae cried.

Christy smiled at the doctor. "Tell us, Doctor. Have you ever come across such a medical condition?"

"Starving for love. Hmmm." The doctor tapped his finger on his chin. "There have been documented cases, although they usually appear in the human male." He grinned at Christy. "Now, in a mammal the size of a horse, I would think it would take, oh, a good two months or so for any symptoms to develop."

"Two months," Christy repeated, winking at the doctor. "That's plenty of time for you to get your schoolwork and chores back on track, Ruby Mae."

"What does he know?" Ruby Mae said. "He ain't no horse doctor."

"By the way, have you started on that English homework I assigned?" Christy asked.

"Not yet," Ruby Mae said sullenly.

Miss Alice came bustling into the room from the kitchen where she had packed some food to take with her. She was carrying a paper sack and her medical bag in her left hand. Her sprained wrist was much better, but she still had her right arm in a sling most of the time.

She pursed her lips. "I do hate to go, what with Neil still running a fever and this trouble with the moonshine. But Janey Cook's had a couple of hard deliveries, and I'd like to be there. I won't be as much use as I'd like, with this arm of mine, but her grandmother will be there, too. Together we should manage."

"Be careful, Miss Alice," the doctor warned. "I'm concerned about retaliation over that moonshine David threw out."

"I can take care of myself," Miss Alice said. She shook a warning finger at the group. "But I want the rest of you to keep an eye out. And David, this might be a good time to let things simmer down a little. Give folks a chance to think."

"Who is it you think is going to be retaliating, anyway?" David asked, sounding defensive.

"Bird's-Eye Taylor is one of the biggest moonshiners in these parts, of course," Miss Alice said. "And I suspect he uses Lundy to help him. But there are others."

"Tom McHone, for one," the doctor added. "And Jubal McSween and Dug—" He stopped in midsentence.

"Go ahead and say it, Doc," said Ruby Mae, her eyes flashing. "Sure, my step-pa's made moonshine and sold it some. Everybody does it around these parts. I ain't defendin' him or nothin'. But there ain't no way else to make a proper living here." She tossed her napkin onto the table. "Not like that'll stop you-all from tellin' the rest of the world how to live their lives and what they can do and can't do and if'n they can be with the one thing that means more to them than the whole rest of the wide world." She pushed back her chair. "Can I be excused?" she demanded. "I got dishes to do, and homework."

"Yes, Ruby Mae," Christy said. "You may be excused."

She watched as Ruby Mae dashed from the room. "I hope she doesn't stay mad forever," she said sadly.

"That's one thing people in these mountains do very, very well," said the doctor with a weary smile. "Stay mad. And get even."

Ruby Mae stared down at the tear-stained diary page. The ink was blurry. The letters melted one into another, but she could still make out her words:

I can't stand it no more. It just ain't fare. Prins needs me as much as I need him. Well, mebbe not as much, but almost. Itz only bin a few owrs and my hart is braking. How kin I go for weeks without seein him, or mebbe even longer?

She wiped her eyes and sniffled. It was very late. The others had gone to sleep hours ago.

With a sigh, she went to the window and opened it wide. The chill air sent a shiver through her. Out there, past Miss Alice's vegetable garden, past the lattice-covered well, past the school, was the little shed where Prince was waiting for her.

Did he miss her as much as she missed him? Creed Allen said animals could feel even more than people could, and she liked to think he was right. (Although Creed also swore that his raccoon, Scalawag, could read his mind, and she had serious doubts about that. After all, Creed was known for the whoppers he liked to tell.)

A sound, a strange rhythmic thud, met her ears. It seemed to be coming from far away, but there was an urgency to it.

Ruby Mae listened, straining to make out the source of the sound. It was coming from the direction of the schoolhouse. Could it be someone had returned to put more moonshine under the school? She hoped not, especially since it wouldn't surprise her to learn her step-pa was involved. Truth was, she didn't rightly see what business it was of the preacher and Miz Christy if her step-pa wanted to make moonshine. But she sure didn't want them getting riled up all over again.

Suddenly, she heard a wild, desperate whinny, like nothing she'd ever heard before.

Prince! It had to be him.

The sound came again, a horrible cry carried on the wind.

He sounded terribly afraid. Whatever was happening to Prince, it was bad, very bad. She had to get to him, and get there fast.

Ruby Mae threw open her bedroom door and flew down the stairs. She ran across the wet lawn in her bare feet. Another terrified whinny filled the air, followed by a series of pounding noises, as if Prince were trying to kick right through the sides of his stall.

She didn't slow down, not for an instant, not even when she realized that there might be someone lurking behind the dark trees, lying in wait.

Breathless and shivering, she finally made it to the shed. The door was slightly ajar. Either the preacher had forgotten to close the door, or someone else had been here.

Or someone might even still be here.

With a deep breath, Ruby Mae flung open the door. "Who's there?" she cried, trying her best to sound like someone big and scary and well-armed.

She took a step inside. The familiar smells of hay and leather and manure greeted her. In the dim moonlight, she could make out something lying on the floor.

It was the preacher's saddle, the one Prince wore! Ruby Mae knelt down, tracing her fingers over the dark leather. Someone had slashed the beautiful saddle with a knife. Long gashes covered the seat. The girth had been ripped out and tossed aside.

A low, sweet whinny of greeting made Ruby Mae look up.

"Prince?" she whispered. "Are you all right, boy?"

Trembling, she stepped closer. And then she saw the answer to her question. The beautiful black stallion was not all right, not at all.

❧ Seven ❧

Lordamercy!" Ruby Mae cried in horror. "Prince, what have they done to you?"

Prince's beautiful flowing tail, mane, and forelock had been sheared off. They lay clumped in the hay by his feet. He looked pathetic, and he knew it. He pawed at the floor, throwing his head up and down in angry protest.

Ruby Mae draped her arms around the horse's broad neck. "Oh, Prince," she moaned, "I could just bust out cryin'. You ain't hurt, is you?"

Carefully she ran her hands over his shoulders and flanks and legs, searching for any cuts or wounds. As far as she could tell, there were none. But the loss of his gorgeous mane and tail was insult enough.

"Ruby Mae?" a voice called frantically.

Miz Christy ran into the shed. She was carrying a lantern. Seconds later, Doctor MacNeill and the preacher appeared behind her.

"We heard your scream—" Miz Christy began. Her eyes fell on the saddle. "What happened?"

"Prince!" David cried, rushing over to the agitated stallion. "What's happened here, Ruby Mae?"

Ruby Mae knelt down and picked up a handful of Prince's silky tail. "I'll tell you what happened," she cried. "Someone hurt Prince to get back at you. If you'da just kept quiet about the moonshine, this would never have happened! It's your fault, Preacher." She turned to Miz Christy. "And your fault, too. Why couldn't you-all have left well enough alone?"

She was crying, but she couldn't stop herself. Hot tears spilled down her cheeks. She buried her face in Prince's neck, and he seemed to calm down, as if he understood that she needed him.

"Are the others all right?" the preacher asked. "Old Theo and Bill?"

Doctor MacNeill looked over the old mule and his own horse. "They're fine," he said, "just a little nervous, what with all the commotion." He stroked Prince's muzzle. "Looks like they didn't waste any time getting even," he said grimly. "It's like I said, David. Revenge is the way of the mountains."

"So this is my fault?" the preacher cried. "I'm responsible for this horrible act?"

"I'm not saying that," said the doctor. "I'm just saying it's time to back off. Call a truce. Let the highlanders have their moonshine, and you get back to the business of being a preacher."

"This *is* part of the business of being a preacher." The preacher sighed. "Look, Doctor, I understand your point of view. Really, I do. But you must understand that it's not my job to just tell people what they want to hear. Sometimes it's my job to tell people exactly what they don't want to hear. No matter the cost."

Ruby Mae watched as the preacher tenderly stroked Prince's withers. She could see the pain in the man's dark eyes. Could it be he was as upset as she was?

"You didn't see anyone, did you, Ruby Mae?" he asked softly.

"No, sir."

"You'd tell me if you had, wouldn't you? Even if it was someone you knew?"

"I didn't see my step-pa, if that's what you're gettin' at." Ruby Mae fought back a sob. "I didn't see anyone." She scratched Prince's right ear. He gave a soft nicker, then lay his head on her shoulder.

"He was so purty, with that long mane of his a-sweepin' back in the wind," Ruby Mae said. "And now he looks plumb unnatural, like a mule—no offense to you, Old Theo. He won't even have nothin' to flick off the flies with." A wave of anger washed over her. "I wish I could knock the livin' daylights out of them that done this. Even if it were my own step-pa."

"I can't believe anyone could be this cruel," Miz Christy said in a sad, faraway voice. She was crying, too, Ruby Mae suddenly realized.

"It could have been worse," said the doctor. "They might have injured him, even killed him." The doctor leaned against the wall. He looked weak and pale. "Getting even is considered a virtue around here. The mark of a strong character. Truth is, you were lucky this time. They let you off easy."

"Easy?" Miz Christy cried.

"You're sitting on a powder keg, Christy," the doctor said. "It only takes one match to set it off. David came close to it with his sermon."

"No doubt you're right about that, Doctor," the preacher said, his voice growing angry again. "There is a powder keg here. But you can't simply wish evil away. You have to stand up and oppose it. You know as well as I do that this illegal liquor is behind at least half the terrible things that happen in these mountains. And I don't see you offering any solutions."

"I don't have any easy solutions to offer," the doctor said, rubbing his shoulder gingerly. "I just know that the Cove people don't see anything criminal about making a little homemade brew. After all, it's know-how that's been passed down through their families for centuries. To them, it's not a moral issue. Especially when they can't find any other way to make a living here in these mountains."

"But it *is* a moral issue, Doctor," said Miz Christy. "You're an educated man. You can see it. Moonshining has horrible results—feuds and terror and even death. How can you ignore all that? How can you ignore that painful wound in your own shoulder?"

"I'm not ignoring any of it," the doctor said. His voice was suddenly full of rage. "I've been taking care of these people a whole lot longer than you and David. The two of you come along and decide you're going to tell people how to live their lives. What gives you that right?"

Silence fell. Ruby Mae gulped. She had never heard this kind of grown-up argufying. Sure, her ma and step-pa fought all the time. But those fights were just made of loud words, flying around the cabin. This fight was about loud words *and* big ideas. Ruby

Mae wasn't sure she understood everything, but one thing was clear—the doctor and Miz Christy and the preacher were nowhere close to agreeing about moonshine.

"I might as well ask you the same thing, Doctor," the preacher said in a low whisper of a voice. "What gives you the right to condone evil? Are you doing these people a favor by defending their addiction to moonshine? The Bible says we must love the sinner, even though we hate the sin. And by hating the sin, and resisting the sin, perhaps we can help to free the sinner. That's why I preached against moonshine. Not because I don't care about these people, but because I *do*."

"Well, I'm just one man, doing what little I can to help," the doctor said. "You can't change the world overnight. Unfortunately, you and Christy haven't figured that out yet. I have."

"How can you be so arrogant?" Miz Christy demanded.

Ruby Mae gasped. She wasn't positive what *arrogant* meant, but she was pretty sure it wasn't the nicest thing in the world you could be.

The doctor started toward the door, then paused. "Funny. I was going to ask you two the same thing." The shed door closed behind him.

"He's awful riled, ain't he?" Ruby Mae whispered.

"We all are," Miz Christy said with a sigh. "Well, there's nothing more we can do here tonight. Come on, Ruby Mae. We'll check on Prince in the morning. He just needs some rest now."

"No!" Ruby Mae cried. "I'm not leavin' him alone."

"You can't stay," the preacher said gently. "It isn't safe out here. I'll keep an ear open for anything unusual. Prince will be fine. I promise."

"Lot of good that'll do me," Ruby Mae said bitterly. "You're the reason we're in this fix." She turned to Miz Christy. She was Ruby Mae's only hope. "Please, Miz Christy. Let me stay here. You know I'll be all right." Tears spilled down Ruby Mae's cheeks. "If'n I'd been here before, Miz Christy, maybe I could have saved Prince."

But Miz Christy just shook her head. "If you'd have been here before, you might have been hurt yourself, Ruby Mae. I'm sorry, but David's right. You head on upstairs. We'll check on Prince in the morning."

"But—"

"No, Ruby Mae. You need your sleep for school tomorrow. And Prince needs to rest up, too."

There was no point in fighting them. She was outnumbered. Ruby Mae kissed Prince gently on the muzzle. "You'll be back to your old self in no time, boy," she whispered. "Don't you worry."

Ruby Mae ran back to her room, crying all the way. She was still crying when she finally drifted off to sleep.

— ~ — ~ —

When Christy got home from school the next afternoon, she found an envelope with her name on it, sitting on the dining room table. "What's this?" she called to Miss Ida.

Miss Ida came in from the kitchen, wiping flour-covered hands on her crisp apron. "A note from the doctor."

"A note? But why would he write me a note? Isn't he upstairs?"

Miss Ida shook her head. "He left for home about an hour ago. I tried to stop him. Told him he looked like death warmed over and that you and Miss Alice would be furious. Besides, it appears there's a big storm coming on. But you know the doctor. Stubbornest man that ever laid foot on God's green earth."

"He left?" Christy dropped into a chair, rubbing her eyes. "This is awful. It's all because of the terrible fight we had last night after we found Prince. I wondered why the doctor didn't come down to breakfast this morning. David and I should have tried to resolve things with him."

"You know the doctor was hankering to get back to his own cabin, anyway," Miss Ida said. "He asked me today how I could believe in a merciful God when He allows Ruby Mae to keep making oatmeal."

The front door opened and David rushed inside. He was wearing his work clothes. His shoes were covered with hay and mud. "Anyone seen the doctor?" he asked breathlessly. "I was just putting Prince out in the pasture, and I noticed the doctor's horse is gone!"

Christy held up the envelope. "Doctor MacNeill left about an hour ago."

"Well, that's a relief," David said, sinking into the chair next to Christy.

"David, how can you say that?" Christy demanded.

"I *meant* it's a relief to know he took his horse," David said. "I was afraid it might have been stolen. You know—the moonshiners up to their tricks again. Although—" he winked at Miss Ida, "I have to admit I won't exactly miss the man."

"The doctor is still sick," Christy insisted. "He should never have left here, especially after our argument last night."

"It's not as if we could have resolved things, Christy," David said. "There are some things people are just never going to agree on."

Christy opened the envelope and read the letter inside:

My dear Christy:

You have been a fine hostess, nurse, and surgeon, but I find I must get back to my patients before you spoil me any further.

I trust that David will keep an eye on you, but please be careful in the days ahead. We may argue about many things, David and I, but about you, at least, we seem to be in remarkable agreement.

Neil MacNeill

P.S. You still owe me a dance.

Christy set the letter aside. "David, we have to go get him."

"What?" David cried. "Go get the doctor? After what he said to us last night?"

"The point is, he's running a high fever."

"He's a doctor," David argued. "He can take better care of himself than we can."

"David. Be reasonable."

He gazed at her pleadingly. "You're not going to budge on this, are you?"

Christy shook her head.

David looked at her intently. "You know, the doctor's cabin is a long ride off. And I can't take Prince. He's way too high-strung to be ridden today. I'd never even get a saddle on him."

"Poor thing," Christy said. "I let Ruby Mae

and Rob go visit him during the noon recess. Ruby Mae said she'd never seen him so skittish. She's still furious at us, by the way."

"I know. She wouldn't say a word to me during math class this afternoon." David sighed. "The point is, I'll have to ride Old Theo. And let's face it, that mule isn't exactly the fastest thing on four legs. Not only that, it looks like it's going to storm."

"Maybe I should go."

"Christy, you know I can't let you do that." David stood and stretched. "Okay, I'll go get the doctor, assuming, that is, he'll come back. The man's more ornery than Old Theo."

"Which is why you're the perfect person to retrieve him," Christy said.

David rolled his eyes. "I'll try to make this quick," he said. "With luck, I may even be back before dark. But in the meantime, you and Miss Ida and Ruby Mae stay close to the house, all right?"

"We will," Christy agreed. "But don't you think the danger's past, now that the moonshiners have gotten their revenge?"

"Maybe so, maybe not. On this, at least, I'm inclined to listen to the doctor."

❧ Eight ❧

Ruby Mae stared at her dinner plate. Usually, she loved Miss Ida's chicken pot pie, but this evening she was in no mood to eat.

She was still furious at the preacher and Miz Christy about what had happened to Prince. And since the preacher was out hunting for Doctor MacNeill, that meant the only person Ruby Mae could be mad at for the time being was Miz Christy. They'd barely spoken all through supper, except for the occasional "pass-the-muffins" or "may-I-have-the-salt."

Still, Ruby Mae knew that she was only going to get what she wanted if she acted at least a *little* polite to her teacher. She could be polite on the outside and mad on the inside, she figured.

"Miz Christy," Ruby Mae said, trying on her

pretend-sweet voice, "can I go out and check on Prince, seein' as how the preacher's not back yet from fetchin' the doctor? It'll be dark soon, and there's a storm a-brewin'. You know how Prince hates thunder. Gets himself all riled up over it. And I already done finished my math homework before supper."

Miz Christy gave her an *I-don't-believe-you* look.

"Looky here, I'll prove it to you," Ruby Mae said. She pursed her lips. "Twelve divided by three is five."

"Twelve divided by three is four, Ruby Mae."

"Well, still and all, I was right close."

With a sigh, Miz Christy got up and crossed to the window. The sky was covered with thick, gray clouds. Flashes of far-off lightning lit the horizon, but there was still no sign of rain.

"Actually, it looks like the storm's going to pass us by," Miz Christy said. "It may have stalled to the west, over that next ridge. I wonder if David and the doctor got caught in it. They should be back by now."

"All the more reason I oughta put Prince in the shed for the night, don't you figure?" Ruby Mae pressed. "When the preacher gets back, he'll be mighty tuckered out."

"You've got some dinner dishes to take care of," Miss Christy reminded her.

Ruby Mae felt her heart sink. What good was using her most polite tone of voice, if

Miz Christy wasn't even going to have the good sense to notice it?

"I can get to 'em when I get back," Ruby Mae offered.

"All right, then," Christy said. "But make it quick, Ruby Mae. I want you back in twenty minutes, understand? And if you see or hear anything unusual, you hightail it right back here."

"I promise!" Ruby Mae cried with relief as she jumped from her chair. "Twenty minutes and not a lick more."

"Oh, and Ruby Mae? Give these to Prince for me, would you?"

Miz Christy reached into the sugar bowl and passed Ruby Mae a handful of glistening white sugar cubes.

"Christy!" Miz Ida cried. "Do you realize how expensive that sugar is? And you're giving it to a *horse*?"

"He's not just *any* horse, Miss Ida," Christy said, smiling at Ruby Mae.

Ruby Mae put the sugar in the pocket of her yellow skirt. "Thanks, Miz Christy," she said gratefully, and for that moment, at least, she wasn't using a pretend voice anymore.

～ ～ ～

On her way to the pasture, Ruby Mae tried to figure out what was going on inside her.

Her heart felt crowded with way too many feelings, and she didn't like it one bit. She felt the way she did when she tried to do division problems—there was one question, but way too many answers. Maybe her step-pa was right. Maybe she really did have chicken feathers for brains.

She started up the path to the pasture. It led through a thick stand of pines, then opened onto the small, cleared area where the mission horses grazed. Way off in the distance, thunder rumbled—a low groan that made it sound like the sky had a bellyache. Miz Christy was probably right. It looked like the storm had moved on. Good thing. Prince hated storms. Always had.

It was hard, staying mad at her teacher. Truth was, Ruby Mae liked Miz Christy a whole heap, and the preacher, too. They were good people. A little big on *dos* and *don'ts*, maybe, but they meant well.

Today during the noon recess, Rob had gone with Ruby Mae to check on Prince. When he saw what had happened to the beautiful stallion, he'd been almost as upset as she'd been.

When Ruby Mae had told him how angry she was at the preacher and Miz Christy, Rob had listened very quietly until she'd said her piece. He'd thought for a good, long while before speaking.

"Maybe," he'd said at last, all slow and

careful-like, "you're even madder at your own self, Ruby Mae. You wanted to take care of Prince, and you couldn't. Maybe you feel kinda like you let him down."

He was right, of course. That's why Rob was such a smart boy. He could look right at someone and see straight into their heart.

Rob had said something else, too. He'd told Ruby Mae she shouldn't let herself feel bad. That Prince was the luckiest horse in the world to have her for a friend.

She wasn't so sure Rob was right about that. But it had made her feel better, just the same.

As Ruby Mae neared the end of the path, she let out a whistle for Prince. It was a little game they had. He would hear her whistle and gallop over to greet her. By the time she emerged from the stand of pines, he'd be waiting by the fence, tossing his head and snorting and carrying on.

Of course, she wasn't sure he'd respond to her whistle. He hadn't been his usual playful self when she'd gone to visit him at recess. He'd seemed jittery, skittish, and afraid of the least little thing.

The path through the pines ended and the pasture came into view. Ruby Mae leapt onto the split-rail fence that the preacher had built to surround the small grassy area.

"Hey, boy—" she began, and then her heart turned cold as stone.

Prince was gone! Even in the twilight gloom, she could tell that he was nowhere in the pasture.

She scrambled over the fence, frantic with fear. "Prince!" she screamed, running through the grass. "Where are you, boy?"

Then she saw the spot. At the far end of the fence, a top rail had been knocked loose.

She knew what had happened. Prince had bolted over the fence. Maybe he'd been scared off by the thunder. Maybe he'd just been so upset over what had happened to him that he'd run away out of pure embarrassment.

Or maybe someone had chased Prince off, or even stolen him.

Ruby Mae checked the sky. It was nearly dark, but she had to find Prince. Ruby Mae figured she was going to be in a world of trouble when she got back to the mission house late.

The only thing that mattered was finding Prince.

~ ~ ~

"Where on earth is that girl?" Christy murmured as Miss Ida handed her a plate to dry. "It's been half an hour, and it's practically pitch-dark out there."

"You know Ruby Mae," Miss Ida said, scrubbing away at a pie tin. "She probably thinks five minutes have gone by. The girl has no sense of time."

"Especially when she's with that horse." Christy set aside her dish towel. "I'd better go get her."

Miss Ida frowned. "What was that? Did you hear something?"

"No, I didn't hear a thing."

"On the front porch. I could have sworn I heard voices."

Christy grinned. "David and the doctor, I'll bet. It's about time!" She grabbed a lamp off the counter and headed for the front door.

Miss Ida followed Christy into the parlor. "Fortunately, there's plenty of pot pie left. I'll just warm it up—"

She was interrupted by a loud, insistent pounding on the door.

"Open up in thar!" came a male voice. "We'uns aim to git in! How 'bout some sweet-heartin', purty ladies?"

Wild, drunken laughter filled the air. Then the voices grew muffled. Christy could hear hoarse whispers. Instantly, she doused the light so the men couldn't see inside the house.

She grabbed Miss Ida's arm. "That sounds like Bird's-Eye Taylor," she hissed. "And he's got others with him. Quick, run and be sure the back door is bolted."

Miss Ida dashed back to the kitchen. Her pulse racing, Christy scanned the room.

Fortunately, the front door was locked tight, but how long would that last? A strong shoulder could break down that flimsy door. She'd even heard of men shooting hinges right off a door. Could they really do that? And in any case, they could easily break one of the windows if they were determined to get in.

She watched as the brass doorknob slowly turned. "Come on out, little teacher-lady," came a slurred voice Christy didn't recognize. "We ain't a-goin' to hurt you."

Again, the horrible drunken laughter.

"Plumb feisty, that one is," someone else said. "Citified as they come. Bet she smells mighty fine."

Christy tried to count the different voices. It sounded like three men, but she couldn't be sure. However many there were, they were undoubtedly armed. There was no way that Christy and Miss Ida could fight.... .

Suddenly, Christy gasped.

"What is it?" Miss Ida whispered as she rushed back into the parlor.

"Ruby Mae!" Christy cried. "What if she comes back?" She closed her eyes and said a quick, desperate prayer aloud. "Please, God, let Ruby Mae dawdle a little longer."

"Amen to that," Miss Ida whispered. "But Ruby Mae knows what happens when these men are drunk. If she does come back, she'll hear the ruckus and keep her distance."

Someone pounded on the door with what sounded like the butt of a shotgun. "Come on, preacher ladies! We got enough moonshine for all of us to share. Git you likkered up, you'll like it just fine!"

The pounding grew louder. It sounded like all the men were beating on the door at once as they screeched with laughter.

Christy nudged Miss Ida. "The bookcase, quick!"

Together, they struggled to drag the bookcase toward the front door. When it was pulled to within a few inches, Christy paused to wipe her brow. Her mind was racing. How long could they fend off the intruders? If only David or the doctor were here!

"How about the dining room chairs and the piano bench?" Miss Ida hissed.

"Good idea. The bigger the barricade, the better."

"But what if they break through a window?"

Christy paused. "Then we'll protect ourselves."

"With what?" Miss Ida moaned. "Our bare hands?"

"You get the rest of the furniture. I'll worry about our weapons," Christy said with determination.

The voices and pounding grew more insistent. "Come on, gals. We knows yer in thar."

Another voice piped up, "And we knows that nosey preacher's not thar to protect you!"

Christy met Miss Ida's gaze. Even in the near-dark, she could see the fear in the older woman's eyes. "How do they know?" Christy asked under her breath.

"Probably saw David on the road," Miss Ida said as she struggled to drag a stuffed chair closer to the door.

Christy ran to the kitchen. She grabbed a cast iron frying pan and a kitchen knife. Back in the parlor, she added two fire pokers to her collection and placed them near the door.

"Our weapons," she whispered to Miss Ida.

Miss Ida reached for one of the frying pans and waved it in the air. "Nothing like a swift whack to the head with one of these," she said.

Christy couldn't help smiling at the prim figure of Miss Ida, thrashing the air ferociously. Christy gave a soft, nervous laugh, and Miss Ida joined in. It helped to break the tension just a little.

"What a pair we make," Miss Ida whispered. "I do hope we live to tell the tale!"

Suddenly the men fell silent. Christy felt her whole body tense. What were they planning? Could they be heading to the back of the house?

"Maybe I should talk to them," Christy whispered.

Miss Ida nodded. "It's worth a try. What have we got to lose?"

Christy cleared her throat. "Who are you,

out there?" she called out in a firm, controlled voice.

"It's the purty one!" one of the men cried.

"I hear tell she's feisty as they come, Jubal," another added.

So Jubal McSween was one of the prowlers, Christy thought. And she was sure she recognized Bird's-Eye's voice. But who was that third man?

"I want you to leave this property right now," Christy said.

"Don't be nervish, now," said Bird's-Eye. "We're not likkered up or nothin'."

"You are too liquored up," Miss Ida cried. "And we want you to leave this instant."

"It's the old 'un!" the third man exclaimed. "Poppin' her teeth and carryin' on!"

"Why are you here?" Miss Ida called out. "What is it you men want?"

"Want to teach you'uns a lesson, 'bout tellin' us how to live," Jubal said. "Want to give you a taste o' moonshine, change yer minds 'bout it."

"Miss Henderson is going to hear this racket," Christy called. "She'll be over here any minute. I'd advise you to leave quietly, before you get into real trouble. She's a fine shot, you know."

"Aw, she's way over yonder, birthin' a babe," Bird's-Eye said. "You cain't fool us, Teacher-gal!"

Christy rolled her eyes in frustration. She knew word traveled fast in these mountains, but never before had that fact been a threat to her very life.

"Open up and we'll have ourselves a real playparty!" Bird's-Eye called.

"A hullaballoo," Jubal added with a cackle.

Christy glanced over at Miss Ida, who was sitting on the piano bench, her frying pan at the ready.

"There's one thing left to do," Christy whispered.

"What's that? We've run out of furniture and frying pans."

"Pray."

Miss Ida nodded. Together they closed their eyes.

"Please, Lord," Christy whispered, "give us the strength to deal with this crisis. And please, please, keep Ruby Mae out of harm's way—"

The sharp, horrifying clatter of glass breaking stopped Christy in mid-sentence. Her eyes flew open. On the parlor floor, she could just make out the outline of a large rock and shards of glass. Chill air blew in through the broken window.

An arm reached through the hole. "Howdy, ladies," someone said.

"Oh, my Lord," Miss Ida cried in terror. "They're breaking in!"

❧ Nine ❧

Christy raised her fire poker high as Jubal McSween kicked out the last pieces of glass in the broken window.

"Please, God," Christy prayed, "give me strength."

Suddenly, a white flash of lightning lit up the room. Christy could see the startled look on Jubal's face as he gazed up at the angry sky. A moment later, the whole house shook with the sound of thunder. Windowpanes rattled. The floor shook. It was like nothing Christy had ever heard before.

And then the rain came. It was not the usual spring storm, either. The rain came down in torrents, in buckets, in rivers. A strong wind came with it, driving the rain in horizontal sheets against the windowpanes. It flooded the porch, drenching the men instantly. Puddles formed on the parlor floor as the rain poured in through the broken window.

"Let's git us on inside!" Jubal cried, still standing by the broken window.

Lightening stabbed the sky again. "Dang!" came the voice of the third man. "The still on Blackberry Crik! Crik's a-goin' to flood somethin' fierce. If'n we don't get thar quick, we'll lose the still fer sure!"

A string of curse words followed. Between the blasts of thunder, Christy could hear the men shuffling and muttering on the wooden porch.

Suddenly, the muzzle of a hunting rifle poked through the broken window. A shadowy figure was lit by another burst of lightning. The hate-filled, grizzled face of Bird's-Eye Taylor came into view.

"Another time, preacher-ladies," he said with a dark laugh. "I promise you fer sure and certain we'll be back."

The voices vanished, and silence fell over the house. The lightning and thunder quickly faded, and the only sound was the steady drum of the rain on the tin roof.

Christy ran to Miss Ida and hugged her close. "We're safe," Miss Ida whispered, trembling. "We're safe, Christy."

"We are," Christy said grimly. "But Ruby Mae may not be. I'm going to find her."

"But those men—"

"You stay here and wait for David and the doctor. I'll be back before you know it."

"There must be something more I can do," Miss Ida said, wringing her hands.

"Do something about that window," Christy advised. "And pray. It certainly helped just now."

———

"Ruby Mae!" Christy called as she made her way through the woods at the edge of the mission property. By now she'd grown hoarse, waiting for an answer.

She had to face the truth. Ruby Mae had run off. Christy had searched all the mission buildings, hoping Ruby Mae might be hiding from the moonshiners. But after seeing the fence knocked down in the pasture, Christy knew all too well what had happened—Prince had run away, and Ruby Mae had gone to find him.

Christy slogged on through the black forest. The pine needle floor was soggy, and even with the thick canopy of trees overhead, the rain poured down without mercy. She was soaked to the bone, and her long, wet skirt clung to her legs, making a swift pace impossible.

It wasn't as if she knew where she was

going. She knew that Ruby Mae often took Prince down to Blackberry Creek, so that seemed as good a goal as any. But it was just a hunch. Prince could have gone anywhere. David had said the stallion had been acting strangely today. And as for Ruby Mae . . . well, who knew where she'd have decided to start looking?

There was just one problem with Christy's hunch. She'd heard one of the moonshiners talk about a still on Blackberry Creek. Obviously, she was heading in the same direction they were, and she did not want to run into those men again—especially not all alone, in the dark woods. At least in the mission house, she'd felt some tiny bit of security. But out here, with the wind howling and the rain pelting down, she was in their territory. Those men knew these woods in a way she never would. And they were drunk and very angry.

Christy paused to catch her breath near the top of a wide ridge. With her skirts weighed down, she was already exhausted. Her feet were cold, her shoes caked with mud.

The icy rain had chilled her to the bone. She could not stop shivering.

Near as she could tell, Blackberry Creek was down the steep incline to her left, another quarter-mile or so. She could make it that far, then decide her next move. Perhaps she might even find some tracks, although that seemed hard to imagine, in this rain.

She started down the ridge. The forest floor was slick, and she had to use trees to support her. Twice she fell. She was climbing to her feet the second time when she heard the unmistakable click of a gun being cocked.

Christy froze. She scanned the darkness, but all she could make out were the dark ghosts of the nearest trees.

"Well, well, well. What have we here? If'n it ain't the teacher-gal!" came Bird's-Eye's voice from somewhere to her right. "Lookin' fer us, was you?"

"Changed her mind about the likker, I'll wager!"

She heard the shuffle of feet through leaves and pine needles, and suddenly the men came into view—Bird's-Eye, Jubal, and Duggin Morrison, Ruby Mae's stepfather. So *he* had been the third man on the porch.

Bird's-Eye came closer. Rain dripped off his felt hat. Christy could smell the sharp tang of tobacco and moonshine. Her stomach lurched.

"Ain't so purty now, is she?" he said. "Looks more like a drowned rat than one of them citified wimmin." He poked at her shoulder with the end of his rifle, but Christy stood tall.

"Let me pass," she said.

The three men hooted. "Let her pass, she

says!" Jubal cried. He put a jug to his mouth and guzzled down some liquor.

"Boys, we got business to tend to," Duggin Morrison said.

"The still!" Jubal said, his voice slurred. "I plumb forgot! Let's take the teacher-gal with us. We'll make sure the still's all right. Then there'll be plenty o' time for sweetheartin'."

Bird's-Eye nudged Christy with the barrel of his gun. "Git a move-on. We got business by the crik."

With Duggin in the lead, the four of them started down the steep incline. Christy could hear the roar of the swollen creek, not far below them. Bird's-Eye kept his gun trained on her back, poking her along when she stumbled. It was almost impossible for her to keep up, even though they were clearly very drunk.

"Imagine a blossom-eyed gal like her, out in a gully-washer storm like this 'un," Jubal said thickly. "Wonder what she were up to."

"Lookin' fer some jollification, I reckon," Bird's-Eye cackled.

"Since you're interested," Christy said, loudly enough to be heard over the steady rain, "I was looking for Ruby Mae Morrison."

Duggin spun around. "I hear you right? Yer a-lookin' for Ruby Mae?"

"She's lost, Mr. Morrison. I think Prince ran off and she's searching for him."

"Aw, don't listen to her, Duggin," Jubal said, taking another swig from his jug. "She's just a-pullin' yer leg."

"It's true, Mr. Morrison," Christy said. "I swear it is."

Duggin paused for a moment, stroking his long beard.

"Could be, I reckon. Ruby Mae do love that preacher-horse somethin' fierce."

"That stepdaughter of yers is as twitter-witted as they comes," Bird's-Eye said. "Wouldn't be a-tall surprised if she's wanderin' round in the dark lookin' for some no-tailed horse!"

A few feet below them, Blackberry Creek rushed furiously.

Duggin paused near the bank, scratching his head.

"You say she run off tonight?" he asked Christy.

"Quit yer frettin' over that no-good gal," Bird's-Eye snapped. "Ruby Mae ain't been nothin' but trouble and woes fer you since the day she first took breath and squalled. Ain't never shut up since, neither."

"Spring's swolled up somethin' fierce," Duggin said softly. "Ruby Mae told me and her ma she come down here with that preacher-horse. Said she liked to think thoughts."

"Actual thoughts," Christy said with an affectionate smile.

"Ruby Mae Morrison?" Bird's-Eye scoffed.

115

"Much as I hate to admit it, the gal can ride. But think? Ain't likely." He poked Christy hard with his gun barrel. "Git movin', teacher-gal."

Just then, Christy gasped, but it wasn't because of Bird's-Eye's threat. She pointed a trembling finger at a bush near the creek's edge.

A swatch of yellow cloth was caught on one of the branches overhanging the rushing creek.

"That piece of fabric," Christy cried. "That's from Ruby Mae's skirt!"

✒ Ten ✒

Duggin knelt by the bank and grabbed the wet fabric. "It's Ruby Mae's, all right. Her ma made this skirt fer her last Christmas."

Christy stared at the raging creek. She knew Duggin was thinking the same thing she was. What if Ruby Mae had fallen in? What if she had drowned? And if she hadn't fallen in, where was she?

"Ruby Mae!" Duggin called out. "Ruby Mae! Is you here, gal?"

Bird's-Eye cocked his gun again. "We got better things to worry about, Duggin. That gal o' yers is fine. She's a tough 'un. Now, let's git to where we're a-goin'."

Duggin stood slowly, his own gun pointed directly at Bird's-Eye's chest. "I'll tell you where we're goin'," he said fiercely. "We're lookin' fer my Ruby Mae."

The two men stood a few feet apart, their guns trained on each other. Christy shuddered. One wrong word, and those guns could go off. That was the way of Cutter Gap.

"Mr. Taylor," Christy said gently. "What if Lundy were lost right now, instead of Ruby Mae?"

"My boy ain't that stupid."

Duggin answered by cocking his gun.

"Maybe I don't understand much about these mountains," Christy said, her voice trembling, "but I do know one thing. Family counts more than anything here. Isn't that true, Bird's-Eye?"

Bird's-Eye took a long, slow breath. His mouth twitched, but he didn't answer.

"Send Jubal to check the still," Christy urged. "You and Duggin and I will look for Ruby Mae."

Bird's-Eye blinked at her in disbelief. "You even know what a still is, teacher-gal?"

"I know."

"Well, I never. Cain't say as I thought I'd ever hear such words from the likes of you."

"Neither did I," Christy admitted.

Bird's-Eye jerked his head at Jubal. "Do what the teacher-gal says and go check the still. Duggin and me'll go searchin' for that dang-fool stepdaughter o' his."

"What about her?" Jubal demanded, pointing to Christy.

"Her, we'll deal with another day. Blood ties come first in these parts. Teacher-gal's got that much right, at least."

With a sigh, Jubal headed off, weaving and swaying along the muddy bank.

"Now what?" Duggin asked. "She could be anywheres. Even . . . " He stared at the raging water mutely.

"You know, Ruby Mae told me once about a cave she goes to near this creek," Christy recalled. "Do you know where it is?"

"Sure," Duggin said. "Just down a ways yonder, on the other side o' the crik."

"It's worth a try," Christy said. "Maybe she went there with Prince to take shelter from the rain."

Christy followed Duggin and Bird's-Eye along the bank. The rain was still coming down hard, and it was difficult to keep up with them. For two men who'd consumed a great deal of moonshine, they were surprisingly nimble.

After a couple hundred yards, Duggin paused. "Cain't see that cave from here, but it's over yonder, behind that brush."

"Ruby Mae!" Christy called. Duggin and Bird's-Eye joined in. After a few moments, they paused to listen.

"Ain't in that cave, I'm afeared," Bird's-Eye said at last. "We're yellin' loud enough to wake the dead."

"You haven't seen Ruby Mae sleep," Christy said.

"True enough," Duggin agreed. "Gal can snore somethin' fierce."

"I'll go see," Christy said.

"Ain't no way yer a-crossin' that creek," Duggin said. "I'm her pa. I'm a-goin'."

"Duggin, you old coot," Bird's-Eye said. "Yer older than the hills. I'll go. 'Sides, yer drunker'n I am."

Duggin cocked his gun again. "Old coot, ya say?"

"Mr. Morrison," Christy said, pushing away the gun. "We don't have time for this."

Duggin hung his head. "Yer right. And so is Bird's-Eye, I'm afeared."

Bird's-Eye handed Duggin his gun. "Here goes nothin'," he said.

Slowly Bird's-Eye made his way across the raging creek.

Halfway across, the water came all the way to his chest.

"Careful, you mean old buzzard," Duggin called.

They watched as Bird's-Eye crawled back up the far bank and disappeared into the brush, where the cave was hidden.

"Mr. Morrison?" Christy said.

"Yep?"

"Are you the one who shaved Prince?"

The old man paused. "Naw. Jubal did that.

Me, I ain't never seen any point in pickin' on critters. It's men I got my feudin' with." He shrugged. "'Sides, I would never a done somethin' to hurt Ruby Mae that way."

"Maybe you should tell her that," Christy said. "When we find her."

"If'n we find her."

They heard Bird's-Eye's cry from the far bank.

"Ya think?" Duggin asked hopefully.

A moment later, the thick brush parted to reveal a sleepy-eyed Ruby Mae on Prince's back. Bird's-Eye came running out behind them.

"Sound asleep they was, in the cave, snorin' away just like you said!" he called.

"Miz Christy?" Ruby Mae yelled. "Pa? What're you doin' out here in the rain? You're soaked to the bone!"

"Come on, Ruby Mae," Bird's-Eye said, "yer goin' straight back to the mission, where you cain't get into any more trouble."

Christy looked over at Duggin. "Are we?" she asked. "Going back to the mission, I mean?"

Duggin nodded. "I reckon so."

He went to the edge of the bank, waiting for Bird's-Eye to return Ruby Mae safely. Christy thought she saw him wipe away a tear. Of course, she realized after a moment, it might just have been a drop of rain. After all, there was no telling what was going on in the hearts of these mountain men. Not long ago, they'd had her fearing for her life. Now, she didn't know whether to fear them, or pity them.

Maybe, she thought sadly, that's how it would always be.

— — —

Late that night, Christy sat by the fire in the mission house. Everyone had long since gone to bed. Only she and Doctor MacNeill were still awake.

"If only I hadn't left," the doctor said for the hundredth time. "None of this might ever have happened. If you hadn't sent David to fetch me, if the rain hadn't slowed down our return . . . "

"Ifs," Christy said as she watched the embers in the fireplace glow. "There's no point in doing this again, Neil. Everything turned out fine."

"This time," the doctor said darkly.

"I feel badly, too, actually," Christy admitted. "I wanted David to bring you back here because of your fever, but getting soaked in that rain couldn't have helped you any."

The doctor smiled. "Come to think of it, I am feeling a bit light-headed. Could be delirium setting in."

Christy reached over to feel his forehead. "You do feel hot."

"Strangest thing. I'm hearing music, too. Think I'm hallucinating?" He stood, grinning down at her, and reached out his hand. "You do still owe me a dance, you know."

"Now that you mention it," Christy said as she got to her feet, "I seem to be hearing music, too."

She gave a little curtsy and the doctor pulled her close, using his good arm. Together, they swept slowly around the parlor, dancing to the music of the rain drumming on the roof.

"I'm so glad you're all right," the doctor whispered.

Christy lay her head on his broad chest. Memories whirled in her mind—frightening memories. The doctor's blood-soaked shirt. The sound of the parlor window shattering. The cold muzzle of Bird's-Eye's gun between her shoulders.

She closed her eyes. The doctor was humming an old mountain tune. The fire crackled softly.

Slowly, one by one, other memories came to her. Miss Alice's graceful smile at her birthday party. Starlight, spilling over Prince's coat that night in the shed. Ruby Mae's musical laughter. Christy's class at recess, filled with high spirits and spring fever—filled with love for these beautiful, dangerous, complicated, God-given mountains.

The doctor paused. "What are you thinking?" he asked.

"I was thinking," Christy whispered, "that I don't want this dance to ever end."

The
Proposal

The Characters

CHRISTY RUDD HUDDLESTON, a nineteen-year-old girl.

CHRISTY'S STUDENTS:
    CREED ALLEN, age nine.
    LITTLE BURL ALLEN, age six.
    WANDA BECK, age eight.
    BESSIE COBURN, age twelve.
    LIZETTE HOLCOMBE, age fifteen.
    SAM HOUSTON HOLCOMBE, age nine.
    WRAIGHT HOLT, age seventeen.
    ZACHARIAS HOLT, age nine.
    VELLA HOLT, age five.
    SMITH O'TEALE, age fifteen.
    ORTER BALL O'TEALE, age eleven.
    MOUNTIE O'TEALE, age ten.
    RUBY MAE MORRISON, age thirteen.
    JOHN SPENCER, age fifteen.
    CLARA SPENCER, age twelve.
    LULU SPENCER, age six.
    LUNDY TAYLOR, age seventeen.

DAVID GRANTLAND, the young minister.
IDA GRANTLAND, David's sister.
MRS. MERCY GRANTLAND, mother of David and Ida.

FAIRLIGHT SPENCER, a mountain woman.
JEB SPENCER, her husband.
  (Parents of Christy's students John, Clara, and Lulu.)

DELIA JANE MANNING, a friend of David's from Richmond, Virginia.

PRINCE, black stallion donated to the mission.
GOLDIE, mare belonging to Miss Alice Henderson.

DR. NEIL MACNEILL, the physician of the Cove.

ALICE HENDERSON, a Quaker mission worker from Ardmore, Pennsylvania.

BEN PENTLAND, the mailman.

❧ One ❧

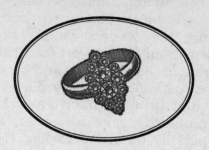

Miz Christy! I got a question to ask you! And it's a matter of life and death—yours!"

Christy Huddleston paused near the edge of Big Spoon Pond. Creed Allen, a nine-year-old who was one of her students at the Cutter Gap Mission school, dashed toward her.

"What is it, Creed?" Christy called. "The Reverend Grantland and I were just about to go for a boat ride."

Creed came to a stop, panting. "I know. That's what I got to ask you about."

"Actually, Creed," David Grantland said with an impatient roll of his dark eyes, "*I* have something to ask Miss Christy, too. Something very important."

Christy looked at David in surprise. Something in his expression sent a shiver through her of excitement mixed with uncertainty. Could it be . . . ?

David had arranged this special evening so carefully. He'd told Christy to dress up, so she'd worn her favorite yellow dress and braided daisies in her sun-streaked hair. David was wearing his Sunday best, and his dark hair was slicked back. They'd had a dinner picnic.

David had brought hand-picked flowers and a homemade cake his sister, Ida, had made especially for the occasion. He'd even brought a candle along in case it got dark. The sun was just now beginning to sink, sending a golden sheen over the pond.

Creed tugged on Christy's arm. His freckled face was tight with worry. "Please, Miz Christy. I need to talk to you, in private. It's for your own good, I reckon."

"David," Christy said, "would you mind giving Creed and me a moment of privacy?"

David sighed loudly. "Creed, do you understand that Miss Christy and I are in the middle of . . ." He hesitated, glancing at Christy. "Of . . . an appointment?"

"Appointment?" Christy teased. "Is that what this is, David?"

"Shucks, Preacher," Creed said apologetically. "I didn't know you was appointin'. I just figgered you was sweetheartin'."

Christy stifled a giggle as David's cheeks turned as red as the setting sun. "Tell me,

Creed," she said, taking the boy aside. "What brings you so far out of your way? What was it you wanted to know?"

"Well . . ." Creed tugged at a ragged overall strap. "It's like this. Can you swim?"

"Yes, I can. But why do you ask?"

Creed lowered his voice to a whisper. "See, me and Sam Houston saw the preacher out here after school, practicin' his boatin'. Now, the preacher's mighty fine at speechifyin', don't get me wrong, but he ain't no boatin' man." Creed glanced at David, then hung his head sadly. "It was like watchin' a hound try to strum a banjo. Just 'cause he tries hard don't mean the Lord meant it to be so."

"Thank you, Creed, for your concern," Christy said, trying very hard not to smile. "But I promise I'll be fine."

"That's a mighty tippy ol' rowboat."

"We are not going to tip over, Creed."

Creed did not look at all convinced.

"Now, you run along," Christy said. "I'll see you on Monday at school."

David was waiting by the boat impatiently. "What was it Creed wanted?"

"He was concerned about my well-being."

"As it happens," David said with a smile, "so am I."

He held out his arm. Christy lifted her long dress and stepped into the little wooden rowboat that belonged to the mission. David gave the boat a gentle push and leapt aboard. The boat rocked back and forth like a huge cradle. He fumbled with the oars for a moment, then settled into an uneven back-and-forth motion.

Christy trailed her hand in the water. The pond was still cold, although the air was surprisingly warm for May. She had only been in the Great Smoky Mountains of Tennessee for a few months, but already Christy had learned that the weather could be very unpredictable.

From far off, a mourning dove cooed its sweet, sad song. Beyond the pond, the mountains loomed—dark and vast, yet somehow comforting. David's oars sent red and gold ripples through the water.

"Sometimes I can't believe how beautiful it is here," Christy whispered. "Fairlight Spencer says it's like God's most perfect painting." Fairlight was Christy's closest friend in Cutter Gap.

David stopped rowing and stared intently at Christy. "Funny," he said softly, "sometimes I feel that way when I look at you, Christy." He reached into his pocket. "There's something I—" He pulled out a white envelope covered with delicate handwriting. "That's not what I was looking for," he muttered. "What *did* I do with that box?"

Christy cleared her throat nervously. Out here alone with David as the first faint stars began to glimmer, she felt very young and awkward. What if David really *was* planning on asking her to marry him? What would she say? She was only nineteen. And they'd only known each other a few months. Was she ready for such a life-changing commitment?

"Who's the letter from?" Christy asked.

"My mother," David said with a grin. "She's coming for a visit soon."

"That will be wonderful!" Christy exclaimed. "I can't wait to meet her."

"Don't be too sure." David gazed up at the darkening sky. "She's a little . . . well, interfering. Especially since my father passed on a couple years ago. She can be rather judgmental, I suppose. But she means well. You know what Ida's like."

Christy smiled. David's sister, Ida, was a stiff, no-nonsense type who took life very seriously.

"Mother's like Ida," David continued, "only she's more outspoken. And she has even higher standards."

"Standards?" Christy asked. "Such as?"

"Such as she thinks her only son should be preaching at a fine city church with velvet cushions on the pews. Not in a schoolhouse filled with people who spit tobacco during his sermons."

"My parents were the same way when I decided to come to Cutter Gap to teach," Christy recalled. "I tried to explain to them that I felt like I had a calling. That there was something I *needed* to do with my life."

"It's not just my work Mother's concerned about." He gave a soft laugh. "She even has a girl picked out for me."

"A girl?" Christy repeated.

"Delia Jane Manning," David said. He looked down at the water, as if he could see her image there. "Very prim, very well-bred. Very boring, too."

"Is she also very pretty?"

"Not to worry, Miss Huddleston. She couldn't hold a candle to you." He took a couple of quick strokes and the rowboat glided to the middle of the pond. It was dark now. The sliver of moon glimmered in the water like a lost smile.

"Did you have 'appointments' with this Miss Manning, too?" Christy teased.

"Oh, we went to some social events together from time to time. Delia loves the opera, the ballet, the theater. And she's a wonderful equestrian."

"That reminds me," Christy said. "Tomorrow you promised me my first jumping lesson on Prince." Prince, the mission's proud black stallion, was a recent donation to the mission.

Christy gave a little shrug. "Of course, it won't exactly be like riding with your friend Miss Manning."

"Thank goodness for that," David said

gently. He leaned closer and reached for Christy's hand. His fingers were trembling. Christy realized that she was trembling, too.

"You know what my mother thinks?" David said. "She thinks I wasn't too happy here at the mission until you came along. She thinks maybe you're the reason I'm staying here."

Christy took a deep breath. "Am I?" she whispered.

David smiled. "What do you think?" He reached into his pocket again and withdrew a small velvet box. Carefully he opened it. "This," he said, "was my great-great-grandmother's." He held out the box. The diamonds caught the moonlight and turned it into a thousand stars.

"Christy," David said, his voice barely audible above the breeze, "may I have your hand—" He stopped suddenly. "No. Wait. This is all wrong. I keep looking into those blue eyes of yours and forgetting all my careful plans." He laughed sheepishly. "I'll bet I've practiced this a hundred times."

Christy felt a strange sensation overtaking her. Dread, fear, joy—what *was* it she was feeling? David was about to ask her to marry him! What should she say? Did she love David? *Really* love him? How did you know such a thing?

Fairlight said love felt like your heart had sprouted wings. "It makes you all fluttery and light inside," she'd promised. Did Christy ever feel that way with David? Sometimes. On the other hand, she'd felt that way with Doctor MacNeill, too, and of *course* she didn't love him!

Most of the time, all she felt for Neil MacNeill was frustration; the man was so ornery. At least with David, there were no highs or lows. He was just a good, steady, reliable friend. Someone she could always count on.

David made her feel safe and secure. He shared Christy's values. And she had to admit he was very charming, not to mention good-looking. He was the kind of man Christy's mother would have called "a good catch." Wasn't he just the kind of man Christy wanted for a husband?

"David," Christy said. "I'm not sure—"

"Wait, wait," David said. He handed Christy the ring as he shifted his position. The boat began to rock. "I want to do this just right."

Awkwardly, David balanced on one knee. The boat seesawed, sending cold spray into Christy's face.

As she wiped it away, Christy noticed a dark figure walking along the edge of the pond. "Who could that be?"

"Hello!" came a familiar, deep voice.

"It's the doctor!" Christy cried.

David glanced over his shoulder. "Just my luck," he groaned. "Ignore him, Christy."

"I try to make a habit of it," she joked.

"I mean it. I have something important to say, and I intend to say it now, before I lose my nerve."

"Go ahead, David. I'm listening."

"Christy Rudd Huddleston—" David swallowed, "may I have your hand in marr—"

"How's the fishing, you two?" the doctor called.

David's eyes widened in rage. He clenched his fists, leapt up, and spun around. "Can't you see we're—" he began, but just then the boat began to sway wildly, taking on water with each rock.

Christy grabbed the sides of the rowboat. She watched David flail his arms as he tried to regain his balance. He looked so ridiculous that she began to laugh.

And she kept laughing even as the boat rocked wildly from side to side. Then suddenly the rowboat turned over, and she realized just how cold the water really was.

❧ Two ❧

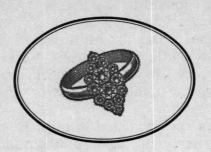

Well, well," said Doctor MacNeill as Christy and David struggled onto the shore. "Seems a little chilly for a swim, all things considered."

"We did *not* intend to swim," David muttered as he pulled off a shoe and emptied it of water. "And we wouldn't have had to, if you had just minded your own business!" He turned to Christy. "Are you all right?"

Christy plucked a wet daisy from her hair. Her beautiful dress hung like a wet blanket around her. Her hair was plastered to her face. Realizing what a pitiful sight she must be, she laughed again.

"I'm fine, David, really I am. And you have to admit—" she exchanged a grin with the doctor, "it *is* kind of funny, when you think about it!"

"Our perfect evening is ruined, the mission's

rowboat is submerged, and my only suit is soggy. Forgive me if I fail to see the humor in this."

"Perhaps I can help," Doctor MacNeill offered. "You see, the humor came in right around the time you went flying—"

"What were you doing here, anyway?" David interrupted. "Why aren't you off somewhere healing the sick?"

"I was out for an evening walk, actually," the doctor said. "I ran into Creed Allen awhile back, over past Turkey Ridge. He said he was worried you weren't quite seaworthy. As it turned out, he was right. I thought you were probably trout fishing—not that you'd find anything this time of year. But Creed explained to me you were *appointin'*."

David's mouth tightened into a line. The doctor smiled back with that charming, annoying half-grin of his.

This wasn't the first time Christy had seen the doctor and David at each other's throats. More than one person had told Christy it was because both men were interested in her. But she knew that wasn't the only reason David and Neil didn't get along. David was a young man of God, anxious to change the world. The doctor, on the other hand, had no use for religion. He was older and more cynical. But despite that, he had a charming sense of humor. When Christy was unhappy or confused, she could always count on the doctor to lift her spirits.

She grinned at the two men. David was tall and lean, with dark hair and wide-set brown eyes. The doctor was a big, burly man. His hair was always messy and his clothes were often wrinkled, as if he had better things to worry about. Most of the time, he did. He was the only doctor in the remote mountain cove.

"If you hadn't come along, this night would have been perfect," David seethed. "I had it all planned—"

"Planned?" the doctor interrupted. "Not much planning is needed for a fishing expedition this time of year." He winked at Christy. "I doubt anything was taking the bait. Or should I say anyone?"

Suddenly, Christy gasped. "Oh, no!" she cried. "No!" She grabbed David's arm. "David! The ring! Your great-great-grandmother's diamond ring! I must have dropped it!"

David closed his eyes. He took a deep breath before he spoke. At last he put his arm around Christy's shoulders. "Don't worry," he said wearily. "We'll find it."

"But how?"

"I don't know how. Somehow, it'll turn up. Come on. I'll take you back to the mission house. You'll catch your death out here." With one last glare at Doctor MacNeill, he led Christy away.

As they left, Christy could hear the doctor chuckling behind them. "Diamond ring, eh?" he said. "Strangest bait I ever heard of. Whatever happened to worms?"

— — —

Christy sat on the mission steps the next morning. A dozen children were gathered around her. It was Saturday, and usually the children would have been helping their parents with chores. But word had spread quickly about the reverend's lost diamond ring. Ruby Mae Morrison, a talkative thirteen-year-old who lived at the mission house, had seen to that.

"For sure and certain one of us can find it," Creed vowed. "And the boat, too, like as not."

"That pond's pretty deep, isn't it?" Christy asked doubtfully.

"Nope," said Sam Houston Holcombe, a blond-haired nine-year-old. "Deepest part's maybe seven, eight feet tops."

"Trouble is, the muddy bottom," Ruby Mae said, curling a finger around a lock of red hair thoughtfully. "That ring could be buried. It's soft down there, and squishy-like."

"We'll go a-divin'!" Creed exclaimed. "It's purt-near summer warm today."

"Well, be very careful," Christy warned. "I don't want anyone going near the water who

141

can't swim well." She paused. "Tell you what. I'll give a reward to the person who finds that ring."

"W—what's a re-ward, Teacher?" asked Mountie O'Teale. The shy ten-year-old was overcoming a speech problem with Christy's help.

"It's a present, in a way. A gift for doing something. How about my copy of *Huckleberry Finn*?"

"That would make a right smart re-ward," said Orter Ball, Mountie's older brother. "Even if'n we can't read it all."

"I'll help you with the hard parts," Christy said. Creed nudged Sam Houston.

"Race ya," he said, and a moment later the whole group was rushing for the pond.

Behind Christy, the front door of the mission house opened and Miss Alice Henderson joined her on the porch. "Beautiful morning, isn't it, Miss Alice?" Christy said.

Alice Henderson was a Quaker mission worker from Pennsylvania who had helped start the mission school. She was loved and respected in Cutter Gap and the communities around it. She had a calm, gentle way about her, but she was strong as the old oaks in the mission yard.

"There's an old saying," Miss Alice said, patting Christy on the shoulder. "'There are no accidents.'"

"What do you mean?" Christy asked.

"Losing David's ring that way." Miss Alice gave a knowing smile. "Perhaps it wasn't entirely an accident?"

"Of course it was! David rocked the boat, and it overturned, and that was that."

Miss Alice walked down the steps and examined the buds on a forsythia bush. "I wonder," she said softly, "what you planned to say to David, if you hadn't been so rudely interrupted?"

"Well," Christy said, "I would have told him I was very flattered, and that I cared for him very deeply, and—" She met Miss Alice's deep-set eyes. "And I'd love to stay and talk, Miss Alice, but I have a riding lesson planned. David's teaching me to take Prince over jumps."

"I'll let you off the hook, then," Miss Alice said as Christy started for the pasture. "Just be careful, Christy. Don't take on more than you're ready for."

Christy paused. "Are you talking about riding? Or my romantic life?"

"Both." Miss Alice smiled. "As dangerous as riding can be, romance can be far more painful."

❧ Three ❧

Well, it's good to see you nice and dry again," David called as he trotted across the field on Prince.

Christy laughed. "Maybe next time we should stick to dry land."

"Does that mean you intend for there to be a next time?" David dismounted gracefully and reached for Christy's hand. "I never did get an answer to my question, Christy."

Christy pulled her hand away, tucking a stray piece of hair behind her ear. "Actually, I don't think you ever finished your question."

David hesitated. "Somehow, this doesn't seem like quite the right time or place—" He was interrupted by a loud, impatient snort from Prince.

"Prince seems to agree," Christy said. She stroked the black stallion's silky mane. "I guess he's anxious for our lesson to start."

"I suppose it can wait. Besides, it's hard to propose without a ring."

"I'm so sorry about that, David. I feel like it's all my fault."

"Don't be silly. I'm the one who tipped the boat."

"Some of the children are diving for the ring right now. I said I'd give them a reward if they found it. A copy of *Huckleberry Finn*."

"It's worth more than that in sentimental value alone," David said grimly.

"I know." Christy patted his back. "But it's bound to turn up. The pond's pretty shallow."

David helped Christy into the saddle and she settled into place. She'd learned to ride as a little girl, but that was always sidesaddle, on gentle, well-trained horses. Since the mission had acquired Prince, Christy had become determined to improve her riding skills. She still felt strange, riding like the men did. But after watching Ruby Mae win a recent horse race, Christy had realized that she could never control a powerful stallion like Prince while riding sidesaddle.

To make things easier, Christy had cut one of her skirts down the middle, then sewn up the split to make what amounted to a pair of very loose trousers. She felt very daring wearing them. Back home in Asheville, North Carolina, they would have caused a scandal. But here in the Tennessee mountains, women often wore men's trousers—for practical reasons, or because they were so poor they simply wore whatever they could get their hands on.

"All right," David called, "let's start by getting warmed up. Take him around the field a few times at an easy trot."

Christy gave Prince a gentle nudge. He responded instantly, trotting her around the field in graceful arcs. He was such a powerful animal, she couldn't help being a little afraid. But she reminded herself that if her students could ride this way, so could she. Besides, jumping was a skill that could come in handy here in the mountains. When she was tending to the sick, Miss Alice often rode her horse, Goldie, to remote areas. Knowing how to take small jumps was important, since there were plenty of creeks and downed trees to get around.

"How about a gallop?" David suggested.

Prince obliged by flying across the field. Christy's heart leapt at his speed. But once she let herself relax into the rolling movement of Prince's gait, she felt thrilled. She smiled at David as she passed him. He was watching her with that look he so often had around her—part admiration, part affection, part confusion.

Suddenly she recalled Miss Alice's question. What *would* Christy have said, if things had turned out differently last night? She imagined saying the words. *Yes, David, I accept your proposal.* She imagined walking down the aisle of the mission church wearing a long white dress—maybe her mother's wedding dress. *And do you, Christy Rudd Huddleston, take this man to be your lawfully wedded husband?*

"Miz Christy!"

Christy turned in her saddle. Creed and Ruby Mae and several other students had gathered by the fence. Their torn, oversized clothes were soaking wet, and their hair hung in damp strings.

"Any luck?" Christy called.

"Nope," Creed reported as Prince came to a stop near the fence. "Not a lick."

"It's awful muddy, Miz Christy," Sam Houston added as he tried to wring out his overalls. "Like tryin' to find a needle in a haystack."

"We'll keep a-lookin', though," Creed vowed. "We just come on over to see your jumpin' lesson."

"Ain't he just the nicest horse you ever laid eyes on, Miz Christy?" Ruby Mae asked as she perched on the fence. She leaned over and planted a big kiss on Prince's muzzle.

"Aw, don't go a-slobberin' all over a fine animal such as that," Creed moaned.

"He's a-goin' to need a bath for sure now," Sam Houston agreed.

With a laugh, Christy nudged Prince back

into a trot. In the center of the field, David had positioned a small jump made of two crossed pine logs.

"Now, the important thing to remember about jumping is that you don't want to get in the way of the horse," David instructed. "Let him do all the work. You're just the passenger."

Christy smiled. "Easy for you to say."

"Hey, I'm not exactly the world's greatest equestrian—"

"No," Christy interrupted, "Delia is."

"I hope the fact that you're bringing her up can be interpreted as a sign of jealousy."

"I just have a very good memory," Christy replied.

"The point is, I'm just telling you the basics."

"That's all I need," Christy said. "Enough to get around these mountains when I have to."

"What I want you to do is take Prince around the field again, nice and easy. Then get a good, straight-on approach to this jump, lean forward, and give Prince lots of rein. He'll do the rest."

Christy took a deep breath. Suddenly, this did not seem like such a good idea. She could see herself tumbling off Prince, doing endless somersaults all the way back to the mission house. It could be very humiliating. Not to mention painful.

"Don't worry, Miz Christy," Ruby Mae called. "It ain't hard, I promise."

On the other hand, it could be equally humiliating to fail at something so simple—something most of her students had been doing since they could walk.

"You won't fall," David said. "I'm looking out for you."

With a grim smile, Christy took Prince around the field. The children applauded as she passed them. "Pretend you're a-flyin'!" Ruby Mae called, and Christy took her advice. She took a deep breath, then another, as Prince approached the little jump.

"Give him rein!" David called.

Suddenly they were there. For a split second, the sound of Prince's thundering hooves vanished, and all Christy could hear was the whoosh of air as they soared over the logs.

The landing was harder. Christy had to grab a handful of mane for extra support. But as she turned back to see David's proud smile, she realized that she'd actually managed her first, official jump.

Ruby Mae let out an ear-splitting whistle. "Atta girl, Miz Christy!"

Christy slowed Prince to a walk. "Well, Teacher?" she asked David.

"Nice work. Very nice. Want to try again?"

Christy nodded. With one jump under her belt, she felt certain the next one would be easier. Again she took Prince around the field. As she neared the children, they applauded.

"You two just flew like a big bird right over that jump!" Ruby Mae called.

Christy waved, then set her eyes on the logs. This wasn't so bad, after all. Her fears seemed silly now. Maybe she would take it a little faster this time—

Suddenly, Prince let out a horrified whinny of protest. He reared back on his hind legs as Christy clung to the saddle, desperately trying to hang on.

"Snake!" one of the children screamed. "Prince is spooked!"

"Hang on, Miz Christy!" Ruby Mae cried, but already Christy could feel her grip slipping.

David was running toward her. "Hang on!" he cried.

"I'm . . . I'm trying," Christy managed. She could sense the huge horse's terrible fear.

Prince lowered his front legs for a moment, and Christy caught a glimpse of a black snake sliding out from a nearby rock. It was just a harmless little black snake, but Prince didn't know that. He let out another terrified, anguished whinny. Again he reared back with even more force, and this time Christy could not hold on.

As she went flying backward through the air, she heard Ruby Mae's screams and David's cries, and then suddenly the world went completely black.

❧ Four ❧

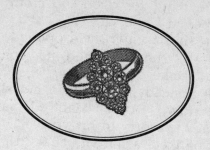

Is she a-comin' to?"

"*She's movin' some. That be a good sign, don't it, Doctor?*"

"*That's some bump Teacher's got on her head, ain't it?*"

"*Christy? Can you hear me?*"

Christy tried to focus on the voices floating through her head. Was that Doctor MacNeill's voice she'd heard?

"Christy? It's Neil. Don't try to move too suddenly. You took quite a spill. You've been unconscious for the last hour or so."

Christy moved toward the sound of his voice. Pain ripped through her head. Her left temple felt raw.

She tried to open her eyes, but there was something covering them—something cool and moist. She reached to touch it.

"That's a cold cloth, dear." It was Miss Alice. "To help keep down the swelling."

A gentle hand removed the cloth. Slowly Christy opened her eyes.

At least, she *thought* she'd opened them.

"The cloth," she whispered, her voice filled with panic, "take off the—"

She felt a steadying hand on her shoulder. "Be still, now," Doctor MacNeill said. She could hear the worry in his voice.

Christy blinked, again and again. Up, down, up, down. There was no difference.

"I can't see!" she cried in terror. She lurched upright and reached out her hands. Where were all her friends? Their voices were so close, but where were *they*?

Her right hand landed on a shoulder, and a warm, strong hand grabbed her fingers. "Don't panic," came the doctor's soothing voice.

"Of course she's panicked." It was David. He sounded frantic. "What's happened to her, Doctor?"

"Calm down, Reverend. It's probably just temporary." The doctor's voice grew softer. "You took a nasty spill off that horse, Christy. Lie back down now, and let me take a look."

Reluctantly, Christy let herself be lowered back down to her pillow.

"Cain't she see nothin' a-tall?"

Christy recognized the little whispered voice as Mountie's. The children were probably just as terrified as she was.

"I'm fine, Mountie," Christy said, forcing cheer into her voice. She reached out her hand and Mountie grabbed it.

"You sure, Teacher?" Mountie whispered.

"Isn't Doctor MacNeill the best doctor in Cutter Gap?" Christy asked.

"Well, I reckon," Mountie said. "Course he's the *only* doctor."

"Come on, children," Miss Alice said firmly. "Let's let the doctor do his job."

"But what if she needs us?" Creed asked.

"She won't be needing you any time soon," the doctor said irritably.

Christy winced at his tone. "You go on, children. See if you can find that ring for me, all right?"

As the children were leaving, Christy lowered her voice. "Tell me the truth, Neil. Why can't I see?"

"First let's decide just how much you can't see. How many fingers am I holding up?"

Christy gazed straight ahead. Her head throbbed. She saw nothing but a vast dark mist. "Thirteen?"

"In other words, you can see nothing."

"It's just emptiness. Like a dark, foggy night."

The doctor sighed deeply. Christy heard some whispering and shuffling, followed by sounds she couldn't quite identify. Fresh air rushed past. Someone had opened the windows in her room.

A few moments later, the doctor returned to her bedside. "I want you to turn your head and body just slightly to the right. Do you see anything?"

Christy did as he instructed. Every inch of movement caused a sharp stab of pain to her temple. She waited. The room was hushed. She could feel the gentle touch of the early afternoon sun on her arms.

She could *feel* its brightness. But she could not see it.

"Nothing," she admitted at last.

Again, the long sigh. "All right, then," said the doctor. "One more thing."

She heard him moving. She could tell he was close by the sweet smell of his tobacco. In the background she heard footsteps marching back and forth, back and forth. Was that David, pacing?

"Look straight ahead for me," the doctor instructed.

Christy did. Darkness stretched before her like a black quilt.

She waited, and then the sharp smell of kerosene met her nose. On one edge of the darkness, something changed. It was as if she were seeing the first faint glimmerings of dawn.

"Anything?" the doctor asked in a calm, steady voice.

"It's . . . it's as if the sun is coming up,"

Christy began. "No, not that strong. But I saw something. Movement, light . . . *something*."

"Then she'll see again!" David cried.

"Not so fast, Reverend," the doctor said. "It's a good sign, but that's all. Just a sign."

"The doctor was moving a lantern very close to your eyes," said Miss Alice. "That was the light you perceived."

"What does that mean?" Christy asked, almost afraid to hope.

Doctor MacNeill took her hand. "Here's what we know, Christy. And I'm no eye specialist, mind you. You've taken a bad fall. When Prince threw you, you hit your head on a sharp rock. There's a lot of damage to the eye and temple area—cuts, bruises, that sort of thing. But that doesn't explain the loss of sight. That could be caused by swelling from your concussion. There may be pressure on the optic nerve."

"So when the swelling goes down," David interrupted, "then she'll be able to see again?"

"Could be," the doctor said cautiously. "But the swelling may have caused permanent damage. We can only wait and hope. I've only seen a couple other cases like this. And they didn't . . . well, they didn't turn out well."

Silence fell. Christy let the words sink in, one by one.

The swelling may have caused permanent

damage. Permanent damage meant she might be blind.

Blind. Forever.

"Meantime," the doctor continued, "I'm going to bandage up those cuts around your eyes and temple to keep them from getting infected." He paused. "Is there a lot of pain?"

Christy smiled. "Yes. In my hand, actually. You're squeezing it too hard."

"Sorry about that."

"How long . . . how long till we know something?" Christy asked. "For sure, I mean."

"It's hard to say. A few weeks, most likely. Maybe even sooner."

"There must be something we can do!" David exploded.

"There is, David," Miss Alice said gently. "We can pray."

"I'm not a praying man myself," the doctor said. "But if I were, now would be the time I'd try it."

The others left while Doctor MacNeill bandaged Christy's eyes.

"Neil?" she asked in a whisper when he was done. "One thing. I was just wondering . . . is it all right if I—"

"What?"

Christy let out a soft sob.

Doctor MacNeill touched her hair tenderly. "It's all right," he said, his voice breaking. "You go right ahead and cry."

❧ Five ❧

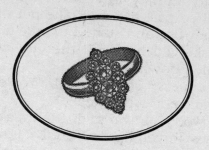

May I come in?"

At the sound of David's voice, Christy stirred. The world was black. She tried to open her eyes, but something heavy made it impossible. Her head stung as she sat up. Gingerly she touched the thick cotton bandages Doctor MacNeill had placed around her head.

"It's me. David."

"I know. I can still hear," Christy snapped. Then, her voice softening, she added, "I'm sorry, David. I didn't mean to sound that way."

"You have every right to sound that way," David said. Christy heard the sound of dishes on a tray. The scent of peppermint tea drifted past.

"Ida fixed you a tray," David explained. "I'll put it here, on your nightstand."

"I'm starving. Tell Miss Ida thanks."

"Here. I'll hand you the cup." David placed the steaming cup of tea into Christy's hands.

Carefully Christy lifted the cup. The hot steam drifted past her chin. She put the china edge to her lips and started to take a sip, but she'd misjudged how full the cup was. Hot tea dribbled down her chin.

"What a mess," she groaned. "You'd think I could manage a cup of tea!"

"Don't worry," David said. "Here's a napkin."

Christy's lower lip quivered. "It's such a simple thing," she said. "Drinking a cup of tea. You never even give it a second thought, but now . . ."

"No use crying over spilled tea," David tried to joke.

"How am I ever going to do all the things I used to do?" Christy asked, trying not to sob. "Teaching, for example. How can I manage the children? I can't even drink a cup of tea. How can I grade a paper or write on the blackboard?"

David was silent for a moment. "The truth is, I don't know, Christy. But if anyone can do it, you can."

"You have more faith in me than I do," she replied.

"I feel so . . ." David took a ragged breath. "This is all my fault, Christy. I was the one who was teaching you to jump. I was the one who promised you nothing would happen."

Christy could hear the pain in his voice. "David, that's crazy. Prince saw a snake. He threw me. That's all. It wasn't your fault in any way."

"There's something I have to say to you," David said. He cleared his throat. "I know this isn't the right time, and I know you probably can't answer me. But I still want you to marry me, Christy. With all my heart I want that. Nothing's changed."

"Oh, David," Christy whispered, "*everything's* changed."

"I love you, Christy Huddleston. I love your good heart and your spirit and the way you laugh. It doesn't matter to me one whit whether you can see or not." He gave a soft laugh. "Truth is, it might be an advantage. I'm not the handsomest catch in the world, after all."

"I have the feeling a lot of women would disagree with that."

"So?"

Christy fingered the edge of her blanket. "David, I need time. Time to think about everything that's happened, and time to sort out my feelings—"

"You're not sure how you feel about me, then?"

"I'm not sure how I feel about *any*thing," Christy said lightly.

"Is there . . . someone else?"

"You know there's no one else."

"Well, I hope not, but you never know. Sometimes I wonder if the Doctor . . ." David's voice trailed off.

"David, please. Neil MacNeill is the most aggravating man I've ever known. He's pig-headed and arrogant and—" Christy stopped herself. "Well, you needn't worry there."

"Good," David said, but he didn't sound entirely convinced. "Well, anyway. I'll give you all the time you need, Christy. I just wanted you to know that my offer stands—ring or no ring."

"You never know. Miracles do happen. Maybe the ring will show up," said Christy.

"Miracles *do* happen. You remember that, all right?"

Christy heard a soft knock at the door, then a familiar voice. "How's the patient?" Miss Alice asked.

"The patient's turning out to be quite a slob," Christy said. "I can't even drink a cup of tea without it turning into a disaster."

"I should let the patient get some rest." David leaned down and kissed Christy on her cheek. "Sleep well."

When he was gone, Miss Alice sat on the edge of Christy's bed. She smelled of pine and balsam and fresh air, as if she'd brought the mountains straight into Christy's bedroom.

Christy had always found it calming to be in Miss Alice's presence. She had such a sense of serenity and grace about her. But tonight, as the dark pressed in on Christy, she felt as if no one could console her—not even Miss Alice.

"Is there anything I can bring you?" Miss Alice asked.

"Some light would be nice."

Miss Alice laughed gently. She reached over toward Christy's nightstand, then took Christy's hand.

Christy recognized the soft leather binding. "My Bible."

"You asked for light. And there it is."

Her tone was both soothing and direct, as it always was. There was no hint of pity. Somehow, knowing that Miss Alice did not intend to treat her any differently reassured Christy.

"Miss Alice," Christy asked, "why did this have to happen now? To me?"

"You're not the first to have her strength tested. And you won't be the last."

"I know that." Christy swallowed back a sob. "But I feel like I was just starting to develop a relationship with the children, to get them to trust an outsider. Now all that's ruined. There was so much I wanted to do here."

"So do it."

"But . . . but I can't! Not now. Not this way."

"Why not?"

The question was so blunt, Christy paused. *Why not?* Wasn't it obvious? How could Miss Alice be so cruel?

"Because I'm blind!" Christy blurted. "Because I may be blind forever, Miss Alice!"

Her words echoed in the little room. Miss Alice sat calmly and quietly. Quakers were fond of silences. They were as much a part of Miss Alice's conversations as words.

"There are many teachers," Miss Alice said at last, "who would look at the one-room schoolhouse in which you teach, and the sixty-seven children, and the poverty and superstition and ignorance, and they would say they could never teach with such handicaps. They would tell you it was impossible. You, of course, did not look at the situation that way. Some see a glass as half-empty. Others see it as half-full."

"But to teach without being able to see . . ." Christy gave a shuddering sigh. "I can get by without paper or pencils. I can't get by without sight."

"You may not be able to teach in the same way," Miss Alice said. "And you most certainly will have to learn to rely on others for help. But then, we all must ask for help from time to time."

"I can't do it," Christy whispered. "I just know I'll never teach again."

"Perhaps not right away. But you will

teach again, when you are ready. The Lord does not give us more than we can handle, Christy." With a gentle hug, Miss Alice left the room.

Christy ran her fingers over her Bible as Miss Alice's words lingered in her ears. Blind, she wasn't going to be the same person she'd been. Miss Alice was wrong. There was no way that Christy could ever teach again.

What would she do instead? She could go home. Back to safe, secure Asheville, where her parents would take care of her. But then what? What would she do with her life? She thought back to that day last summer at the church retreat where she'd first heard about the need for teachers in the Great Smoky Mountains. Something deep in her heart had told her that she'd found the place where she belonged. Teaching here in Cutter Gap, she'd felt certain, was her calling. But how could it be now?

Christy fumbled for her nightstand. She nearly knocked over her plate of untouched toast before her hand grazed her little diary. Her pen was tucked inside. It took several more minutes for her to find her inkpot and prepare to write. At last the diary was perched on her lap. She opened to the last page she'd written in, marked with a silk ribbon. At the top of the page, she began to write. Each letter she wrote with great care, slowly and evenly, imagining the lines and curves in her mind. She felt like one of her students practicing penmanship.

Saturday, May 4, 1912

The Lord does not give us more than

we can handle.

Christy paused, her head tilted down, her bandaged eyes aimed toward words she could not see. She tried to make them come alive on the page. She tried to hear Miss Alice's confident tone as she'd spoken them. But in her heart, Christy knew that they were smudged scribblings, and nothing more.

❧ Six ❧

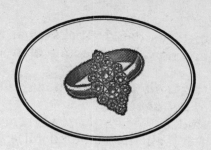

"Miz Christy! What are you doing out of bed?" Christy was dressed and sitting on the edge of the bed combing her hair.

"It's Sunday morning, Ruby Mae," Christy said calmly. "I'm getting ready for church."

Christy heard the clatter of dishes. The smoky scent of bacon filled the room. Ruby Mae must have brought up a breakfast tray. Well, that was very thoughtful. But Christy intended to eat downstairs in the dining room, just like she always did. She could at least manage that much.

"Did I hear you right? Did you say church, Miz Christy?"

"Yes. Church. You remember—sermons, hymns, prayers?"

The bed bounced as Ruby Mae plopped down near Christy. "I don't see how you can go to church," Ruby Mae said earnestly. "I mean, seein' as how you're in a cap that's dated."

"I'm *what*?"

"In a cap that's dated. That's what Miz Ida says you are now. On account of not seein' nothin'."

Christy thought for a moment. "Oh! You mean *incapacitated*."

"Like I said."

"Well, if it's all the same to Miss Ida, I'll decide what I can and cannot do. And I'm going to have breakfast downstairs, then go to church. After all, I got dressed all by myself this morning. It took nearly a half-hour, but I did it." Christy stood. "As you can see, I'm ready."

"Well . . ." Ruby Mae hesitated. "I don't mean to be a botheration, Miz Christy. But you ain't *exactly* ready."

"Why? What's wrong?"

"Well, to begin with, your skirt's all turned which-a-ways. And your colors are kinda . . . colorful."

"You mean they don't match?"

"I guess that all depends. I mean, the colors in a rainbow don't rightly match up, neither. But when you look at them together-like, it's a heap of purtiness just the same."

Christy dropped onto the bed with a sigh. She'd awakened this morning feeling determined to make the best of things. But what could she possibly accomplish in this world if she couldn't even manage to get dressed by herself?

"Don't you worry yourself none, Miz Christy," Ruby Mae said firmly. "I'll git you fixed up as purty as a spring rose."

"Thanks, Ruby Mae. I guess I need more help than I thought."

Ruby Mae bustled about the room. "Now, I ain't no fashionable city-gal, but I figger these look church-right." She placed a pile of clothes in Christy's lap.

"Thanks," Christy said quietly, wondering if she should trust Ruby Mae's fashion tastes. "When I've changed, will you help me down the stairs so I can have breakfast?"

"Yes'm." A long silence followed. Somehow, Christy could feel Ruby Mae's intense dark gaze on her.

"Miz Christy?" Ruby Mae said at last. "Can I ask you somethin'? Somethin' personal-like?"

"Of course."

"What's it like? Bein' blind, I mean?"

"I'm not blind, Ruby Mae," Christy said sharply. She took a deep breath. "What I mean is, I'm not sure that this is permanent. Doctor MacNeill says that when the swelling goes down, I may be as good as new."

Ruby Mae reached for Christy's hand and gave it a shy squeeze. "I hope so, Miz Christy.

Truly I do. And I'm sorry I asked such a fool question."

"It wasn't foolish, Ruby Mae. The truth is, it's hard to describe what it's like not to see. You know how it is when you look down the well in the mission yard? How the dark just seems to go on and on forever? It's like that, a little."

"Lookin' down that well gives me the cold shivers."

Christy sighed. "Me, too," she said softly.

A few minutes later, Ruby Mae led Christy down the stairs. Even holding onto Ruby Mae's arm, every step felt like a gamble. It was like walking off a cliff while wearing a blindfold. Being so helpless was a strange and awful feeling. Christy was Ruby Mae's teacher. Yet here she was, being dressed and guided by her thirteen-year-old student.

At the bottom of the stairs, Christy heard the clink of silverware. The sharp smell of coffee wafted past.

"Christy!" Miss Alice exclaimed from the direction of the dining room. "How wonderful to see you, dear." A moment later, she was at Christy's side, helping her to the table. "Do you feel up to this?"

"I'm fine, really I am," Christy insisted as she sat down in her usual spot.

"She got dressed all by herself," Ruby Mae announced.

Christy fumbled for her napkin. "Actually, I required a little fashion advice."

"Are you sure you should be up so soon?" David asked.

"I fixed a fine breakfast tray," Miss Ida said. "It doesn't seem right, you walking around like this."

"Would you all stop fussing?" Christy demanded. "I'm having breakfast, that's all. It's not like I'm trying to climb Mount Everest, or—" she paused, "or teach school."

"Christy's right," Miss Alice said. "It's her decision."

A chair scraped on the wooden floor. "I'll start another plate of eggs," Miss Ida said.

"I'm sorry to be such a bother," Christy apologized.

"Not at all," Miss Ida said, putting a comforting hand on Christy's shoulder. "Anything I can do, you just ask."

It was all Christy could do to keep from crying. Miss Ida was usually so gruff! The pity in her voice was almost more than Christy could bear. But perhaps she was going to have to get used to the pity of others.

Breakfast was an ordeal. Christy insisted on doing everything herself, which meant that half her scrambled eggs ended up in her lap. She was only slightly more successful with her toast.

She was almost done eating when Doctor MacNeill entered the mission house. "What on earth are you doing out of bed?" he demanded as he strode into the dining room.

"Making a huge mess of the breakfast table," Christy replied.

"I want you to go straight back up to your room," the doctor said, sounding furious. He knelt beside Christy and examined her bandages. "Any dizziness? Nausea?"

"I feel perfectly fine."

"Pain?"

"My head still hurts some. But not much, I promise." Christy crossed her arms over her chest. "And there's no use arguing with me, Neil. I am going to church."

"I can't allow that," the doctor said. "You've had too much trauma. You need to rest for several days."

"You look like *you* need to rest, Neil," Miss Alice said. "You may not have heard, but there's a new-fangled idea floating around these parts. We call it 'sleep.'"

"I was up all night reading medical books." Doctor MacNeill pulled up a chair. "I was hoping . . . well, I just wanted to be sure there wasn't anything I'd missed."

"What did you find out?" Christy asked as she struggled to locate her glass of juice.

"There are cases of sight recovery after concussion. And then there are other cases . . ." The doctor's voice trailed off. "We'll just have to wait and see," he said simply.

"And pray," David added.

"Thank you, Neil," Christy said. "Thank you for trying. Now go home and get some sleep."

"That is, unless you'd care to join us in church, Doctor," David said. "There's always room for one more."

"Not for a wayward soul like me," the doctor said. "I can't talk you out of this, Christy?"

"I need to go, Neil. I can't explain it. I just know I'll feel better there."

"Well, I can see I'm outnumbered." The doctor pushed back his chair. "I'll check on you again soon."

"I'll keep an eye on her," Miss Alice said.

"And tomorrow at school, I'll watch out for her like a mama hen with her chicks," Ruby Mae vowed.

David cleared his throat. No one spoke. Someone—Miss Ida, probably—began clearing up the dishes, one by one.

Christy knew what they were thinking—there wasn't going to be school tomorrow, at least not with Christy teaching.

"Why's everybody so all-fired tongue-tied all of a sudden?" Ruby Mae demanded.

"We're going to have to wait and see about school, Ruby Mae," David explained.

"Christy is in no condition to teach," the doctor added.

Again, Christy felt the pity flowing around her, tugging at her like an ocean current. It was as if, in the space of one terrible moment, she'd lost the person she was. She wasn't Miss Christy Huddleston, teacher, anymore. She was just another helpless somebody to whisper about.

Who could blame them? The truth was, she felt sorry for herself, too.

She started to sob. Just as she pushed back her chair to leave, she heard someone knocking at the mission's front door. "Preacher?" someone called. "It's Ben Pentland."

"Mr. Pentland!" David exclaimed. "Is this about the service today? Or have you taken to delivering mail on Sundays?"

"It ain't mail I be deliverin'. I done brought you a visitor—"

"And I must say it was the most uncomfortable buggy ride of my life!" came a high-pitched, woman's voice.

"Mother?" David cried.

"David, sweetie pie!"

℘ Seven ℘

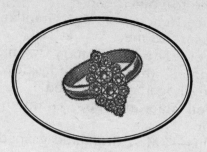

Christy heard the swish of petticoats as Mrs. Grantland rushed to embrace David.

"*Sweetie*-pie?" Doctor MacNeill whispered loudly.

"But I thought you weren't coming until next week!" David said, sounding a little shocked.

"I changed plans. I knew you wouldn't mind," Mrs. Grantland said briskly.

"Well, welcome to our humble abode," David said.

"Humble, indeed! I've seen outhouses with more style." Mrs. Grantland clapped her hands. "Ida, dear girl, come here and give your mother a kiss."

"It's good to see you, Mother," Miss Ida said.

"What have you done to yourselves? You

both look positively rural." Mrs. Grantland clucked her tongue. "Aren't you going to introduce me to your friends?"

"I'm Alice Henderson, Mrs. Grantland. It's a great pleasure to meet you at last."

"Oh, yes. The missionary woman from Pennsylvania," Mrs. Grantland said. She did not sound altogether impressed.

"I'm Neil MacNeill, Mrs. Grantland," said the doctor.

"And this—" Mrs. Grantland gasped. "Don't tell me this is Miss Huddleston, the one you've written me so much about?"

"Oh, no'm. I'm Ruby Mae Morrison."

Mrs. Grantland gave a relieved sigh. "Ah, yes. David mentioned you in his letters."

"Proud to meet you," Ruby Mae said. "I never rightly figgered the preacher *had* a mama. But I guess everybody does, even preachers—"

"Yes, well, delighted to meet you," Mrs. Grantland interrupted. "And who might this unfortunate soul be?"

Christy realized with a start that Mrs. Grantland must be referring to her.

"This," David said, "is Christy Huddleston, Mother."

Christy extended her hand out into the air, but Mrs. Grantland didn't take it. "It's nice to meet you, Mrs. Grantland. David's told me so much about you."

"Is she *blind*?" Mrs. Grantland asked David, as if Christy were deaf as well.

"Christy had an accident, Mother," David said tensely. "She can't see, but we're all praying that it's just temporary."

"Oh, my. Poor dear. What a shame."

Christy felt a hand patting her on the head. Suddenly she felt the need for air. "We were just on our way to church, Mrs. Grantland," she said as she stood. "Will you be joining us?"

"I was hoping to freshen up first. Not that it would matter much here," Mrs. Grantland added with a dry laugh. "The church—would that be the wooden building I noticed on the way in?"

"It's the schoolhouse as well," Miss Alice said. "David built most of it himself, from the ground up."

"He always was a talented boy."

"Indeed," the doctor muttered under his breath.

Mr. Pentland cleared his throat. "There's a couple big trunks out yonder."

"I'll help you with them," David volunteered.

"Me, too," Ida said.

"I'd better supervise." Mrs. Grantland rushed off, skirts swishing.

"Is she gone?" Christy asked in a whisper.

"Yep," Doctor MacNeill said in a low voice. "She's not one to mince words, is she?"

"David warned us she could be rather blunt," Miss Alice said. "Now I see what he meant. Of course, she's probably very tired after her long trip."

"I thought she was kinda mean about Miz Christy and all," Ruby Mae said.

Christy sighed. "I could use a little fresh air. Doctor, would you mind escorting me over to the church?"

"As long as you don't ask me to stay," the doctor joked.

Christy took his arm and they headed out into the sunshine. She could hear Mrs. Grantland's voice on the far side of the mission house, directing David to be careful with her bags. She could hear the squeak of the springs in Mr. Pentland's wagon, and the babble of the mockingbirds in the nearby oak tree.

Christy paused near a stand of pines. She rested her hand on one of the trees and held up her head toward the sun. "Do you think I'll ever see the sky again, Neil?" she whispered.

"I hope so, Christy. With all my heart, I hope so."

They stood for a moment, arms linked. Mrs. Grantland's harsh voice floated over the breeze.

You can't possibly be thinking of marrying her now, David.

Christy clutched Doctor MacNeill's arm tighter. "She's talking about me!"

"Come on," he said. "You don't need to be hearing this."

But Christy stood firm. She could hear David replying in hushed tones. Then she heard Mrs. Grantland again.

But she's blind, David. What kind of a wife would a blind woman make?

Christy's heart seemed to stop. Mrs. Grantland was right, of course. What kind of wife would Christy make now? What kind of teacher? What kind of *person*?

Miss Alice had been wrong to encourage Christy last night. She'd just been trying to be kind. Mrs. Grantland was only saying what everyone else was thinking.

Doctor MacNeill pulled Christy along toward the church. "Ignorant old crow," he muttered. "You'd make a fine wife for any man. I hope you know that." He gave a short laugh. "Well, not *any* man. Not the Reverend, certainly."

"And why not David?"

"You're a fine woman, Christy. You don't have to settle for less. Remember that when you answer the Reverend. Don't make a choice you'll regret the rest of your life because . . . because you're selling yourself short now."

Christy was surprised when his voice broke.

He led her up the stairs to the schoolhouse and helped her settle on a front bench. Then he left without another word.

— — —

Church was a new experience. Without being able to see, it became a picture made of sounds and sensations and scents. It was the familiar smell of chalk and wood smoke and tobacco. It was the sound of rustling Sunday school papers and the coos of babies and the whispers of restless children. It was the vibration in the wooden floor, as the congregation tapped their feet while singing an old hymn.

Oh, for a faith that will not shrink, they sang, and Christy listened to their voices surround her like a warm embrace. Here, with her mountain friends, she felt safe and secure. One by one as they'd entered the church this morning, they'd come to her. The children had climbed in her lap and hugged her. The women had brought her cakes and cookies and breads—things they could hardly afford to give away. The men had been more awkward, but they, too, had come forward. Their words were simple—*Powerful sorry to hear about your troubles, Miz Christy*, or *I done prayed for you last night*. But what she'd heard in their voices wasn't pity. It wasn't anything like the tone she'd heard in Mrs. Grantland's harsh words. It was love.

When the room grew hushed, Christy knew that David was about to start his sermon. She heard his steady footsteps as he walked to the small pulpit.

"The preacher's a-comin," whispered Mountie, who was sitting next to Christy on the hard wooden bench. She was serving as an extra pair of eyes for Christy, informing her about what was happening in the room.

"That's my son," Christy heard Mrs. Grantland whisper in a pew behind her.

The memory of her hurtful words came back to Christy. *You can't possibly be thinking of marrying her now, David.*

They were strong, blunt words. Words that stung. At first, they had made Christy want to cry. But now, surrounded by her friends, she began to feel angry.

What kind of a wife would a blind woman make?

"Hebrews, 11:1," David began in his clear, strong voice. "'Faith is the substance of things hoped for, the evidence of things not seen.'" He paused. "'The evidence of things not seen.' What does that mean? What does that mean to each of us as we struggle through the trials of life?"

Christy listened intently. Somehow she felt as if David were speaking directly to her.

"There are many ways of seeing," he continued. "We can see with our eyes, of course. But that doesn't begin to paint the whole picture. Even the most perfect, shiny apple can have a worm inside. So how else can we see?"

Christy heard steps, and she knew that David was moving down the aisle that separated the men and women. He liked to move among the congregation as he spoke to them.

"We can 'see' with our other senses, too," David continued. "We can hear and smell and taste and touch, but we're never going to know the true nature of a thing that way. Sight can blur. Hearing can go bad. You have only to look at Jeb Spencer's old coon dog, Magic, to know that. Jeb tells me that hound couldn't sniff out a skunk in a patch of pokeweed." The room broke into laughter. "No, only the heart can detect the evidence of things not seen."

He paused. Christy could tell he was only a few feet away, near the end of her bench.

"We cannot touch faith. We can't see it with our eyes, or hear it with our ears. But we can know it, as sure and solid as the earth beneath our feet, if we use our hearts." David's voice wavered. "You don't need eyes to have faith. You don't need anything but a good and loving and open heart."

Christy felt Mountie's small fingers lace into

hers. When Christy had started teaching, Mountie had barely spoken more than a few garbled words. She'd had a terrible speech problem, and the taunts of her classmates had left her almost mute. But a tiny gesture of caring from Christy—sewing a few old buttons onto Mountie's worn and tattered coat—had been the beginning of a miraculous change.

"We can see the world in a whole new way," David said softly, "when we use our hearts, instead of our eyes."

Soon the room was full of song again. *Amazing grace*, they sang, in that boisterous, full-of-life way they had. Christy sang, too, letting the words move her.

Slowly, other words came back to her— Miss Alice's words. *You will teach again, when you are ready.*

For the first time since her accident, Christy felt a glimmer of hope. What kind of a wife would she make? What kind of teacher? What kind of person?

She wasn't sure, but she knew she wanted to find out.

✎ Eight ✎

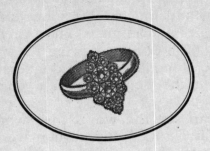

I must say that was a fine sermon," Mrs. Grantland said that evening at the dinner table. "Although the circumstances left a great deal to be desired. I don't know how you do it, David, dear. The primitive conditions! I mean, really. *Pigs* living under the floor!"

"Them's hogs, Miz Grantland," Ruby Mae corrected.

"Thank you for clearing that up."

Christy smiled. All through dinner, Mrs. Grantland had been talking that way. Poor David! Christy didn't know how he managed to keep his tongue. The only time he'd lashed out was when Mrs. Grantland had suggested Christy might be more "comfortable" eating in her room, where she could make a mess without being embarrassed.

It hadn't even bothered Christy. Ever since

church that morning, she'd been filled with a sense of hope and resolve.

"And the *smells*!" Mrs. Grantland continued. "I thought I was going to faint. Thank goodness I had my perfumed hankie with me."

"You get used to it after a while, Mother," Miss Ida said.

"Goodness, me! I certainly hope not, dear. I keep telling David he needs a ministry back home in Richmond. He belongs in a big, fine church with a congregation that understands what he's saying. A church without any tobacco spitting or mangy dogs or pigs."

"Hogs, ma'am," Ruby Mae corrected again.

"The congregation here may not be the best dressed or the most educated, Mrs. Grantland," said Miss Alice, "but you can be certain they understand and respect David. He's made great strides since coming here to Cutter Gap."

"But don't the souls in Richmond deserve saving just as much as the ones here?" Mrs. Grantland persisted.

"I believe the Lord's work can be done anywhere," Miss Alice said. Christy could hear the edge in her voice. It was the tone Miss Alice reserved for a wayward child.

"This is my calling, Mother," David said. "I belong here in Cutter Gap."

"Nonsense!" Mrs. Grantland cried. "You belong where you'll be properly appreciated."

"Isn't it really . . ." Christy paused. She felt strange, interrupting a conversation when she couldn't see the participants. "Isn't it David's choice, Mrs. Grantland? My parents weren't eager for me to come here, but in the end, they understood how important it was to me."

"Indeed. And look what happened to you."

Christy took a deep breath. "Still, I don't regret coming here. I've made so many friends—"

"I'm afraid," Mrs. Grantland interrupted, "that may be David's problem."

"And what problem is that, Mother?" David inquired.

"Oh, you know. Friends can keep you rooted to a place when it's time to move on." Christy had the strange feeling that Mrs. Grantland was looking right at her.

"Well," Miss Ida said after a moment of awkward silence, "I think it's time for me to clear the plates."

"I'll help," David said quickly.

"No, let me," said Miss Alice.

"Me, too," Ruby Mae chimed in.

"All of you stay put," Mrs. Grantland commanded. "There's something I must do. I've brought you all gifts."

"Presents!" Ruby Mae cried.

Christy could hear Mrs. Grantland swish across the dining room. She always seemed to move in great, flowing movements that made Christy think of an actress dashing across a stage.

"It was so hard to know what to bring," Mrs. Grantland said. "Now I see I could have brought everything but the kitchen sink. You *do* have a kitchen sink, don't you?"

"Yes, Mother," Miss Ida said, laughing.

"And a proper pump right outside," Ruby Mae added.

"Haven't you people heard of indoor plumbing?"

"We have, Mother," David replied. "But we think it's more fun tromping out into the yard in sub-zero temperatures to get a bucket of near-frozen water. It builds character."

"Don't you get sassy with your own mother," Mrs. Grantland chided, but it was clear she was laughing, too.

"This was very generous of you, Mother," David said.

"Oh, you know me. Any excuse to shop."

Christy heard the clasps of a trunk pop open, then the rustle of paper.

"I've brought plenty of books and magazines, of course," Mrs. Grantland began.

"Books!" Christy exclaimed. "That's wonderful! You have no idea how desperate the school is for reading material."

It occurred to her with a sudden pang that she might never again read another book. *No,* she told herself firmly. *No more thinking like that.*

"And I brought these for the mission house," Mrs. Grantland said.

Ruby Mae gasped. "Those gotta be the biggest diamonds in the world!"

"Actually, they're crystal, Ruby Mae," said Miss Alice. "Beautiful crystal candlesticks."

"They seem silly now," Mrs. Grantland said, for the first time sounding a little less sure of herself. "With all you need . . ."

"Quite the contrary," Miss Alice said gently. "They're a reminder of all the beauty in the world. A touch of magic. Thank you, Mrs. Grantland. It was very kind of you."

"And for Ida, a new dress. Goodness knows you need one."

"Oh, Mother! It's beautiful," Ida exclaimed.

"It's all shiny and blue with little stripes and bows and such," Ruby Mae whispered to Christy.

Mrs. Grantland placed a hand on Christy's shoulder. "And for you and Ruby Mae, I brought these lovely hats."

"For me?" Ruby Mae screeched. Christy felt the table jiggle as Ruby Mae leapt out of her chair. "You ain't havin' fun with me, are you, Mrs. Grantland?"

Mrs. Grantland laughed. "Of course not. Here. Try it on. And here's yours, Miss Huddleston."

"Please, call me Christy." Christy accepted the hat. She could feel the straw edges. Around the brim were what felt like little silk roses.

"They're all a-covered with these pretend flowers, Miz Christy," Ruby Mae cried with excitement. "Sort of a pinkish color, like the sun when it's just comin' up." She paused. "Miz Grantland, I don't know if this would be rightly proper, considerin' that you're a preacher's mama and all, but would it be all right if I gave you a hug to say thank you kindly?"

"That's all right, dear—" Mrs. Grantland began, but David interrupted.

"Sure, Ruby Mae," he said. "Go on and give Mother a hug. Sort of an official welcome to Cutter Gap."

Christy heard footsteps, a rustle of skirts, then a slight *ugh* as Ruby Mae squeezed Mrs. Grantland.

"Miz Christy, ain't you goin' to try yours on?" Ruby Mae asked.

Carefully Christy placed the hat on her head. "I wish you could see how purty it looks!" Ruby Mae said.

Christy pulled off the hat and set it on the floor. "Thank you, Mrs. Grantland. That was very thoughtful of you."

"I hope it . . . I mean, if I'd known about your injury, perhaps I might have brought something more appropriate."

"Just because she's blind don't mean Miz

187

Christy can't wear purty things," Ruby Mae pointed out.

"Of course not," Mrs. Grantland said, her voice softening a little, "I only meant . . ." She paused, rummaging around in her trunk. "Anyway, last, but not least—for David, a new suit. From Whitman's in Richmond. Remember that tailor your father always used? I do hope you haven't lost so much weight you can't wear it."

"It's wonderful, Mother," David said. "Very impressive. And there are fine seamstresses here in the Cove who can alter it if need be. Thank you."

"It seems a little silly," Mrs. Grantland said with a sigh. "You could wear overalls to give your sermon and who would notice? That suit would be much better suited to a ministry back home."

David was silent. Miss Ida cleared her throat.

"Well, now that the gift-giving is over, I suppose we should get down to work, Christy," Miss Alice said at last. "That is, if you're feeling up to it. David and I want to go over your lesson plans. We're going to need to divide up the teaching work load. I expect we'll have to cut back quite a bit on school. Perhaps we'll shorten the school days so we can keep up with our other duties."

Christy let the words sink in. *Divide up the teaching work load.* Giving up her teaching duties felt like giving away part of herself. She felt a decision brewing, like a bubble in a pond slowly rising to the surface.

"You know, Mother was a teacher for many years," David said. Christy could almost *hear* the smile on his face. "Perhaps she wouldn't mind helping out a bit."

"David!" Mrs. Grantland objected. "I simply couldn't. I haven't set foot in a classroom in years. And those were *civilized* children— well-bred, with manners."

"What do you think about it, Christy?" David asked.

"In my experience," Christy said thoughtfully, "children are children, no matter where you go."

"I wouldn't hear of it," Mrs. Grantland said. "Sorry, David. You'll just have to recruit someone else. After all, you'll need to find a permanent replacement, anyway."

The room fell silent. The only sound was the clink of silverware as Ruby Mae finished her pie.

"I have an announcement to make," Christy said. Even as she slowly stood, she wasn't quite sure what she was going to say. But she felt something in her heart, urging her to speak.

"There won't be any need for a new teacher," Christy finally said. "Or for Miss Alice and David to divide up my teaching duties. I am going to continue teaching, as I always have. And I don't want any argument from anyone about this."

"Yahoo!" Ruby Mae cried.

"And there's one other thing," Christy added as the words rushed out. "David and I will be staying here in Cutter Gap permanently. As man and wife."

First, Christy heard gasps.

Then she heard a sigh.

Then she heard a very loud thud.

"What was that?" she asked.

"Miz Grantland," Ruby Mae replied. "She done took the news a little hard. She's plumb fainted straight away!"

❧ Nine ❧

How's your mother?" Christy asked David a few minutes later.

"Miss Alice is tending to her on the couch. You'll have to forgive Mother. I told you she takes things *very* seriously." David sat down at the dining-room table with Christy. She could hear Ruby Mae and Miss Ida in the kitchen, talking in shocked whispers.

"Apparently I've caused quite a sensation," Christy said.

"You certainly have where I'm concerned. I'm not going to ask you why you made this decision," David said. "I'm only going to tell you how very glad you've made me."

"I'll tell you, anyway," Christy replied with a smile. "It was your sermon today. Listening to you, I realized that even if I have lost my sight forever, I can still be a teacher or a wife. I don't have to give up on my dreams. There are many ways to see. You're right about that. And now I'm going to prove it."

David fell silent for a moment. "So I'm a sort of experiment? Is that it?"

"No, no, not at all!" Christy cried. "It's just that today, listening to your beautiful words, I realized how deep my feelings really are for you, David. You're a strong and kind and gentle man, a good man." She smiled shyly. "And of course, you've got an awfully cute smile."

With trembling hands, David cupped Christy's face and gently kissed her.

"Oh. Oh, my. Excuse me—" It was Miss Ida, sounding very embarrassed.

"It's all right, Ida," David said. "Come on in. I am allowed to kiss my fiancée, aren't I?"

"Miss Ida," Christy said, "I'm so glad that we're going to practically be sisters."

"Welcome to the Grantland family," Miss Ida said stiffly, and then Christy heard her march off.

"Don't worry," David said. "She'll warm up to the idea."

"But she knows me," Christy said. "If Miss Ida's that set against it, how will I ever win over your mother?"

"With your incredible charm," David teased.

"Don't hold your breath," Christy said. "Why did you suggest she take my place teaching, anyway? Wasn't it obvious what she'd say?"

"Wishful thinking. I suppose I was hoping that if she got to know the students, she'd see why we love it here so."

"It's hard to imagine her having the patience to teach."

"Actually, she was quite good at it. But after my father died, she just sort of closed herself off. I know it's hard to believe, but she used to be much more . . . tolerant." David sighed. "I'd better go check on her. Want to come?"

"You think she can handle the strain?"

David took Christy's hand. They settled in the living room on two chairs across from the couch. "How are you feeling, Mother?" David asked.

"She'll be back to normal in no time," Miss Alice said.

"I'll be fine, with the grace of God," Mrs. Grantland said in a quavery voice. "No thanks to you two."

"I'm glad you're feeling better," Christy said.

"Miss Huddleston, my dear," said Mrs. Grantland. "Come here."

David helped Christy over to the couch, where Mrs. Grantland took her hand. "My dear girl, you must understand," she said. "I have nothing against you personally. I'm sure you're a fine girl. And I'm sure you'll go far in this world, even with your . . . your problem. But David is my only son. And I have such high hopes for him. Plans, great plans. He belongs in the right place, with the right people."

"You mean with Delia?" Christy asked with a smile.

Mrs. Grantland pulled away her hand. "As a matter of fact, I've always been very fond of Delia Manning. So refined and well-bred. And such a beauty! But that's not all I meant. I meant David doesn't belong here. Nor Ida. Nor you and Miss Alice, I'll wager. You're all decent folk. This is no place for your kind."

Someone knocked on the front door. "Come on in," David called. He lowered his voice. "We can only pray that it's decent folk."

The door flew open. Evening air, scented with spring flowers, cooled the room.

"Creed!" David exclaimed. "And Zach! What brings you two here?"

"We got some bad news, Preacher."

"Try to top what I just heard," Mrs. Grantland muttered.

"We done swum all afternoon over to the pond," Zach said. "Fished up the rowboat finally. It's right muddy but I 'spect it'll float again."

"I thought you said it was bad news," David said. "That's great."

"The bad news is we poked around every last inch o' that pond. We found two bullets,

194

a belt buckle, and a moonshine jug. But there just ain't no sign o' that diamond ring anywheres."

"Diamond ring?" Mrs. Grantland repeated. "What diamond ring might that be? Who in this awful place owns a diamond ring?"

"The preacher did, ma'am," Creed answered. "He was sweetheartin' Miz Christy with it when he done dunked hisself and Miz Christy too and they—"

"Thank you for that very helpful information, Creed," David interrupted quickly. "Now, you boys need to be heading on home before it gets dark—"

"Sweetheartin'?" Mrs. Grantland repeated slowly. Christy felt her leap off the couch. "Great-great-grandmother Grantland's wedding ring? You *lost* her ring?"

"He didn't exactly lose it on purpose," Zach offered. "The way I hear tell, it was Miz Christy who was a-holdin' it—"

"You! YOU lost it?"

"Well, it was an accident, really—" Christy began, but she was interrupted by another loud thud.

The room went still.

"It seems," David informed Christy, "that Mother's fainted yet again."

"Is she dead?" Creed whispered.

"No, Creed," Christy replied with a sigh. "Just dead set against me."

"You think I'm completely crazy, don't you?" Christy asked Miss Alice the next morning as they walked up the steps to the school. Christy wanted to get there well before the students started arriving.

"What are you referring to?" Miss Alice said as she held open the door. "Your return to the classroom? Or your engagement to David?"

"Either. Both," Christy said, laughing.

They stepped inside. Instantly Christy felt the warm reassuring feeling she always had when she was here. *This is where you belong*, the room seemed to say. *This is home.*

Christy let go of Miss Alice's arm and began making her way toward her desk. In her mind she tried to picture the arrangement of desks and benches. The blackboard would be just over to the right. Zach's desk was just a foot or two away, and over there was the bench where Ruby Mae and Bessie Coburn and Lizette Holcombe always sat.

Slowly she navigated her way through the maze of obstacles. "See how easy it is?" she asked. "I know this room like the back of my hand."

"You do indeed. But I think you're going to have to realize something, Christy. It's not a sin to ask for help."

"I don't need any help," Christy said firmly.

She bumped into a long desk and realized she'd reached her destination. Lovingly she ran her fingers over the rough wood, with its carved initials and gouges.

"Everyone needs help sometimes."

Christy put her hands on her hips. "You're the one who said I could teach again."

"And I still think so. But I think you're going to have to do it differently."

"I am going to be the same teacher I always was, Miss Alice." Christy settled into her chair. "Any less would be cheating the children."

Miss Alice was quiet for a moment. "Well, I am here, if you need me. We all are."

"Thank you," Christy said. "Really."

"Are you sure you don't want someone to stay with you today? I've got a patient to tend to, but perhaps—"

"No. I want to do this myself. All by myself."

Christy heard Miss Alice walk toward the door. Suddenly she felt very alone. "Miss Alice?" she called. "What do you think about David and me getting married?"

"I think," Miss Alice said gently, "that only you can know what's in your heart, Christy. But when we make a commitment, a big commitment, it's important to be sure we're doing it for the right reasons."

The right reasons? What does she mean by that? Christy wondered.

"Why, hello there, Neil," Miss Alice said suddenly.

Christy heard the sound of boots on the wooden steps.

"You're making a mistake, Christy," the doctor said darkly.

"Word certainly travels fast in these parts," Miss Alice commented. "I'll leave you two to talk."

"A mistake?" Christy repeated as the doctor approached her desk. "You mean about teaching?"

"About teaching and a whole lot more," the doctor barked. "You're trying to prove that nothing's changed. And you're making a mistake that could ruin the rest of your life."

"I'm ready to teach, Neil. I have to teach."

"Maybe. Maybe not. But you're not ready to marry. At least . . . at least not him."

Christy tapped a pencil against the desk, trying to control her anger. "Who are you to tell me what I'm ready to do? Who are you to tell me whom I should marry?"

The doctor grabbed her by the shoulders. "I know you, Christy," he said, with such intensity she could practically see the pain in his eyes. "I know you want to prove you can take on the world. But this is not the way to do it."

"Why does everyone doubt me?" Christy cried. "Miss Alice just got done telling me I can't teach without help. Now here you are, marching up to tell me that I can't marry David because you think I don't love him."

"I didn't say that," the doctor pointed out. "You did."

"Of *course* I love him. I feel safe with David. And I admire him. And I know he loves me."

"And me?" the doctor asked softly. "What about me?"

"Neil, you make me feel happy, and I like talking to you. But you can also make me angrier than anyone I know. David is predictable. But you, Neil, just make me feel . . . too many things at once. And at the moment you're making me very angry."

The doctor took a step backwards. "I hope you'll be very happy," he snapped.

"You're invited to the wedding, of course," Christy said, trying to sound happier than she felt.

The doctor gave a harsh laugh. "I plan to be busy that day," he said, and with that, he was gone.

✎ Ten ✎

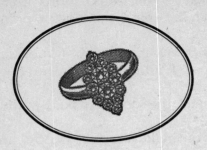

When the doctor had left, the only sound was the soft whoosh of the pine trees swaying outside the window. Christy stood, trying to rein in her anger.

She could picture the schoolhouse perfectly in her mind. To her right sat the girls; to her left, the boys. She imagined the first row of girls. Ruby Mae, Bessie, Lizette, Clara. Or was it Clara, then Lizette? They changed places so often, it was hard to know.

Carefully Christy paced off the distance to the blackboard. One, two, three, four, five. Five steps, and if she reached out her arm, there was the board. Would she be able to write on the board legibly? Yes, if she really concentrated. She'd always had excellent penmanship. She'd just have to imagine the letters, one by one.

You're making a mistake. She heard the doctor's voice in her head as if he were still there in the room. Never had he sounded so angry. Well, he had no right to tell her what to do. This was her life, after all.

"There she is!"

"David?" Christy turned toward the voice. "Is that you?"

"I've brought you a visitor."

Christy caught a whiff of the rose perfume. "Mrs. Grantland! What a . . . surprise."

"How did you—"

"Your perfume." Christy took five careful steps back to her desk. She bumped her chair with her knee, then sat down. "David, I really don't think today is a good day for visitors . . ."

David perched on her desk. "I was going to stay and help you myself," he said, lowering his voice to a whisper, "but Ida just informed me that the pump's not working, and unless I fix it, we're going to be mighty thirsty come evening. I thought Mother could stick around and help you out, just in case things get hectic."

"David!" Christy said. "I just don't—"

"I want you two to get to know each other," David insisted under his breath. "If she knows you better, she'll understand why I love you so much. Besides, I'll feel a lot better knowing there's someone here in case you need help."

"I want to do this myself, David." Christy sighed deeply.

"I know. She'll stay out of your way, I promise."

"If she annoys me, I'm going to ask her to leave."

"Fair enough." David took her hand. "Are you sure you're up to this?"

"Absolutely."

"All right, then. Oh. I almost forgot." Christy felt him slip something onto the ring finger of her left hand.

"What's this?"

"A makeshift engagement ring. It's just a piece of red ribbon from Ida's sewing box. The best I could do on short notice."

"It'll do very nicely till we find the ring."

David kissed her cheek. "*If* we find it. Now, if you need anything, you just yell, all right? And don't hesitate to ask Mother for help. She was a teacher, after all."

When David left, the room was silent. If it hadn't been for the perfume, Christy would have been sure his mother had left with him.

"Mrs. Grantland?"

"Yes. I'm still here."

"I know David meant well, asking you to stay. But I really don't need any help. I intend to do this myself."

"Young lady, I don't want to be here any more than you want me. But my son insists that you two are going through with this betrothal. Moreover, he insists I spend time with you. And since I do not know anything about repairing pumps, and since my daughter is busy tending to chickens, of all the disgusting things, this is the only recreation left to me. You would think after I came all the way from Richmond, my children would at least have the decency to entertain their poor mother."

"Well, you're welcome to take a seat and observe," Christy said coolly. She had enough to worry about without taking care of David's mother. She knew he meant well, but having an audience was just going to make Christy *more* nervous.

"Miz Christy! You really *are* here!"

Christy recognized the voice instantly as Lulu Spencer's, a sweet six-year-old who was one of Fairlight's daughters. An instant later, Lulu was in Christy's lap, offering her a warm hug. "I was afeared you weren't comin', on account of your eyes not working."

"I'm here, all right," Christy said. "I can still teach even if my eyes aren't working, don't you think?"

Lulu thought for a moment. "I reckon so."

Within minutes, the schoolroom was buzzing with children. Each one came over to greet Christy. They seemed fascinated by her bandages. Christy tried to keep a mental count of the students as they arrived, but she lost count after thirty.

Although she couldn't see, it amazed her

what she could hear. It was as if her ears were working harder, to compensate for her lack of sight. She heard marbles on the floor in the southeast corner. She heard sniffles coming from the second row on the boys' side. Was that Little Burl Allen, with yet another cold? She heard whispers coming from the back of the room—no doubt Lundy Taylor and Smith O'Teale, the class bullies. She heard an argument brewing in the back of the room—two of the younger children, fighting over a rag doll. She heard two other children playing tic-tac-toe on the blackboard.

It was so much information! She didn't know what to do with it all. With her eyes, she could make sense of the classroom. She could tell where a real fight was starting, and when it was just a silly squabble she could ignore. She could tell who had dark circles under their eyes from staying up late doing chores, and who was gaunt from hunger. Those were students who wouldn't be able to concentrate, and she would know to take it easy on them.

But she couldn't know any of those things. Not anymore.

The noise in the room swelled. A paper airplane hit her in the shoulder. The children knew that was against the rules, since they couldn't afford to waste a single piece of paper. She felt a wave of panic. This was insane! She couldn't handle all these children! No one could!

Calm down, she told herself. Hadn't she thought exactly the same thing on her first day of teaching? Her knees had been shaking so hard that even the children had noticed.

"All right, children," Christy said in her best stern-teacher voice. "Settle down." She gripped the edge of the desk for support. "I want you all to take your seats."

She heard the shuffle of bare feet on the wooden floor. Shouts turned to whispers.

All right, that was a good sign. At least they were still willing to obey her.

"Now, today is a special day for two reasons," Christy began. "First of all, we have a visitor. The Reverend Grantland's mother is here, all the way from Richmond, Virginia. So I want you to all be on your best behavior."

"She smells like roses, Teacher," Creed said.

"Yes, Creed. That's called perfume. It's made from flowers."

"Well, do I got to sit next to her all day? It's like sittin' next to a rosebush in full bloom. My nose will like to burst!"

"Creed, that is very rude," Christy chided. "Don't you think you should apologize to Mrs. Grantland?"

"Gee whiz, Miz Grantland, I didn't mean no offense—"

"Apology accepted. Perhaps, Miss Huddleston, if you taught these children some basic hygiene skills, they wouldn't object to the scent of perfume."

"Thank you for the advice, Mrs. Grantland." Christy turned to the left, where the map of the United States was tacked to the wall.

"I wonder if someone can find Richmond on a map of the United States?" she asked.

"Me, Teacher!"

"Pick me, Teacher!"

"I knows it for sure!"

When the children all spoke at once, it was very hard to tell their voices apart. And although she'd taught them to raise their hands, that wouldn't help her now.

"Sam Houston? Did you want to point out Richmond?"

"No'm. I ain't got my hand a-raised. Try Wraight."

"Wraight?"

"He knows I ain't got my hand up no ways," Wraight cried. "Sam Houston Holcombe, I'm a-goin' to whop you good at recess for that!"

"Boys, that's quite enough," Christy said sternly. If she wasn't careful, she was going to lose control of the class. "John Spencer, why don't you show all of us where Richmond is located?"

John, one of her best students, was a safe choice. She heard him walk over to the map. Suddenly she realized there was no way to know whether he was correct. It was likely, since he was a good student. But how could she be sure?

The questions multiplied in her head. How was she going to grade papers? How was she going to write up tests?

How was she going to discipline students at recess? How was she going to bandage a scraped knee?

How was she going to know if John had just pointed out Richmond or not?

Panic surged through her like lightening. In her heart, she'd known these problems were waiting for her. She just hadn't wanted to admit it. *This is crazy,* a voice in her head cried. *You can't do this. Not in a million years.*

"I . . . I, uh . . ." Christy stammered.

"Correct," came a shrill voice from the back of the room. "What was your name again? John?"

"Yes'm, Mrs. Grantland."

Christy sighed with relief. She'd gotten through that minor crisis, but not without some unwelcome assistance.

"Very good, John," she said. "You may go back to your seat."

"Miz Christy?"

"Yes? Is that Creed?"

"You done said there were two reasons this day was special."

"So I did. The other reason is that this is the start of an experiment. An experiment is a sort of test, to see if something is true or false.

And what I am trying to find out is whether or not I can teach without my sight. I think I can—at least, I *hope* I can. So you see, in a way, you are part of the experiment."

"Miz Christy?"

"Yes, Creed."

"We done brought you something for the 'speriment."

A moment later, Christy felt something pressed into her hands.

"It's a cane," Creed explained. "Zach and Sam Houston and I made it outa oak."

"Like my granny's!" Mountie exclaimed.

Christy felt the carefully smoothed wood. "Boys, I can tell it's beautiful. Thank you very much. I needed one. And I will be proud to use it."

In truth, Christy had talked herself into believing she could get by without a cane. But she had to admit that was silly. Even if she memorized every square foot of the mission property, how was she going to navigate through the yard when it rained or snowed, unless she had a cane?

"Miz Christy?"

"Who was that?"

"Me, Lizette. Is it true about you and the preacher gettin' hitched?"

Mrs. Grantland let out a loud sigh.

"Yes," Christy said, "it is true. And you're all invited to the wedding."

Mrs. Grantland let out a much louder sigh.

"Miz Christy?"

"Yes, Creed?"

"Is there somethin' wrong with the preacher's mama? She's breathin' awful funny."

"There's nothing wrong with me that a little dose of reality couldn't cure," Mrs. Grantland muttered.

Christy cleared her throat. *Penmanship*, she told herself. *That's a good idea. Don't think about all the things that could go wrong. Don't think about the doctor yelling. Or David's mother sighing. Or the fact that Lundy Taylor is undoubtedly tossing spitballs from the back of the room by now.*

"I think we'll start today by working on our penmanship," Christy said. Carefully she headed to the blackboard. One, two, three, four—

With a thud, she hit the board, nose-first. The pain was horrible. The board teetered back and forth on its wobbly wooden legs.

"Look out!" someone yelled.

Christy tried to grab it, but it was too late. The board went crashing to the ground. Slate shattered into pieces that skittered across the floor.

The children were silent. Even Mrs. Grantland kept quiet.

"Miz Christy?" Creed whispered.

Christy rubbed her head. "Yes, Creed?"

"Does this mean the 'speriment's over?"

"No, Creed," Christy said wearily. "It just means it's going to be a *very* long experiment."

⮂ Eleven ⮀

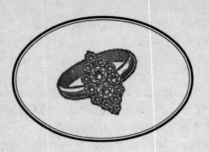

It was awful," Christy said at dinner that evening. "Just awful. I broke the blackboard. I tripped over the water bucket. I stepped on one of the hogs at recess. I gave a math quiz and couldn't grade it." She shook her head. "I looked ridiculous."

"To whom?" Miss Alice asked gently. "To the children? Or to yourself?"

Christy shrugged. "Both, I guess."

"You didn't look foolish to none of us, Miz Christy," Ruby Mae said. As usual, her mouth was full of food. "I mean, a couple kids snickered some when you sat on your sandwich at lunchtime. Mostly Lundy and them older boys. But it weren't so bad."

Mrs. Grantland let out a long sigh. Christy had heard that sigh so many times today, she knew it like her own voice. Still, she had to admit that Mrs. Grantland *had* come to her rescue several times—not that Christy had wanted her to.

"Personally, I think it's insane for you to try to teach—sight or no sight," Mrs. Grantland said. "That's the most awful excuse for a schoolroom I've ever seen! And the filthy children! No shoes, no clean clothes, no manners, no proper English, no respect for authority . . ."

"I ain't dirty," Ruby Mae said proudly. "I wash behind my ears and everything. Wanna see?"

"I'll take your word for it, dear."

"Are all city folks as prissy as you, Miz Grantland?" Ruby Mae asked.

"Prissy?"

"You shoulda seen her, Preacher," Ruby Mae said. "Creed done brought a black snake to school. When he handed it to your mama, she musta jumped halfway to heaven."

David laughed loudly.

"David!" Mrs. Grantland scolded.

"Sorry, Mother," David said. "It's just that I was remembering that time when Ida and I brought home a toad. I couldn't have been more than eight. We named him Harold, remember, Ida?"

"Mother was none too happy about Harold," Ida recalled.

Mrs. Grantland even laughed a little. "Well,

you were generally very well-behaved children. That was just . . . the exception that proves the rule. But these children are another story altogether."

"I'm very sorry about the snake, Mrs. Grantland," Christy said. "If I'd known . . ."

"No matter," Mrs. Grantland said. "It's just an example of why you're taking on more than any person could possibly handle. When I was a teacher, the children knew their place. No talking back, no—what are they called?—salivaballs—"

"Spitballs, ma'am," Ruby Mae interrupted politely.

"—and certainly no snakes. And the sheer number! Sixty-seven students, of all ages and abilities. Why, that's enough for three classrooms. It's madness."

"Suppose we all take shifts, Christy?" David asked. "Ida and Miss Alice and I—and maybe Mother, too, while she's here? We could act as assistants, like Mother did today. Just help out till you get things under control."

"I can't ask you to do that," Christy said. "You've all got your own work to do. And I'll wager your mother has seen all she needs of my classroom."

"Goodness me, yes!" Mrs. Grantland exclaimed.

"If I'm going to do this," Christy vowed, "I'm going to do this myself."

Mrs. Grantland leaned across the table and touched Christy's hand. "I'm just telling you the truth, my dear. It's impossible. You simply can't handle that group of hooligans all by yourself."

"What's a hooligan, Miz Christy?" Ruby Mae asked.

"It's what you'll be if you don't help me clear these dishes," Miss Ida said sternly. Then under her breath she explained, "It's a troublemaker."

Christy leaned back in her chair while Ruby Mae cleared away her plate. "What do you think, Miss Alice?" she asked. "Is Mrs. Grantland right?"

"I believe she's right that you have set before you a very large task," Miss Alice said, choosing her words in that slow, careful way she had. "But I also believe you can handle it, *if* you recognize your limitations. As I said, it's no sin to ask for help, Christy."

The Lord does not give us more than we can handle.

Christy thought of the words she'd scribbled in her diary the night of her accident. No, she was not going to ask for help. She was going to prove that she was everything she ever was. She was going to do this alone.

Otherwise, it would mean admitting what she'd lost.

"No, thank you, Miss Alice," Christy said

firmly. "I have to try to do this by myself. You can understand that, can't you?"

Miss Alice didn't answer right away. "I came across a book among the many Mrs. Grantland brought us. It's called *The Story of My Life*, by a woman named Helen Keller."

"I remember reading something about her in the newspaper back home in Asheville," Christy said.

"She was left blind and deaf after an illness," Miss Alice explained. "But with the help of a gifted teacher named Anne Sullivan, she was able to learn to communicate. Now she travels the country, giving speeches and raising money on behalf of the handicapped."

"So you're saying if she can accomplish that, so can I?" Christy asked.

"Yes, I'm saying that. And I'm also saying she didn't get where she is today without the help of others."

With a sigh, Christy reached for her new cane and pushed back her chair. "If you'll excuse me," she said, "I'll be heading off to bed. I've got a busy day planned for tomorrow. We're having a spelling bee."

"I'll say one thing for that girl," Christy heard Mrs. Grantland comment as she walked away, "she's certainly as stubborn as they come!"

By Friday, Christy felt like the week had held a hundred days in it. She was exhausted and bruised. Her morale was shaken. She'd broken, bumped, or tripped over more things than she'd ever imagined possible. She'd never realized how full of obstacles the world was.

As she sat on the schoolhouse steps at recess, she tried to tell herself that things were improving. That she was getting the hang of being a blind teacher to sixty-seven difficult students. That she was just as good a teacher as she'd ever been.

But she knew it wasn't true.

This morning, when she'd sat down at her chair, she'd known it all over again. She'd heard the delicate crack of an egg, then felt the gooey insides soaking her skirt.

It was a harmless prank, no doubt Lundy Taylor's doing, but it was the kind of thing that never would have happened in the old days.

Worse than that sort of embarrassment was the feeling she couldn't reach her children as well. Without being able to see their beautiful faces, she couldn't know all the stories hidden there. Pain, hunger, and sometimes joy—their eyes revealed it all. But she couldn't see them anymore.

"I'll git you for that, you slimy little tree toad!"

Christy heard a shout, then a scream, then the sound of scuffling in the schoolyard. She grabbed her cane.

"Teacher! Teacher! Come quick! Lundy's a-beatin' on Creed somethin' fierce!"

Christy started toward the noise of the fight, but her skirt caught on a shrub and she tripped.

"Awwoww!" came a boy's scream. "Stop it, Lundy! I give, I give!"

"Lundy!" Christy cried as she struggled to her feet. "Lundy Taylor! You stop that this instant!"

"And what're you goin' to do, blind lady?" The voice was coming from her right, about twenty feet away. "Whop me with your cane?"

Christy heard the terrible sound of a fist meeting flesh. Creed howled with pain.

Frantically, Christy ran toward the crying boy. She hit a solid wall that turned out to be Lundy. She grabbed him by the shoulders and shook him with all her might, even though he stood several inches taller and weighed far more than she did.

"You ain't a-goin' to hurt me," he sneered. "You're blind as a bat!" He took a step backward and she lost her grip on him. "What're you goin' to do now? Whop me with your cane? I can beat up on this whole school and there ain't no way you're a-goin' to stop me."

Nearby, Creed was sobbing on the ground.

Christy heard what sounded like a sharp kick, and Creed cried out again.

"Lundy!" Christy screamed. "Stop it, now!"

"You don't scare me none," Lundy said.

The sense of helplessness was more than she could bear. Filled with rage, Christy lifted the cane high into the air, ready to strike.

Then she heard a shout. "No! Don't do it!"

✺ Twelve ✺

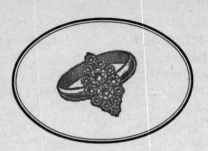

Please, Miss Huddleston, stop!"

It was Mrs. Grantland. There was a busy rustling of skirts, and a moment later, the scent of roses filled the air.

"What on earth is going on here, young man?" Mrs. Grantland demanded. "Lundy, isn't that your name?"

"Teacher's a-beatin' on me with her cane," Lundy whimpered in a pathetic voice. "You seen it."

"I'll wager you did something quite abominable to warrant your teacher's wrath," Mrs. Grantland said. "Not that I'd blame her one whit for taking a switch to you."

Christy lowered her arm. She felt horrified at her own actions and humiliated that Mrs. Grantland had seen her.

"Mrs. Grantland, I can handle this," she said shakily.

But Mrs. Grantland wasn't listening. "Lundy, did you hit this little boy?" she demanded.

"He had it comin'—" Lundy began.

"I want you to apologize to him this instant," said Mrs. Grantland.

"You ain't my teacher. And I ain't sayin' sorry to someone who's lower than a snake belly in a wagon rut—"

"Apologize," Mrs. Grantland commanded. "Now."

Christy could hear Lundy's breathing. She could hear Creed's sobs. Then, to her amazement, she heard Lundy mutter, "Get up, you twit-wit. I'm sorry, I reckon."

Mrs. Grantland clapped her hands firmly. "The rest of you, back into the classroom. And I do not mean maybe."

Christy listened to the whispers as the children filed sullenly back into class. "Creed?" she called. "Are you all right?"

The little boy ran up to her. "Right as rain, Miz Christy. I'll have a mighty fine bruise, though. Ain't bad. Lundy's done beat me up much worse." With that, he ran off whistling, as if nothing were wrong.

But something was very wrong. Suddenly, the enormity of what had happened hit Christy.

It was bad enough that Mrs. Grantland, of all people, had stepped in to control Lundy. It was far worse that Christy had raised her hand in anger at one of the children—even if it *was* Lundy Taylor, a vicious bully.

Worst of all was the fact that she hadn't been able to protect one of the children. Creed had been in danger, because of her.

"There now," Mrs. Grantland said briskly. "All settled. Everyone's back inside. That Lundy creature is a torment, isn't he? How you handle him is beyond me."

"I couldn't handle him, obviously. You did."

"Oh, he was just startled by the sound of my disciplinarian voice." Mrs. Grantland laughed. "Haven't used that in many years. I have to admit, I rather enjoyed it."

"What were you doing here, anyway? Did David send you to check up on me again?"

"No, I was just going for a walk. These mountains are rather interesting. Richmond's so flat by comparison." She hesitated. "If the truth be told, I've walked past the school every day this week, right around this time."

"Spying on me," Christy said bitterly.

"Not exactly. I just . . ." Mrs. Grantland's voice trailed off. "I suppose I was intrigued."

"Intrigued by what?"

"By how you were managing. It's not that I *care*, one way or the other," she added stiffly. "It's just that, as a former teacher, I kept wondering how it was possible you could pull it off. Professional curiosity, you might call it."

"And now you have your answer," Christy

snapped. "I can't! I was fooling myself, thinking I could do this. You knew and David knew and Doctor MacNeill knew. But no, I had to be The Great Christy, capable of magically pulling off the impossible." Her throat tightened. "My own vanity put these children at risk. I've been dealing with Lundy for months, and I've never been that out of control. What if I had hit him? What if he had really hurt Creed?"

Mrs. Grantland did not say anything.

"You know I'm right," Christy said.

"The truth is, dear, I don't think anyone could do what you tried to do. If you must know, I'm not particularly pleased at being right."

"Of course you're pleased," Christy cried. "You don't want me to marry David. If I can't stay here and teach, then you think he'll return to Richmond with you."

"I have hopes, certainly . . . but I'm starting to think it's not quite that simple," Mrs. Grantland said softly. "He seems to really care about these people."

"Well, if you won't say it, I will. I shouldn't be a teacher. I can't be a teacher."

"I know we aren't exactly allies, Miss Huddleston. But whatever my feelings about your engagement to David, I'm very sorry about what's happened to you."

Christy tossed her cane across the yard in disgust. She winced when she heard the sharp crack as it hit a tree.

"Tell them class is dismissed," she told Mrs. Grantland. "I'm sure you'll enjoy that duty."

— — —

"I was totally out of control," Christy confessed the next day as Doctor MacNeill checked her bandages. "I've never been so angry."

Why was she confiding in the doctor? When he'd checked on her throughout the week, they'd barely spoken. She knew he was still angry about her engagement to David. Still, he somehow seemed like the only person who would understand her anger.

"It's natural," the doctor said. "You're upset about what's happened to you. You've been holding it all inside. It was bound to come out, sooner or later."

"But I was so rude to Mrs. Grantland. I apologized this morning and she told me she understood, but I don't see how she could have. I wanted to lash out at someone, and she seemed like the perfect target. I was just mad because she was right about my trying to teach."

"Come on," the doctor said suddenly.

"What?"

"We're going for a walk, you and I. Fresh air will do you good. Doctor's orders."

"I thought . . . I thought you were mad at me. About the engagement."

"I am," the doctor said flatly. "But you need a friend today. And it looks like I'm elected."

Christy took the doctor's arm as they walked through the woods. The birds were in full chorus. The sun teased her shoulders. The smell of pine was as refreshing as a splash of icy water on her face.

"I've noticed one thing about not having my sight," Christy said. "I do 'see' things differently. The sounds, the smells—they're so much more intense. It's as if I'm experiencing the world in a whole new way."

"I suppose you are."

"Neil?"

"Hmm?"

"When can we take the bandages off?"

He stopped. "Another week, perhaps. When the swelling is down a bit more."

"I almost took them off last night," Christy admitted. "I just wanted to know for sure. To be done with it."

"You need more time."

The doctor resumed walking, and Christy fell into step beside him. "I wish . . ." he began. "I wish there were something more I could do about your eyes. I feel so inadequate."

The anguish in his voice made her heart ache. "This is in God's hands, Neil. There's nothing more you can do."

"There are other ways I feel inadequate," the doctor continued. His voice was so soft she could barely hear it over the chattering of the birds. "I wish . . . I wish I could tell you—"

"Tell me what?"

"Remember that night? That night when Ruby Mae was lost and you went out to find her in the storm? I was so worried about you! And then when you came back safely, and we sat by the fire, and we . . . we danced together . . ."

"I remember," Christy said softly. "You danced very well even with one arm in a sling."

"I guess it *was* a bit awkward." The doctor gave a rueful laugh. "But I just want you to know, Christy—that night will always be with me."

"Me, too," Christy said softly.

"If you aren't going to teach anymore, does that mean you're leaving Cutter Gap?"

"I don't know," Christy said. "I suppose that depends on what David wants to do."

At the mention of David's name, Christy felt the doctor stiffen. "You need to learn to listen to your own heart, Christy Huddleston," he said. "I love the stubbornness in you, but sometimes it just plain gets in the way of your hearing what you need to hear."

They walked in silence after that. Christy listened to the crackle of sticks beneath their feet, and the flutter of wings overhead. But mostly she listened as the doctor softly hummed an old Scottish folk song about lost love.

Somehow, the sweet, sad tune seemed to be coming from her very own heart.

❧ Thirteen ❧

On Monday morning, Christy did not bother getting dressed. She stood at the open window of her bedroom in her robe and listened to the shouts and laughter of her students floating on the breeze. Miss Alice and David were taking over her teaching duties until another teacher could be found.

It had all been decided at dinner last night. David felt it was for the best. Miss Alice had not expressed an opinion. Neither, for that matter, had Mrs. Grantland—much to Christy's surprise.

The knock on her door startled her. "Christy?"

"Miss Alice! Come in. I thought you were teaching this morning."

"I've been called away. It seems Ben Pentland broke his ankle last night, and

Neil's busy over at the Holcombes with their sick baby. David's in El Pano this morning, picking up that delivery of medicine, which leaves Mrs. Grantland."

"Mrs. Grantland!"

"She'll have to do. She's all we've got."

"But—" Christy stopped herself. It was not her classroom, not anymore. Whatever her faults, Mrs. Grantland would make a much better teacher than Christy.

"I must be off. Is there anything I can get you before I go?" Miss Alice asked.

"Nothing. I'm fine. Be careful," Christy said.

She returned to the window. The bell in the steeple was ringing. The children would be running to their desks. Creed, of course, would be showing up late, no doubt with some new wild animal in tow. Ruby Mae would be giggling with Bessie about their latest crushes. John Spencer would have his head buried in the book of poetry Christy had lent him.

Would Mrs. Grantland know to be gentle with Mountie? She embarrassed so easily. Would she know that Zach had trouble with his eyesight? Would she . . .

Stop it, Christy told herself. They weren't her students anymore. She was not their teacher anymore. And it was a good thing, too.

She climbed back into bed. For a change,

she could sleep in. She could sleep in every morning, from now on.

She closed her eyes. The laughter of the children traveled on the breeze like the chatter of birds. Try as she might, she could not seem to sleep.

— — —

It wasn't until afternoon that Christy finally bothered to get dressed. Miss Ida had already stopped by twice to make sure she was all right.

Christy was just lacing up her shoes when she heard a shy knock on the door. "I'm all right, Miss Ida," Christy said. "I'm actually getting dressed, you'll be pleased to hear."

"Teacher! It's me, Creed!"

"Creed!" Christy rushed to the door, fumbling for the knob. "Is something wrong at school?"

"You just gotta come quick-like, Teacher! It's plumb awful! Lundy Taylor's done tied up Miz Grantland to her chair. And Sam Houston let the hogs loose in the schoolroom. And Ruby Mae and them girls are havin' a square dance, a-singin' and carryin' on. I swear it's true! It's like the whole school's gone plumb crazy!"

Christy hesitated. What could she do? Maybe she should send Miss Ida instead. After last

Friday, Christy knew better than to presume she could handle things alone. Still, if Mrs. Grantland really *was* tied up, that called for quick action.

Christy allowed Creed to lead her by the hand across the yard to the schoolhouse. Strangely, as they got closer, she couldn't hear any noise coming from the school. As a matter of fact, the place was eerily quiet.

"I thought you said they were having a square dance."

"Yes'm, they is." Creed hesitated. "I mean, they was, and if they isn't, well, it's probably 'cause that Lundy's done somethin' powerful mean."

"Creed." Christy stopped and knelt down. "There's something I need to say to you. I am very, very sorry that I broke the cane you made me. Sometimes even adults get angry and have temper tantrums. I felt angry at myself because I wasn't able to protect you from Lundy. And I'm very sorry that I broke that beautiful cane. Can you forgive me?"

"Shucks, Teacher. It weren't nothin'. I have powerful good tantrums my own self."

Christy laughed.

"Besides, we already made—"

"What?"

"Nothin'. Come on." He tugged on her arm. "Miz Grantland's gotta be goin' plumb crazy by now."

Slowly, Christy ascended the wooden schoolhouse steps with Creed's help. She thought she heard vague whisperings, but that was all.

"Mrs. Grantland?" Christy called from the doorway. "Is everything all right?"

Suddenly the entire room burst into song:

> For she's a jolly good teacher,
> For she's a jolly good teacher,
> For she's a jolly good teacher,
> Which nobody can deny!

Christy gasped. "What in the world?"

"Sorry, Teacher," Creed said. "I kinda told a fib to get you here. Well, a bunch o' fibs. See, it's a 'speriment."

"I don't understand."

"You will, soon enough." It was Mrs. Grantland's voice.

"Mrs. Grantland? Are you . . . are you by any chance tied to a chair?"

"Goodness, no. Although if I gave these hooligans half a chance, no doubt they'd try it. Creed, take Miss Christy to her seat."

She started toward her desk, but Christy felt a tug on her arm. "Follow me, Teacher. We done made some changes."

Christy followed Creed to her desk. No longer was it located on the raised platform she'd tripped on so often last week. Now it was on the lower level, where the students' desks were.

She sat down obediently. "Mrs. Grantland," she began, "this is all very nice, but I really don't—"

"John Spencer, why don't you begin?" Mrs. Grantland interrupted.

Christy heard John clear his throat. "We got together and sort of come to the conclusion that we wasn't helpin' any with your experiment, Miz Christy," he said. "We put together some ideas we kinda wanted to run by you. To start with, we got ourselves some—what was they called, Miz Grantland?"

"Monitors."

"Yeah. We got us some monitors. First off is Ruby Mae Morrison. She's the noise monitor, on account of she's usually the one making it."

Everyone laughed.

"My job is to get the class to hush, Miz Christy," Ruby Mae announced. "And I aim to do it, too!"

"Next off is Sam Houston," John said. "He's the hand monitor."

"Hand monitor?" Christy repeated.

"I tell you who-all's waving their hands, Teacher. And if you want, I can pick who answers, too. Like as not, I can tell who's done homework and who's just a-fakin' it."

"Lizette is board monitor," John continued,

"on account of she's got the best handwriting. 'Ceptin' for you, Miz Christy. And I'm map monitor. On account of I know where all the states is."

Christy began to smile, in spite of herself.

"Me! Don't forget me!" came a loud, boy's voice.

Christy recognized it as Wraight Holt's. "What's your job, Wraight?" she asked.

"I'm the recess monitor," Wraight explained. "Which is most likely the most important monitorin' goin' on. I round up all the little ones when you says it's time. *And* I break up all the fights."

"'Less'n he started 'em," Lundy Taylor said.

"Actually," Mrs. Grantland broke in, "I think Mountie O'Teale has the most important job."

"And what might that be?" Christy asked.

"I'm the bell monitor," Mountie proclaimed in her gentle voice. "If'n Lundy does some bullyin' or we all get too hard to handle, I get to pull the church bell so the preacher or Miss Alice can come a-runnin'."

"What about me?" tiny five-year-old Vella Holt demanded.

"What is it you're monitoring, Vella?" Christy asked.

"I'm the chair monitor!" Vella exclaimed proudly. "I check it for eggs or tacks or anything else that might be a-lurkin'."

"There's more, too," Mrs. Grantland continued. "We've done some rearranging to make things easier. Your desk is off the platform, for one thing. And the desks are arranged so that all the children are in a semi-circle. I thought it might be easier for you to address them that way. The children are seated alphabetically, too."

"Boys and girls together?" Christy cried. She hadn't yet been able to convince the children to stop dividing up, with boys on one side and girls on the other.

"It's a mighty big favor to be askin'," Creed said, "seein' as I'm stuck next to Wanda Beck. But we did it for you, Teacher."

"Creed!" Sam Houston urged. "The present!"

"I almost forgot!"

Christy felt something placed in her lap. Instantly she knew. It was a new cane, even smoother and larger than the last one.

"It's beautiful, children," Christy whispered. "I don't know what to say."

All this planning, for her! It was so thoughtful, and she knew the children meant well. But what kind of teacher would she be, relying on her own students for such help?

"Was this your doing, Mrs. Grantland?" Christy asked.

"Quite the contrary. The children came up with the idea last Friday after you left. I just added some pointers."

"The thing is, Miz Christy," John said, "we want to help make the experiment work. I mean, seein' as we're a part of it and all, it only seems right."

They *were* a part of it, Christy realized. She'd been so busy thinking about her own need to prove herself, she hadn't thought about *their* need to be involved.

"I've never seen such goings-on for a teacher," Mrs. Grantland said. "All I ever got was an apple or two. Of course . . . maybe I didn't give as much, either."

"I don't know what to say," Christy admitted.

"Say you'll do the 'speriment, Teacher," Creed pleaded.

Christy took a deep breath. This wasn't how she'd wanted it to be. But then, maybe it was even better, in a way.

"Get out your history books," she announced, and the whole class cheered.

❧ Fourteen ❧

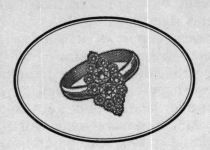

When school was over Friday, Christy asked David to go for a walk with her around Big Spoon Pond.

"Hoping the engagement ring washed up on shore?" David teased as they walked past the water's edge.

"I wish I *could* find it," Christy said. "Your mother would be so relieved. And it seems like the least I could do, after the way she helped me at school."

"I think she enjoyed feeling useful," David said.

"I still can't get over how smoothly teaching went this week, David!" Christy gave an embarrassed laugh. "If I hadn't let my stubborn pride keep me from asking for more help, I could have avoided a lot of pain."

"Actually, I've noticed the difference myself," David said. "When I teach the Bible and math classes, the children are more organized than I am these days. Yesterday afternoon we were working on multiplication, and John Spencer actually suggested I could use my time more efficiently if I divided the class into groups, according to ability."

"I have to admit, I'm glad to have Vella acting as chair monitor. I haven't sat on an egg all week!" Christy paused. She could hear the water lapping gently at the rocky shore. "Sometimes I think my blindness may be a blessing in disguise. I've learned a few things since losing my sight."

"Such as?" David reached for her hand, lacing his fingers through hers.

"Well, how wrong I can be, I suppose. I was so sure the only way to succeed at teaching was to do it all myself. Anything less would have been an admission of failure. But my pride and stubbornness were wrong. I should have relied on God and my friends. It wasn't so hard to let others help me after all."

"Miss Alice says the doctor thinks it's time to remove your bandages," David said softly.

Christy nodded. "He's coming tomorrow morning. You know, I think I'm prepared, David. No matter what happens. If my sight never returns, I truly believe I can accept it and move on with my life."

David cleared his throat. "Christy, there's something I wanted to mention to you. I heard about that walk in the woods you took with Dr. MacNeill, and I—" He paused. "Well, I just don't think that sort of thing is appropriate, now that you're engaged."

"Appropriate?" Christy echoed.

"It just doesn't look right. You understand."

"I'm not sure I do, actually." Christy hesitated. There was something else she wanted to say, but she simply didn't know how to begin.

"Miss Alice said something to me, David, after I accepted your proposal. She said it was important to be sure I was doing it for the right reasons."

"The right reasons," David repeated. He let go of her hand. She heard him scoop up a handful of stones. A moment later, she heard one skip lightly over the surface of the pond.

"I'm not sure . . . I'm not sure I made my decision for all the right reasons, David. I'm afraid maybe I was trying to prove something to myself. I wanted to prove that nothing had changed."

Another stone dropped into the water. "So," David said, his voice a whisper, "you're saying you don't love me?"

"I care for you deeply, David. I'm happy and content when I'm with you. I feel safe when I'm with you. But I'm not sure that's all there is to love."

"You're calling off the engagement," David said flatly.

Christy bit her lip. "For now. Just for now, until I can be sure about my reasons. I don't want you to marry me out of pity. And I don't want to marry you just to prove that my blindness hasn't changed me. The truth is, I *have* changed. But I'm beginning to accept that. Teaching this week, with the children pitching in, has helped me to see that I don't have to prove anything. The 'speriment, as Creed puts it, is over, I suppose."

"And you expect me to just accept that calmly? You betrayed me, Christy! You lied to me about how you felt!"

"I didn't lie, David. I just didn't know *what* I felt. I thought it was love. Maybe . . ." She took a shuddery breath. "Maybe it still can be. But I know I need more time. I was wrong about teaching, David. I don't want to be wrong about marriage, too. I hope you can find it in your heart to forgive me."

"I can forgive," David said angrily. "I'm just not sure I can forget."

~ ~ ~

"Now, I don't want you to expect too much," Doctor MacNeill cautioned Christy the following morning. "All the windows are covered, so it's quite dark in this living room. Assuming you can see anything, it's going to take awhile for your eyes to adjust."

"Assuming I can see anything," Christy repeated with a smile. She could tell that Doctor MacNeill and the others were even more nervous than she was. She felt oddly calm. There was a great comfort in knowing that whatever happened, she was prepared to deal with it.

She heard the mission door open. "Am I too late?"

"David!" Christy cried. She was surprised he'd come. They hadn't spoken since yesterday. "I'm so glad you're here."

"Of course I'm here," he said softly.

"It's almost time for the great unveiling," Christy said.

"How she can joke at a time like this is beyond me," Mrs. Grantland muttered. "I'd be a nervous wreck."

"This will be like the other times I've changed your bandages," the doctor said to Christy. "Except that this time, I'll remove the dressing over your eyes, and I want you to very gradually open them."

"Wait a second, Doc," Ruby Mae said. Christy heard shuffling and the sound of furniture being moved.

"What *are* you doing, Ruby Mae?" Miss Alice asked.

"Movin' my chair up front, so as I can be the first thing Miz Christy sees."

Christy laughed. "Well, what are we waiting

for, Doctor? I've dearly missed the sight of Ruby Mae's bright red hair."

Doctor MacNeill put a hand on her shoulder. "I don't want you to get your hopes up, Christy. There's still some swelling. It may be too soon . . ."

"I understand. Really I do," Christy assured him.

Slowly the doctor began to unwrap her bandages. Christy could feel his fingers trembling.

At last the gauze that had been wrapped around her head was off, and all that remained were two large pieces of cotton dressing over her eyes.

"How do I look so far?" Christy asked.

"Pretty black and blue around your eyes," Ruby Mae reported.

"Kinda yellow and green, too," Creed added. "It's a mighty fine bruise, Teacher."

"All right, now, Christy," the doctor said. "I'm going to remove the cotton. The area around your eyes is still a bit swollen, so there may be some pain when you open them."

"Whatever happens," Christy said, "I want to thank you all for helping me through this."

"Here we go, then," the doctor said.

She felt the rough tips of his fingers as he gently pulled away the cotton. Her eyes felt strange, but she knew that was just because of the swelling.

Christy swallowed past the tight lump in her throat. Slowly she willed herself to raise her lids.

Nothing. There was nothing at all, nothing but darkness.

She took a deep breath. It was all right. She was going to be all right, no matter what.

It surprised her, how easily the feeling of peace and acceptance came to her.

"Well?" Ruby Mae asked in a hushed voice.

"I'm afraid I can't—"

Something changed. At the edges of the black mist, shadows formed and broke. The mist grew grayer, softer, like an early evening fog. "Wait," Christy whispered. "I see . . . I see light."

"Blink slowly a couple times," the doctor urged. "Don't try too hard to focus. Just let it happen."

Christy waited. Not a sound could be heard. Were they all holding their breath, just like she was?

A round, gray, shadowy form moved. Another came into her field of vision and left. Beyond the shadows was a square of some kind. It was a lighter color, almost a pale yellow.

A window? Was that a window?

Christy let her lids drop. Her whole head ached with the effort.

"Maybe it's too soon," Miss Alice suggested gently.

"No," Christy said. "I want to try again."

Again she opened her eyes. Shapes and colors blurred and danced. "Colors!" she whispered. "Blue! I see blue! And . . . red!"

She closed her eyes again and when she opened them, the tears began to fall.

It *was* red she'd seen. It was *very* red.

It was the tousled, wild, beautifully red hair of Miss Ruby Mae Morrison.

Christy turned her head slightly. She made out the slightly blurred image of a big man with a big smile.

"Neil," she whispered, "I can see!"

Without thinking, she threw her arms around him. He held her close, and in a voice only she could hear, whispered, "I'm so glad, Christy, so very glad."

She looked up and realized with a start that tears were streaming down the doctor's face. She'd never seen him cry before. She hadn't even though it was possible, somehow.

"Oh, Miz Christy," Ruby Mae exclaimed, "it's a miracle, is what it is. You must be feelin' as happy as a robin on the first day of spring!"

Christy pulled away from the doctor's arms, suddenly self-conscious. She *did* feel happy—gloriously happy—and so much more. What had made her throw her arms around Neil that way? Was it relief? Excitement? Or was it something more?

In an instant, everyone seemed to be hugging Christy at once. When she glanced over at the doctor, he was watching her with a tender smile as he wiped away his tears.

❧ Fifteen ❧

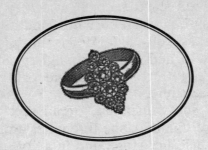

On Sunday afternoon after church, Miss Alice had a farewell picnic for Mrs. Grantland, who was leaving the next day. Everyone from Cutter Gap was there to enjoy good food and the beautiful spring afternoon. Each family brought something, however simple, to eat. Even Creed and Zach had contributed the three small fish they'd caught in the pond that morning before church.

Christy wandered the mission grounds as if she were walking through a spectacular dream. Doctor MacNeill had insisted that she wear a large sunbonnet to protect her eyes, but she could see all she needed to see. The grass had never been so green. The sky had never been so blue. Every sight, no matter how plain, was a gift.

But it was the faces of her students that

held the most magic. Had Creed's freckles always been so charming? Had Little Burl's eyes always been so deeply blue? How had she missed so much? Never again would she look at her students without marveling at their precious and unique beauty.

"Having my sight return is such a blessing," she said to Doctor MacNeill as they stood on the schoolhouse steps.

"I'm so glad for you, Christy."

"I feel so . . . so lucky."

"As it happens, so do I." The doctor gave her a knowing smile. "I heard you called off your engagement to David."

Christy gazed off at the mountain vista beyond the mission house. "I was doing it for the wrong reasons," she said at last. "But I couldn't admit it to myself." She shrugged. "Someone once told me I can be very stubborn."

"A wise man, indeed."

"I want to thank you, Neil."

"For what?"

"For being there when I needed you. And for being honest with me." Christy laughed. "I feel like I have so many thank-you's to say." She pointed across the yard, where Mrs. Grantland and David were talking. "Take Mrs. Grantland, for instance."

"David's mother? Are we talking about the same woman who disapproved of you from the start?"

"In spite of her feelings, though, she helped me. And I'm a better teacher because of her. Which reminds me . . . I have a presentation to make. Could you give me a hand?"

With the doctor's help, Christy gathered the children together and herded them over to Mrs. Grantland.

"My, what a procession!" Mrs. Grantland exclaimed. She gave David a questioning look. "What is all this about?"

"Ask Christy," David said. "I have no idea."

"Better yet," Christy said, "ask the children. Creed, why don't you explain?"

"We got somethin' for you, Miz Grantland, 'cause you're a-goin'," Creed announced.

"We made it last week," Ruby Mae added. "Instead of spelling lessons."

Mrs. Grantland looked at Christy. "You needn't have made them do this."

"I didn't. It was their idea completely."

"It's sorta to say thanks with the 'speriment and all. 'Cause you helped us talk Teacher into stayin'," Creed explained.

"Who's the gift monitor?" Christy asked.

"Me!" came a tiny voice. Vella stepped through the crowd. In her hand was a simple wooden box.

"Here, Miz Grantland," she said, holding out the box.

"Why! Why, it's a . . ." Mrs. Grantland examined the crude box, looking very confused.

"Well, it's a fine box, children. And I will most certainly think of a use for it. Perhaps . . . perhaps I could put pins and needles in it? Or maybe—"

"Naw, Miz Grantland, it ain't for puttin' into," said Zach. "It's already *got* stuff in it."

"Oh! My mistake." Mrs. Grantland opened the box. She stared at the bits of dried flowers and grasses inside. "Weeds!" she said, mustering a smile. "Well, I always say you can't have too many weeds—"

Christy could see how hard she was trying to be kind. "Smell them," she urged. "I think you'll understand."

Mrs. Grantland curled her lip a bit, but she bent toward the box and inhaled. Her eyes went wide.

"Roses!" she cried. "It smells just like roses!"

"It's dried wild rose petals and flowers and herbs and such," John Spencer explained.

"We knowed you'd like 'em on account of you always stinking like roses," Creed added helpfully.

Mrs. Grantland laughed, then breathed in the sweet-smelling box again. Christy was amazed to see a glimmer of tears in her eyes.

"In all my years of teaching, I've never had such a fine gift," Mrs. Grantland said. "Thank you, children."

"Thank you," Christy said. "I don't know what I would have done without your help.

To tell you the truth, to this day, I don't know why you helped me."

Mrs. Grantland shrugged. "I don't know. I suppose I liked feeling useful. With David and Ida all grown up, and my husband gone, it was nice to be needed for a while."

"You could always start teaching in Richmond again, Mother," David suggested.

"You could always start preaching in Richmond," she replied with a wink.

"I'm happy here," David told her gently.

"I can see that now," Mrs. Grantland said with a resigned sigh. "But a mother can still hope, can't she? Just think of all you're missing, David. The fine restaurants and fancy stores and—"

"And Delia Jane Manning," Christy added with a grin.

"She is a *fine* girl," Mrs. Grantland said wistfully. "She'd make some man a beautiful wife . . ."

"Well, it *does* seem I'm available once again," David said, avoiding Christy's eyes.

A frantic figure clad in a white apron rushed out of the front door of the mission house.

"Mother! Mother! David! Come quick!" Miss Ida screeched. She waved something silver in the air.

"That thar's one of our fishes!" Zach cried.

"Ida, dear!" Mrs. Grantland cried. "What's happened?"

"The ring! The ring!" Miss Ida cried frantically. She held up a tiny band with a cluster of diamonds on it. "I found it inside this fish!"

"Great-great-grandmother Grantland's ring, inside a fish!" Mrs. Grantland fanned her face, as if she might faint yet again. "We can only thank the good Lord she's not here to witness this!"

"Zach and I done caught the fish," Creed cried, "so we get the reward!"

"It looks like I'll have to come up with *two* copies of *Huckleberry Finn*," Christy laughed.

David took the ring from Miss Ida. It glimmered in the sun like a radiant promise. He gazed at Christy, shaking his head. For the first time, he began to smile.

"You don't suppose," he said, "that this is a good omen, do you?"

Christy smiled back. "Miracles do happen, David," she said. "At least, that's been my experience."

Christy's
Choice

The Characters

CHRISTY RUDD HUDDLESTON, a nineteen-year-old girl.

CHRISTY'S STUDENTS:
    CREED ALLEN, age nine.
    BESSIE COBURN, age twelve.
    SAM HOUSTON HOLCOMBE, age nine.
    RUBY MAE MORRISON, age thirteen.

DAVID GRANTLAND, the young minister.
IDA GRANTLAND, David's sister.

ALICE HENDERSON, a Quaker mission worker originally from Ardmore, Pennsylvania.

DR. NEIL MACNEILL, the physician of the Cove.

LETY COBURN, mother of Christy's student, Bessie.
KYLE COBURN, Bessie's father.

FAIRLIGHT SPENCER, a mountain woman.

GRANNY BARCLAY, the midwife of the Cove.

MR. HUDDLESTON, Christy's father.
MRS. HUDDLESTON, Christy's mother.

GEORGE HUDDLESTON, Christy's brother.

LANCE BARCLAY, a young man from Asheville.
MR. BARCLAY, Lance's father.
MRS. BARCLAY, Lance's mother.

MABEL BENTLEY, **MELISSA BENTLEY**,
ELIZABETH DEERFIELD, **and JEANETTE GRADY**,
Christy's friends from Asheville.

THOMAS WOLFE, a boy from Asheville.

❧ One ❧

*S*queal! *Squeeeeal!*

Christy Huddleston was standing in front of her class writing on the blackboard, when suddenly the hogs began squeeling at the top of their lungs.

Squeeeeeal! Squeeeeeeal!

"What on earth?" Christy wondered aloud.

"Teacher, them ol' hogs is scared somethin' awful," Sam Houston Holcombe said.

"Must be a varmint got in with them," nine-year-old Creed Allen agreed. "Them's the sounds of hogs that are mighty afeared."

Squeeeeeal! Squeeeeeeeeal!

Christy put down her chalk. She sighed and rolled her eyes up to heaven. "Why me?" she whispered. She had to be the only teacher in the world who had hogs living under her classroom.

The hogs lived in the cool, dark mud beneath the school building, which also served as a church on Sundays. In rustic Cutter Gap, high up in the Great Smoky Mountains of Tennessee, the mountain people were too poor to afford two separate buildings.

Since the building provided some shelter for the hogs, Christy had learned to accept them—even though sometimes their smell was quite unpleasant.

Squeeeal! Squeeeeeeeeeal!

Suddenly, a loud banging came from underneath the floorboards. The hogs were squealing louder and louder. They were making so much noise that Christy knew she couldn't continue with her lessons.

Christy walked down the aisle toward the trapdoor that led down to the hogs. "I suppose we had better see what's going on," she said.

"Ma'am, you might best be careful," Creed warned. "Them hogs is acting downright fitified!"

"Well, I have to see—" Christy started to say.

Suddenly the trapdoor jumped upward with a bang. Christy took a step back.

With a second blow, the door flew open. A huge hog came leaping up from below. It was in a panic. It scrabbled on the wooden floor, then ran right for Christy.

"Look out!" Sam Houston yelled.

Christy snatched up her skirts just in the nick of time. The hog went flying through her legs, leaving a smear of mud on Christy's stockings.

Squeeeal! The hog tore around the room, banging into everything in its path.

"It's after me!" thirteen-year-old Ruby Mae Morrison cried. She jumped up on a chair. "Keep away, you old hog!"

Then a second hog seemed to explode up from below. A third hog followed.

"Look out!" Christy yelled. "Everyone be careful!"

Now there were *three* crazy hogs racing madly around the classroom. Children jumped out of their way. Desks were overturned. Books went flying. Papers were blown every which way.

Sam Houston stuck his head down in the hole and said, "I reckon I know why them hogs is so scared, Miz Christy. There's a fox down in there with them."

"Someone grab these hogs!" Christy said. "They are destroying the classroom."

"Dumb old hogs," Sam Houston said. "Can't no little fox hurt them none."

Squeeeal! Again one of the hogs ran straight for Christy.

She jumped aside. But when she jumped, she bumped into a second hog, which knocked her off-balance.

"Look out, Teacher!" Creed Allen yelled.

Christy teetered on the edge of the opening in the floor. Down below, she could see the quizzical look of the little fox. He was looking up at her. Christy windmilled her arms, trying to keep her balance. But it was no use.

"Aaaaaah!" she cried.

Down she fell. Down through the hole in the floor. Down into the mud.

She landed with a plop. The fox took one look at her and ran.

When she looked up, Christy could see the faces of her students peering down at her.

Then, one by one, three more faces appeared. The first was David Grantland, the handsome young preacher who ran the mission.

He smiled.

"Is this some new teaching method, Christy?" he asked.

The second face belonged to Miss Alice Henderson, the Quaker missionary who had founded the mission. She poked her head over the huddled students. Christy could tell she was trying very hard not to grin.

"Why, Miss Huddleston," said Miss Alice. "Whatever are you doing down there?"

The last face to appear belonged to Doctor Neil MacNeill. He didn't even try to hide his smile. Instead, he laughed outright.

"No, no, Christy," he said. "It's supposed to be *you* in the classroom and the *hogs* down below. Not the other way around."

"Very funny, all of you," Christy said through gritted teeth.

David stuck his hand down. "Come on, I'll help you up."

Christy tried to climb up out of the hole. But the sticky mud held on to her skirts and resisted her attempt to escape. She slipped and fell back again. One of her shoes was so stuck she had to unlace it to get free.

Finally, after several tries, she emerged back into her classroom. The three hogs had been shooed outside. But it was too late to save Christy's dress, or her dignity. She was covered from head to toe with mud.

"You're not setting a very good example for the students," David said with a laugh, as the others joined in.

"I'm glad you're all enjoying this," Christy said.

"Actually, we came to discuss a serious matter with you," Doctor MacNeill said. Then he wrinkled his nose. "But I think first you might want to see about a bath."

"I'll watch the class," David volunteered.

Christy left David in charge of the class and marched out of the schoolhouse to the mission. She was definitely not in a happy mood.

257

Miss Ida, David Grantland's older sister, was in the doorway of the mission house. "Surely, Miss Huddleston, you don't intend to track all that mud into my clean parlor!" she exclaimed.

Christy just glared at her. Miss Ida decided it might be best to step aside.

Twenty minutes later, Christy felt almost human again. She had taken a very hot bath, using plenty of soap, and had put on a fresh skirt and blouse. She found Doctor MacNeill and Miss Alice in the parlor, waiting patiently for her.

Christy set down the basket she was carrying, filled with her muddy clothes. It was going to take hours to get them clean. They seemed to have picked up ten pounds of mud.

"Feeling better, Christy?" Miss Alice asked.

"Yes, Miss Alice, I am. I apologize if I seemed ungracious before."

"Ungracious?" Doctor MacNeill said. "You looked like you would have bitten the head off anyone who crossed your path."

"I believe Christy had reason enough to be snappish," Miss Alice said kindly. "Perhaps you had best tell her your news, Neil."

The doctor grew serious. He leaned forward in his chair. "It's Bessie Coburn," he said.

At the mention of Bessie, Christy's face clouded with concern. Bessie, who was thirteen, was Ruby Mae's best friend. The two of them were inseparable. Since Ruby Mae lived right in the mission house, Bessie was often there, too. That is, until very recently, when she'd become ill.

"Is Bessie's condition worse?" Christy asked the doctor.

"Yes. I'm afraid it is," Doctor MacNeill said. "Much worse."

❧ TWO ❧

Bessie is in increasing pain," Doctor MacNeill continued, "and it will only get worse. I am certain now that we are dealing with some sort of a cyst or abscess. I don't believe it's life-threatening, at least not yet. But it is very painful. It will have to be removed."

"Surgery?" Christy asked. "Poor Bessie. She's just a child."

"Yes, we'll have to perform surgery. And it is more than I can handle here in Cutter Gap. I need the facilities of a *real* hospital. And I would dearly love to consult with Doctor Hugo Mecklen. He is a surgeon who specializes in this area of medicine."

"Whatever it takes to help Bessie," Christy said. "Only . . . what about the money?"

"Naturally, I'll contribute my services free of charge," Doctor MacNeill said. "And I believe Hugo will as well."

"But there are still the costs of the hospital itself, and of medicines," Miss Alice said. "We all know that the mission doesn't have much money. But I don't see how we can avoid this expense. It will mean no more books or school supplies for a while." Miss Alice smiled confidently. "But we have always managed."

Christy bit her lip. No books! Already the children were sharing books between two, and sometimes even three, students. But, of course, Bessie's health came first.

"I've already spoken to some friends on the railroad, and they've generously agreed to let Bessie and her companions travel for free," Miss Alice said.

"We'll be leaving as soon as we can get Bessie's parents to agree," Doctor MacNeill said. "Once that's arranged, we'll only have one problem."

"What problem?" Christy asked.

"It's not a very big problem," Miss Alice said, with a grin. "It's simply that we'll need someone to travel with Bessie. Her mother can't go. Not only is she expecting another baby soon, but she's needed to help plant the corn crop. Anyway, we thought perhaps you might wish to go."

"Me?"

"The hospital I'll be taking Bessie to is the one in Asheville," the doctor explained with a smile. "You could turn it into a visit home."

Home.

Christy glanced at the basket filled with her muddy clothes. Her mind traveled back to her home in Asheville. There in her room was a large oak wardrobe, a lovely armoire. Inside hung a dozen or more dresses. Clean dresses, clean blouses, clean everything.

Here in Cutter Gap, it seemed, nothing was ever truly clean. No matter how hard they all tried.

She pictured her tidy, well-decorated room. There were lace curtains on the windows and rugs on the floors.

Here at the mission, her room was almost a cell by comparison.

Most of all, she pictured her bed. Her big, fluffy, soft feather bed.

Had she ever been able to sleep as well here, on her lumpy secondhand mattress?

"So will you go with the doctor and Bessie to Asheville?" Miss Alice asked.

"And *me*," David added as he strode into the middle of the room. "I'll be going, too."

"I take it all's well at the schoolhouse?"

David grinned. "The children are on their way home, and the hogs are back where they belong. I just stopped by to see how Christy was doing."

"Well, she's no longer covered in mud, if that's what you mean." The doctor grinned, then added, "And I don't see any reason why we need *you* along on the trip, Reverend."

Christy exchanged a knowing glance with Miss Alice. The doctor and David were both "sweet on" Christy, as Ruby Mae liked to say. "The doctor and the preacher are like two hungry old coon dogs, circling around one bone," she'd told Christy once.

Christy wasn't sure she liked being compared to a bone. But she supposed there was some truth to what Ruby Mae said. In fact, David made no secret of his affections. He had even proposed marriage. Christy had turned down his offer, but with the understanding that she might reconsider at a later time. David was very special to her.

As for Neil MacNeill, well, he clearly didn't want her to marry David, but most of the time it was hard for Christy to know what was going on in *his* mind. Her feelings toward him were usually equal parts affection and annoyance.

"I'll be going to Asheville on mission business," David said. "I've been invited many times to visit some of the churches there and tell them about our work at the mission." He looked at Miss Alice. "I know we never ask for contributions, but if I were to go to Asheville and tell the people there about our work, and if they happened to want to help us . . ."

"We would never decline help," Miss Alice agreed. "As long as it's freely given, from the heart."

"I see," Doctor MacNeill said skeptically. "All of a sudden, just because Christy is going to Asheville, you are moved by an urgent need to visit your fellow preachers? Isn't that just a bit of a coincidence?"

"I have as much right to go to Asheville as—" David began.

Miss Alice interrupted him. "Gentlemen, gentlemen. Please. I don't believe Christy has even agreed to go."

"Oh, she'll go," said the doctor. "If I am not mistaken, she is already seeing visions in her head of clean sheets and cozy fires and meals that do not involve possum stew."

Christy started, jerked out of her daydream. It was very annoying, the way Neil could sometimes read her mind.

"I'll go to see my family," Christy said frostily. "And to help Bessie. She's the only thing that's really important here. *Not* because I'm thinking of those other things, Neil."

"There is still one problem," the doctor said. "As I mentioned, I haven't yet obtained permission from Kyle and Lety Coburn to perform the operation on Bessie."

"But why would they object?" Christy questioned in surprise.

The doctor shrugged. "I suppose it's a combination of things," he said. "Fear of losing their daughter. I've admitted to the Coburns that no operation is ever one hundred percent safe. And then, there's the usual problem—the Coburns are a very traditional clan. Kyle Coburn still believes in the old ways, the mountain cures."

"So Bessie might have to suffer?" Christy was outraged. She had tried to learn to respect the traditions of the mountain people, but to turn away from modern medicine at a time like this was simply foolish.

"Don't worry," David said. "I'm sure Kyle Coburn will come around, in the end."

"Yes, I'm sure you're right, Reverend," the doctor said. Then, with a sly grin at Christy, he added, "You'll get your trip to the city yet, Christy."

"Let me make this clear, Neil," Christy said. "My only concern is for Bessie. I just want her to get better. The fact that the hospital happens to be in Asheville is unimportant." She stood up. "Now, if you'll excuse me, I have work to do."

She grabbed the basket of muddy, hog-smelling clothes. What she'd told the doctor was true—Bessie was all that really mattered to her. Still, she thought as she wrinkled her nose at the smell, it wouldn't really *hurt* to enjoy a few nights in her old room.

After she had cleaned the hog smell out of her dress, Christy decided to go visit Bessie and see how she was doing. Perhaps she would get an opportunity to talk some sense into Kyle Coburn.

"Can I come along?" Ruby Mae asked. "I ain't seen Bessie since yesterday."

"Sure, Ruby Mae. That is, if Miss Ida doesn't need you."

"No, Miz Christy. I tried to help her with her cooking, but she said I was just chitter-chattering so she couldn't hardly hear herself think. That's what she said."

Christy smiled. Ruby Mae did have a tendency to talk constantly, while Miss Ida preferred peace and quiet.

"All right, Ruby Mae, I'd be pleased if you'd come along with me."

It was late in the afternoon, but now that it was practically summer, the days lasted longer. Christy hoped to make it to the Coburn cabin and get back before it was dark, in plenty of time for dinner.

It was a pleasant walk. The day was warm, and wildflowers were blooming yellow and blue and pink in the grassy meadows.

Christy was long-since accustomed to Ruby Mae's stream of chatter. She listened with one ear to Ruby Mae, and with the other to the songs of the birds that were arriving back in the mountains after their winter escape to warmer southern climates.

They were close to the Coburn cabin when

something Ruby Mae said seemed to jump out at her.

"What was that you just said, Ruby Mae?" Christy asked.

"I was just sayin' as how when we're in Asheville it would be fine if we could look into some of those shops where you get your citified clothing."

"When *we* are in Asheville?" Christy repeated.

"Yes, Miz Christy. Didn't you know? I'm a-goin', too."

"Who says *you're* going? Did Doctor MacNeill ask you to go along?"

Ruby Mae looked thoughtful. "I don't recollect rightly if it was the doctor. I just know I'm a-goin'."

"Ruby Mae, I don't think—" Christy began.

Suddenly there came a low, sad moan, carried on the wind.

Christy pointed. "It's coming from the Coburn's cabin!"

"That's Bessie!" Ruby Mae cried.

"Ooooh, it hurts," the girl groaned. "Somebody help me, please!"

❧ Three ❧

Christy ran toward the cabin, with Ruby Mae right behind her.

"Oooh, it hurts," the voice wailed.

Christy stumbled up the uneven wooden steps and burst in the door.

Inside, Bessie lay on a simple cot. Her blond hair was matted and tangled. Strands of it were glued to her forehead by sweat.

"Bessie, what's wrong?" Christy cried.

Bessie's mother suddenly appeared in the doorway behind them. She had an armful of small branches and twigs. She ignored Christy and Bessie and ran to her daughter. "Is it bad again?" she asked.

"Yes, Ma, it hurts somethin' fierce."

Mrs. Coburn dropped the wood near the fireplace. Close by was a small, handmade cupboard. A table, three crude chairs, and the one cot were the only other furnishings. The cabin was orderly and clean enough, but still smelled of smoke and cooking odors. The only light filtered through a single window, which was covered with oiled paper instead of glass.

Mrs. Coburn went to the little cupboard and pulled out a bottle and a spoon.

"Here you go, sweetie," she said. She poured a spoonful from the bottle and gave it to Bessie.

Christy cleared her throat. She felt awkward, having just barged uninvited into the Coburns' cabin. "I'm sorry to come in uninvited, Mrs. Coburn," she said, "but we heard Bessie crying out for help."

"You're welcome here anytime, Miz Christy," Mrs. Coburn said wearily. "I was out gathering wood for the fire. The nights are still cold."

"Is that some kind of medicine in the bottle?" Ruby Mae asked. She eyed the bottle suspiciously. "Does it taste just awful, Bessie?"

"It do," Bessie acknowledged in a gasping voice. "Only it sort of dulls the hurtin', too. So I reckon I don't mind the taste."

"Doctor says she should take a bit, but only when the pain gets to be considerable," Mrs. Coburn explained. "He says it's laudanum, and it makes folk get a craving if'n they ain't careful."

Christy was shocked. Laudanum was a very powerful drug. Bessie must be in terrible pain for Doctor MacNeill to have prescribed it.

Christy pulled Mrs. Coburn aside. "Mrs. Coburn, has Doctor MacNeill told you that he wants to take Bessie to Asheville for an operation?" she asked in a low voice.

"Yes'm, he talked about that to me and Kyle." Mrs. Coburn bit her lip and looked worried. "Kyle, he don't take no stock in all this medicine of the doctor's. He says if'n it's the Lord's will to take Bessie, then there ain't nothing that folks can do, and it'd be a sin to try."

"But Mrs. Coburn, the Lord also gives us our intelligence, so that we can help ourselves."

She nodded. "That's what I told Kyle. Only he don't take easy to newfangled ideas and such. He says he reckons he'll stick to the old ways."

Christy felt her anger rising. It was difficult to keep it in check sometimes. The mountain people resisted even the things that would clearly help them.

"But your husband can't just let Bessie lie there in pain!" Christy argued.

The mountain woman raised a hand. "Don't you be a frettin', Miz Christy. That man can't stand no argufyin', so he went off to hunt up some meat to help Bessie get her strength back. Generally, if I keeps at him, he comes around."

"Are you saying you think he'll let Bessie go for the operation?"

"Well, I reckon as how there'll be a bit more argufyin' and thrashin' out, but yes'm, he'll end up by letting her go." She smiled at her daughter. "Leastways, he would if'n Bessie herself was to ask him. He's a stubborn old coot, but he does love his little girl." Her eyes darkened. "Unless he was to start to drinkin' tonight. He gets right ornery and stubborn as a mule when he's been at the jug."

Christy took a deep breath to steady her emotions. So Bessie could probably have the operation—but only if her father stayed sober.

Patience, Christy ordered herself. Patience. Miss Alice had warned her, ever so gently, of course, that too much pushing and prodding would just create greater resistance. The mountain people had lived alone, without help from the world outside for many, many years. It was only natural that they were suspicious of outsiders, and set in their own ways.

Unfortunately, their own ways included bootleg liquor and ignorant superstitions.

"Doctor MacNeill has asked if I will go along to Asheville with him," Christy said. "And Reverend Grantland may be coming, too."

"I'd be much obliged to you," Mrs. Coburn said. "It's fittin' that a woman would take care of my Bessie. It pains me mightily 'cause I cain't be going with Bessie myself. But our new baby will be comin' most any time now. Besides, plantin' season came late this year, and we have to get our corn in."

"Of course," Christy said. She knew that a family that didn't plant its crops in spring would starve in winter. Life in the mountains was harsh and unforgiving.

"Don't you worry none, Mrs. Coburn," Ruby Mae said. "Me and Miz Christy will see to Bessie."

"Are you going, too, Ruby Mae?" Bessie cried.

"Sure I am," Ruby Mae said.

"No, she's not," Christy said at the same instant.

"But I got to go, Miz Christy," Ruby Mae pleaded. "Who's Bessie gonna talk to?"

"Who am I gonna talk to, Miz Christy?" Bessie echoed.

"What do you mean, who's she going to talk to?" Christy said. "Why, to me, of course. And to the doctor and Reverend Grantland."

Bessie and Ruby Mae exchanged a look.

"Miz Christy, it ain't the same," Ruby Mae pointed out. "You bein' a teacher and all."

"I don't reckon I could even go all the way to Asheville, less'n I had Ruby Mae to keep company with," Bessie agreed solemnly. "I don't even reckon I could ask my pa to let me go, unless . . ." Bessie gave Christy a sideways look.

Christy almost laughed. Bessie was blackmailing her! She was threatening not to have the operation unless Ruby Mae could go, too. The laudanum had obviously relieved Bessie's pain enough to allow her to instantly fall in with Ruby Mae's plan.

"Bessie would be all alone in the big city, with not a single friend," Ruby Mae added in a pleading voice.

"Powerful lonely is what I'd be," Bessie agreed. "I don't reckon a person can mend properly, if they's all lonely and such."

"You hear that, Miz Christy?" Ruby Mae wailed. "Bessie could just up and die if'n I ain't with her."

Christy rolled her eyes. "I have the distinct feeling," she said with a sigh, "that I'm outnumbered."

~ ~ ~

That night as she lay in bed, Christy couldn't fall asleep. The wind had picked up as night fell, and now it whistled through every chink in the mission house. A loose board rattled and banged.

Rain began to fall. On the tin roof, it made a sound like gravel being thrown against a drum. She knew that in a few seconds, if the rain kept up, it would find its way through the roof and begin leaking from the ceiling.

She thought of the Coburns' cabin, so much rougher and cruder even than the mission house. Surely there, the wind was even more of a problem. Surely there, and in all the simple cabins of the poor mountain folk, the rain was pouring from a dozen leaks.

Christy knew she should be grateful for all she had. But at the same time, she kept recalling her room in her parents' house back in Asheville. So quiet, even in the midst of a spring storm. So warm. So clean. The bed so soft.

She heard the sound of water. Drip . . . drip . . . drip. With a sigh, she threw back her covers and padded on bare feet across the cold wooden floor.

"Oww!" A nail had worked its way up from the planks. She hobbled over to her dresser and grabbed the pot she kept handy. Then she limped over to the corner, where the rain was dripping in a steady stream. She stuck the pot under the drip.

The noise it made was like fingernails on a chalkboard.

"I'm far too awake now to fall asleep," she muttered.

She struck a match and lit a smoky oil lamp. Then she pulled her diary out of her nightstand and opened it.

June 7, 1912

It's been four months since I came to the Cutter Gap mission to teach school. Today I learned that I will be returning to Asheville for a visit. It will only be for a few days. Doctor MacNeill says they will do Bessie Coburn's operation the day after we arrive there. Then, if all goes well (and I pray it will), we will spend a few days there while Bessie recovers before returning.

It will be good to see Mother and Father and George, if he isn't away at school. I have so much to tell them. We've written each other every week, but it's impossible to tell everything in a letter. There's so much to catch up on. I wonder what has been happening in Asheville. I wonder what my old friends have been up to. And I know they are all curious about me.

And yet, in some ways, this trip scares me. Just a little.

I've grown accustomed to life in the Cove. I've grown used to the hostility of so many of the mountain people because it has been balanced by the affection of so many others who have become my friends. And I've grown used to the simple, everyday hardships because I know that for most of the people here life is much harder than what I have experienced.

I suppose I have even grown accustomed to the fact that a little girl's life might be held hostage to superstition and suspicion and bootleg whiskey. Although it makes me angry beyond words.

Still, as I think of visiting my home again, all the old memories come rushing back . . .

What will it be like to be clean again? Clean, all of the time!

What will it be like to talk with people who can talk of world events and art and poetry? Most of the mountain people speak little, and then, only of the necessary things: of crops and hunting and mending broken plows. What will it be like to once again talk of Paris fashions and New York literature?

Will I seem backward and rustic to all my old friends? And what will they make of Ruby Mae or David or Neil?

I should be looking forward to this trip. And yet it makes me uneasy. It makes me think of all I have given up to be here.

When I left Asheville, my head was full of romantic notions. I knew nothing about blood feuds and moonshine; I understood nothing about the ignorance and fear that still live in these mountains. And I never thought about money—about whether this mission could even be kept alive!

Many of my romantic notions have been lost. I love my students, and I am devoted to the mission. But, knowing all the harsh realities, will I be able to leave my home and my family a second time? If I return to Asheville now, will I still have the devotion to come back to Cutter Gap?

❧ Four ❧

"Miz Christy, Miz Christy," Ruby Mae yelled. "Where are you, Miz Christy?"

"I'm right here, Ruby Mae," Christy said. It was Saturday morning, and Christy was walking toward the school with her arms full of flowers in every color of the rainbow. Fairlight Spencer was with her. "I just got back. What's the matter?"

"Howdy, Miz Spencer," Ruby Mae said. "What are all them flowers for?"

Fairlight was Christy's closest friend among the mountain people. Five of her children, including John and Zady, were in Christy's class. Fairlight was a simple woman, only now learning to read. But she had the bearing of a princess, and Christy admired her sense of wonder about life, as well as her common sense and decency.

"They're for the altar, for services tomorrow," Fairlight explained. "Aren't they lovely, Ruby Mae?"

"Yes'm, I 'spect they'll give me something to admire in church when I start to fall asleep during the sermon."

Fairlight and Christy exchanged an amused look. Fortunately, David was not around to hear Ruby Mae's opinion of his sermons.

"I got to talk to you, quick-like, Miz Christy," Ruby Mae said, tugging on Christy's sleeve. "It's Bessie's pa. He got back all liquored up and he and Mrs. Coburn, they got to argufyin' fit to wake the dead. And now he's got it all stuck in his head that Bessie can't be going to Asheville or having no operation, neither!"

Christy thought for a moment. She wished Miss Alice were there. But Miss Alice rode out regularly to check on the health needs of people in several small mountain communities, and she was away for the day. "Ruby Mae, go and saddle up Prince for me. I'm going for the doctor."

"Yes'm," Ruby Mae said. "Only how am I gonna keep up if you're on a horse?"

"I'm going alone. Just for once, don't argue, Ruby Mae."

"I'll take care of the flowers," Fairlight said. She put her hand on Christy's arm. "You be careful. Kyle Coburn is a decent man when he's sober. But if he's been at that jug, don't you be messin' with him."

~ ~ ~

Doctor MacNeill was on the roof of his house, nailing new wooden shingles. He saw Christy riding up, threading the twisting trails, then galloping across the meadow.

He had a pretty good idea why she was coming. News traveled with amazing speed in the Cove. Sometimes he thought they would never need telephones in these hills, the way they could pass along gossip.

He took a moment to enjoy the sight before him—the mountains looming all around; the nearby brook that bubbled and leapt with new-melted snow; and the rather beautiful sight of Christy, her hair flying free in the wind as she galloped toward him on the mission's big black horse.

He climbed down from the roof and went inside for a shirt and his medical bag. When he came back out, Christy was just reining Prince to a halt.

"Well, good morning, Christy," he said.

"Doctor," she said, a little breathlessly. "It's Bessie. Her father—"

"Yes, I know all about it."

"You do?"

"Yep. In fact, I was just on my way to see

Granny Barclay. I thought she might offer me her professional opinion on the case."

Neil paused, enjoying the look of confusion on Christy's face. "Prince is tired, by the look of him," he said. "We'll go on foot."

"But why on earth would we go to Granny Barclay?" Christy protested.

"Before I got here, Granny Barclay was the closest thing to a doctor this cove had seen. Would you prefer that I went stomping up to the Coburns' cabin to lecture Kyle Coburn on what he *should* do?" Neil asked. "That would just get his pride up, and then there will be no moving him."

"Well, we certainly have to do something."

"Yes. But not always the most direct thing," Neil said. "You can come along, if you wish."

With that, he set out at a brisk pace. He was not at all surprised that Christy followed him.

It was a mile to Granny Barclay's simple cabin. The old woman was sitting on her porch on a rocking chair made of bent sticks and wrapped with vines. Her face was deeply wrinkled. Most of her teeth were gone. But her green eyes were still bright, attentive, and shrewd. She showed no surprise at seeing Neil and Christy.

"Morning, Granny," Neil said. "May we have a word with you?"

"I'd be right proud to have you sit a spell with an old woman," Granny said.

"I find I have a little problem, of a medical nature," Neil said. "It's Bessie Coburn. I was wondering if you might be so kind as to come with me to take a look at her."

Neil could see the shocked look on Christy's face.

"I reckon I could," Granny said. "I could do with a stretch."

Without another word, Granny set off in the direction of the Coburn cabin.

"Doctor, it must be two miles from here to the Coburn place, most of it either straight up or straight down," Christy whispered in Neil's ear as they followed the old woman. "Granny is eighty years old! She can't possibly walk that far."

"I think you may be mistaken about that, Christy," Neil replied. "First of all, she's closer to ninety. Now, let's hurry, or we won't be able to catch up with her."

Granny Barclay set a pace that soon had Christy and Neil panting and sweating. A dozen yards from the Coburns' cabin, Granny finally stopped. She made a show of rubbing her shoulder. "I guess these old bones o' mine ain't got quite the life they used to. I don't 'spec I could walk more'n another two, three hours at this pace."

Christy wiped the sweat from her brow and groaned. "Granny isn't quite as frail as she looks," Neil said.

Christy laughed ruefully. "So I've noticed."

Granny Barclay cackled happily.

Inside the Coburn cabin, they found Bessie still in her bed. Lety Coburn was wiping her brow. Kyle Coburn sat in a corner, looking angry and sullen.

Neil took a quick look around. There was no liquor jug in evidence. And Kyle appeared to be sober, if a bit hung over.

"Kyle, Lety," Neil said, "I've asked Granny Barclay if she would be so kind as to consult with me on Bessie's case."

Kyle stared hard. "*You* askin' for Granny's help?" he demanded suspiciously. "I was a-fixin' to ask Granny to come over myself. She midwifed at Bessie's birth. And she helped me that time I had the fever."

"Let me see the child," Granny said, bustling over to Bessie's bedside.

"I didn't think you city folk put no stock in Granny's medicine," Kyle said doubtfully.

"Granny has delivered more babies than I've ever seen," Neil said honestly. "And she has a great store of wisdom."

Kyle nodded. "And Granny don't go around cuttin' folks open, neither. No good comes of cuttin' a body open. That just stands to reason."

"Yes," Neil agreed, "it is dangerous to perform surgery."

Kyle sat forward suddenly. "So you admit

right out it be dangerous! My little girl could die."

This was the real reason Kyle was resisting the surgery, Neil knew. He was just worried about his daughter.

Neil looked Kyle straight in the eye. "Yes, she could die," he said gently. "There could be complications."

Granny patted Bessie on the head and stood. "There's a lump inside that girl where don't no lump belong," she announced. "That's what's causing the pain and the fever."

"Cain't you do nothin' to make it go away?" Kyle pleaded.

"I can help ease the pain, but only a little," Granny said. "I can give her some bark tea and some other potions that will take the edge off'n the hurt. But that won't help for long. The pain will go right on getting worse till it overcomes all medicine."

Kyle looked shattered. "There ain't nothing you can do, Granny?"

"There's something I can do," Neil said. "I can take her to Asheville, to a real hospital. And I can get the best man in the area to help me do the operation."

"Kyle, you got to let them try," Lety urged, fighting back tears.

Kyle looked tortured. "I have to send my little girl off to some city and not even know whether she's livin' or dyin'? What am

I supposed to do? I can't just sit here a-doin' nothing."

"Kyle, you have to trust to modern medical science," Neil said. But the man looked unmoved.

"There is something you can do," Christy said, speaking for the first time. "You can pray that God will guide Doctor MacNeill's hand and keep Bessie well."

When Neil and Christy went back outside several minutes later, they had received Kyle's permission to do the operation. Granny stayed behind to brew up her pain-fightin' bark tea.

"That was very clever of you, Doctor," Christy said. "You knew Kyle was holding out hope that Granny could save Bessie from having to undergo surgery. So you brought Granny over."

"It's something you should learn, Christy. The head-on approach isn't always the best. I could have argued myself blue, but by asking Granny's opinion, I made Kyle realize he had no choice."

"It seemed to me that Mr. Coburn was still doubtful about the operation, even then," Christy said. "He needed to feel he could be involved in some way."

"You mean the thing about praying?" Neil nodded. "Yes, I suppose that did make him feel as if he were doing something to help his daughter."

"But you don't believe it."

"What? That God is guiding my hands when I'm performing surgery? No. I believe in medicine and science. When my knowledge and skill are sufficient, I am successful."

"I see," Christy said, arms crossed over her chest. "So your advice to Mr. Coburn would be to believe in Almighty Doctor MacNeill rather than Almighty God?"

Neil had to laugh. "Well, when you put it that way, I suppose it does sound just a wee bit egotistical."

Christy shook her head, giving him a grudging smile. "Yes," she agreed, "just a wee bit."

❧ Five ❧

The train whistle blew shrilly. It was so loud that even though she was sitting in the next-to-last car, Christy covered her ears. It was an exciting sound, full of promises of adventure. But the sound was also full of memories. It had been this very train—Old Buncombe, they called it—that had first carried Christy away from home last January.

It was Monday morning. Yesterday, after church, they had carried Bessie to El Pano, the nearest town on the railroad line. Miss Alice had arranged for them to stay overnight with a friend. Bessie had rested fairly well last night. Then, early this morning they had caught the train for Asheville.

Christy was sitting beside David. Behind them, Bessie lay across both seats, with the doctor nearby across the aisle. Bessie looked very pale and weak, but the combination of the doctor's medicine and Granny Barclay's tea seemed to have her pain under control.

Ruby Mae seemed unable to sit anywhere for more than two seconds.

"Are we going yet?" she asked excitedly, leaning over Christy and David to look out the window.

The train lurched forward and sent Ruby Mae sprawling over Christy's lap.

"*Now* we're going," Christy said with a laugh.

"Sorry, Miz Christy," Ruby Mae said breathlessly, taking a seat behind Bessie. "I ain't been on no train afore. It's got me as jittery as a bug on a hot skillet."

The train began to pick up speed and pull away from the little station house at El Pano.

"Lordamercy!" Ruby Mae said. "We're practically flying! Look at how the trees just shoot right past till they's nothin' but a blur."

"I'd guess we're going at least twenty miles per hour now," David said. "We'll get up close to forty on the flatter stretches of track."

"It don't seem possible," Ruby Mae said. "Aren't you excited, Bessie? Ain't this just the best thing ever?"

Bessie managed a tired smile. "It is a wonder," she agreed.

"You let me know if the pain gets worse," Doctor MacNeill told her.

Ruby Mae chattered on, remarking on every

new twist and turn in the railroad track. And there were plenty of twists and turns. Sometimes it was impossible to see any ground outside the window, because the track ran right along the edge of sheer drops that plunged down hundreds of feet.

Here and there, Christy caught sight of tumbledown shacks stuck back in the trees. They were gray and shabby, just like the homes of most of her students. No running water, no telephones, no indoor plumbing, none of the luxuries that people in the cities took for granted. Sometimes it seemed as if these small cabins had been marooned there, trapped by the sheer walls of the mountains and unable to escape.

The train wound through tunnels and across narrow bridges over the swollen river below. At times it climbed slowly, straining against the force of gravity drawing it downward. But with each turn, the mountains opened a bit wider. The flat stretches grew longer. The curves grew less extreme.

They had only been traveling for seven hours, but it seemed to Christy that Cutter Gap was a million miles behind them.

And then she saw it—Asheville.

It, too, was nestled in the valleys between mountains. But these mountains were small and tame. Here, the houses were white-painted clapboard or dark brick. There were proper chimneys poking through steep shingled roofs. Streets were paved in most areas, with curbs and shade trees in neat lines. Everywhere she looked, Christy saw telephone wires strung on tall poles.

As the train slowed to enter town, it ran parallel to a road. A beautiful dark blue Deusenberg motorcar, driven by a white-gloved chauffeur, kept pace for a while.

"Look at that!" Ruby Mae exclaimed. "That's one of them automobiles! My, don't it look fine?"

"Yes, it's probably heading for the Biltmore Estate," Christy said. The Biltmore Estate, which belonged to the famous Vanderbilt family, was more of a palace than a home. It rivaled anything ever created by French kings or English lords.

"Do you know the Vanderbilts?" Doctor MacNeill asked.

Christy blushed. "Of course not. I've never met Mr. Vanderbilt. Although I have seen him in Pack Square on occasion. I don't suppose he will be in town at this time of the year. The high season doesn't begin until summer."

"Ah, yes. When all the idle rich who live off the labor of others escape from sweltering New York and steamy Richmond and stuffy Washington, D.C.," Doctor MacNeill said gruffly. "They come to the mountains to breathe fresh air for three months."

Somehow, Christy got the impression the

doctor did not entirely approve of Asheville's wealthier residents. She noticed him looking critically at a frayed patch on his jacket. Was he actually feeling unsure of himself? Was he self-conscious about looking rustic? It didn't seem possible that Neil MacNeill could ever feel uncertain about anything.

She glanced over at David. He was looking out of the window. His gaze seemed to be drawn to each church steeple that came into view. His face looked troubled and a little wistful.

"That's the church I was baptized in," Christy said, pointing to a particular stone steeple. "I used to sing in the choir. Badly, I'm afraid. That's the church where you've been invited to speak."

"A church that size must have quite a congregation," David said thoughtfully.

Christy noticed that even Ruby Mae had fallen silent. She, too, was staring out of the window, looking just a little intimidated.

"Are you excited to be here at last?" Christy asked her.

"Folks has all got so much here," she answered. "Automobiles and fine houses and such. I seen some of the women as we passed by. They was all dressed fit for a wedding or a funeral. I don't s'pose these fine ladies would even stoop to speak to someone who looked like me."

"Ruby Mae, that's not true," Christy said earnestly. "This is where I come from. And have I ever been haughty to you?"

"No, Miz Christy," Ruby Mae said. She smiled in relief. "I 'spec you're right. Folks is just folks, no matter how they look on the outside."

"I'm sure you'll have a good time in Asheville, Ruby Mae," Christy assured her. Still, she couldn't help recalling the way some residents behaved cruelly toward mountain people visiting the city. They called them hillbillies or hicks, among other names.

"I'll tell you what, Ruby Mae," Christy said. "I have more dresses than I could ever need. We'll find something that will fit you just fine, if you like. And we'll get something nice for Bessie, too. Pretty soon she'll be back on her feet, and we'll all be having a wonderful time together."

But as she smiled reassuringly at her friends, all she saw in their faces was worry.

～～～

They were met at the station by Christy's parents.

"Christy!" they cried in unison.

"Father! Mother!" Christy ran to their open arms. "You haven't changed, either of you," she said, when at last they released her.

"Of course not," Mr. Huddleston said. "It's

been less than six months. What did you expect? To find me with a white beard down to the ground?"

"It seems as if so much time has passed," Christy said. She turned to her friends. David and Neil were busy helping Bessie from the train onto a stretcher.

Christy felt a pang of guilt. She should have helped Bessie first, *before* rushing to see her parents.

"This is one of my students, Ruby Mae Morrison," Christy said.

"Ruby Mae!" Mrs. Huddleston practically yelled in excitement. "It's Ruby Mae!"

Ruby Mae looked startled.

"You must understand, Ruby Mae," Mr. Huddleston explained, "Christy writes us letters full of all the events in Cutter Gap. She always mentions you in those letters. We feel as if we know all about you."

"You write about me in letters?" Ruby Mae asked Christy.

"I only tell people the good parts," Christy teased.

"And that must be Doctor MacNeill and David Grantland," Mrs. Huddleston said.

The two men carried Bessie on a stretcher toward a waiting ambulance for the ride to the hospital. The doctor helped make her comfortable inside, while David joined Christy and the others.

"Very pleased to meet you both," David said, extending his hand.

"Reverend, we'll be going now, if you're coming," Doctor MacNeill called out. "Oh, and pleased to make your acquaintance, Mr. and Mrs. Huddleston. I must apologize for hurrying off, but—"

"We understand perfectly," Mr. Huddleston said quickly. "The young lady's health is infinitely more important than introductions. Please, we'll all meet later at the house."

"I should go with them," Christy said.

"Are you coming, Reverend?" the doctor asked again.

"I'll be right there," David called.

"I'm coming, too," Christy said.

"I'm sure the two men can manage quite well," Mrs. Huddleston said. She put a hand on Christy's arm. "Why don't you and Ruby Mae come with us? Your father is dying to show you his new toy."

"What new toy?"

Christy's father grinned. "I bought one of Mr. Ford's Model T's."

"You bought a new automobile?" Christy cried in surprise.

"I did indeed," Mr. Huddleston said, beaming.

"Miz Christy! Miz Christy! I ain't never rode in an automobile," Ruby Mae said excitedly. "Lordamercy! A train and an automobile, all in the same day. Won't the others back in the

Cove just curl up and die o' green envy when I tell them?"

"Go ahead, Christy," Doctor MacNeill said. "Ruby Mae will never forgive you if she doesn't get her Model-T ride. And there's no room in the ambulance, anyway. It'll be cramped, as it is. You can stop by and visit Bessie later."

As Neil, David, and Bessie pulled away in the ambulance, Christy felt a strange sensation. It seemed wrong, somehow, to let them go without her. Still, it was certainly true that she wasn't needed at the hospital. And she and Ruby Mae would both be there for the operation.

Just the same, Christy felt she'd made a mistake, as if she'd failed some test for which she was unprepared.

"Come along, dear," her father said, reaching for her arm. "Let's take you home."

❧ Six ❧

The ride in the Model-T was exciting, especially since Christy's father was bursting with pride in the new machine. They took the "scenic route," as Mr. Huddleston called it. It took twice as long to get home as it would have if they had simply walked. He drove all over town, showing Ruby Mae the sights.

Ruby Mae never seemed to run out of energy, but Christy was soon tired. They'd been up since long before sunrise, and it was now late in the afternoon.

Finally, they arrived at Christy's home. To her surprise, it felt familiar, yet somehow alien. It was as if she had never left, and yet, at the very same time, as if she'd been gone forever.

When she went inside and climbed the stairs, Christy found her room completely unchanged. It was just the way she had left it.

There was the desk where she had done her school lessons when she was younger. It sat nestled against the window, so she could look out over the street and watch the horse wagons and automobiles pass by.

There was her armoire, door open to reveal the dresses, skirts, and bright blouses, she hadn't been able to take with her to Cutter Gap. On the shelves above were hat boxes.

And there was her oak vanity with the oval mirror. The brushes and combs she had chosen not to take with her were still neatly laid out on a starched lace doily.

Christy sat down on the velvet stool and looked at her image in the mirror. It was startling. There weren't any major changes in her reflection, just so many small ones. Her hair had not been properly cut in some time, and it was somewhat dull and lifeless. When she had lived here at home, she had brushed it a hundred strokes each night. But that habit was hard to keep up at the mission, where she often simply collapsed in exhaustion at the end of a trying day.

Her face was windburned and red from the sun. And her hands were no longer as soft as they had been. She often did her own laundry now at the mission, in harsh lye soap.

"Miz Christy?"

Christy saw Ruby Mae appear in the mirror behind her. She turned around. Ruby Mae looked awestruck, like someone who was entering a great cathedral.

"Come in, Ruby Mae," Christy said.

"Was this your room?"

"Yes, this *is* my room."

Ruby Mae wandered around slowly. She touched the books in their shelves. She went to the armoire and just stared, dumbfounded.

"Are all these yours?" she whispered.

"Yes, they are," Christy said. "I know it seems like an awful lot of things. . . ."

But Ruby Mae wasn't listening. She went to the bed and reverently stroked the soft down comforter.

Suddenly Christy felt terribly uncomfortable. Ruby Mae lived at the mission now, but before that she had lived in a cabin as rough and simple as any in the Cove. All her life she had seen nothing but simple, crude furniture, and homespun, hand-me-down clothing. Most of the children in the Cove didn't even wear shoes. Most didn't *own* a pair of shoes.

"Come on, let's go back downstairs," Christy said brightly. "Mother will have tea ready for us."

"I ain't never seen nothin' near to this," Ruby Mae said, sweeping her arm around the room. "This is like some palace where those far-off kings of old lived, like you told us about at school."

"It's certainly *not* a palace," Christy said. "It's no grander than the other houses on this street."

Ruby Mae shook her head. "Miz Christy, if you collected every fine thing in all the Cove and put it all together, you couldn't touch this one room."

Christy stood up suddenly. Ruby Mae was starting to annoy her now, making her feel guilty.

"There's only one thing I plumb don't understand," Ruby Mae said.

"What's that?"

"With all this . . . how come you ever leaved?"

The question surprised Christy. She took Ruby Mae's hand and pulled her toward the door. "Let's go downstairs and have that tea, shall we?" she said quickly.

———

Ruby Mae followed Christy down the stairs. Even the stairs were amazing! There were framed pictures on the walls, all the way down. And the stairs were actually carpeted. Rugs on the stairs! Who ever heard of such a thing?

"Did you find everything as you left it, Christy?" Mr. Huddleston asked.

"Just as if I'd never left," Christy said.

"It was the purtiest room I ever did see," Ruby Mae said. "For sure, I ain't never seen the like."

"I'm glad you liked it," Mrs. Huddleston said. "We've fixed up the guest room for you. I hope you'll find it pleasant as well."

"This whole house is like goin' to heaven, only I ain't dead, and there ain't no angels," Ruby Mae exclaimed.

Mr. Huddleston laughed loudly. Ruby Mae grinned, but then it occurred to her that maybe Mr. Huddleston was laughing *at* her. No, that wasn't likely, on second thought. He seemed like a very fine man.

"Will you take some tea, my dear?" Mrs. Huddleston asked. She held the teapot poised over a tiny cup.

"Yes'm," Ruby Mae said nervously.

"Milk, sugar?"

"No, ma'am, tea. Like you said."

"She means would you like your tea with milk, or with sugar, or maybe both," Miz Christy explained.

Ruby Mae swallowed hard. It was like one of Miz Christy's tests at school—there had to be a right answer, and there had to be a wrong answer.

"I reckon I'll have whatever y'all have," Ruby Mae said warily.

"That would be sweet," Mrs. Huddleston said. "Christy has always had such a sweet tooth. It's amazing she's managed to keep her figure."

"Yes, ma'am," Ruby Mae said. "Only she don't eat much most of the time. I reckon that's on account of the preacher and the doctor."

"Ruby Mae, I don't think—" Christy said suddenly.

"Both of them are sparkin' to Miz Christy something amazing, so it wouldn't do for her to be gettin' all fat and puffed up." Ruby Mae's nervous chatter was beginning to embarrass Christy.

The pink blush that spread up Christy's neck didn't surprise Ruby Mae. Her teacher was always blushing whenever anyone talked about the way the preacher and the doctor both were hankering for her.

Mrs. Huddleston just laughed and sent Ruby Mae a wink. But Mr. Huddleston looked a little troubled. He smiled, all right, but Ruby Mae could tell it wasn't a *real* smile.

Just then, there was a knock at the front door.

"I'll get it for you," Ruby Mae said. She opened the front door to reveal the preacher and Doctor MacNeill.

"Well, howdy," she said. Then, in a low whisper, she added, "reckon you both better wipe your boots off real good. This is a mighty fine home."

The two men glanced at each other. If Ruby Mae hadn't known better, she'd have sworn they looked as nervous as she was feeling. They each carefully wiped their feet on the mat before entering.

Christy jumped up. "Mother, Father, this, of course, is David Grantland whom you met at the station. And this is Doctor Neil MacNeill."

"Pleased to formally make your acquaintance," the doctor said, shaking Mr. Huddleston's hand. "I'm sorry we had to run off at the station."

"We understand, Doctor," Mr. Huddleston said. "How is your patient doing?"

"Bessie made the trip rather well. She was sleeping when we left the hospital," Doctor MacNeill said. "We'll be able to perform the operation first thing tomorrow morning."

"Did she ask where I was?" Christy asked.

"Bessie understood that you were with your parents," he said. "I reassured her that you *and* Ruby Mae would be with her tomorrow."

"Would you gentlemen join us for some tea?" Mrs. Huddleston said.

"Perhaps they would like to go straight upstairs and check out their room," Mr. Huddleston said.

The preacher looked surprised. "Mr. Huddleston, we've made arrangements to stay at a boarding house."

"Nonsense," Mrs. Huddleston said. "Christy's

brother George is away at boarding school, and his room is sitting empty. You must stay here with us."

"If they've already made arrangements, perhaps they'd rather . . ." Mr. Huddleston began to say.

Mrs. Huddleston cut him off. "They'll stay with us. And I'm sure they would both *love* a cup of tea before they go up to see the room. And they will of course be joining us this evening for the soiree."

"What soiree?" Christy asked.

"Why, the Barclays are having a few friends over, Christy," Mrs. Huddleston said. "It's in honor of your homecoming. I believe Lance will be there, too. Lance is home from college for a while."

Ruby Mae saw Christy jerk in surprise at the mention of the name *Lance*. At the same time, she saw the doctor raise his eyebrows and the preacher narrow his eyes. The two of them looked mighty curious.

"Lance Barclay?" Mr. Huddleston sent a doubtful look to his wife. "Maybe Christy would rather just have a quiet evening at home with her parents, whom she hasn't seen in months."

"We've already told the Barclays we would come," Mrs. Huddleston replied.

Ruby Mae hid a smile behind her hand. It was pretty clear to see that Mrs. Huddleston was pleased to have her daughter surrounded by courters, including this Lance fellow, whoever he was. She was just like any matchmaking mother back in the Cove.

And it was just as plain that Mr. Huddleston wanted no part of the preacher or the doctor or the fellow named Lance. Just the same as any nervous father back in the Cove.

Her first instinct had been right, Ruby Mae realized. Folks *were* just folks, even if they lived in fine houses.

"You will come, won't you, gentlemen?" Mrs. Huddleston asked. "I'm sure you'd both enjoy getting to know all of Christy's old friends. Especially Lance. He's such a pleasant young man."

The doctor and the preacher looked at each other suspiciously. Then they each looked at Christy, even more suspiciously.

"I'd be happy to go," the reverend said tersely.

"Oh, yes, we'll definitely be there," the doctor said with a twinkle in his eyes.

Ruby Mae couldn't help grinning to herself. This visit was getting more interesting by the minute.

❧ Seven ❧

My, don't we all look so fine?" Ruby Mae
said that evening. "If Bessie could just see me
in this dress! Wouldn't she be green with
envy?"

Christy and her mother had done some
quick alterations on one of Christy's dresses.
The dress was silk and lace and came with a
small matching clutch purse and shoes with
heels. Christy watched nervously as Ruby
Mae balanced in the painfully tight shoes.
They were planning to walk the two blocks
to the Barclay home.

"I feel like a regular princess," Ruby Mae
said. "Like out of a book."

"Are you sure your feet are all right?"
Christy asked.

"Oh, yes, Miz Christy. It just takes some
getting used to. It's kind of like the way you

305

have to walk real careful and sort of on your toes when you cross the creek on the old log bridge."

"Silly, impractical things, women's shoes are!" Doctor MacNeill chuckled.

The evening air was warm and scented with flowers. As they neared the Barclay home, Christy noticed beautifully-clothed passengers climbing out of expensive automobiles.

The Barclays weren't as rich as the Vanderbilts, but they were well-to-do. Their house was larger than the Huddleston home. It had its own carriage house, with servants' quarters above it.

There were lanterns strung in the trimmed bushes and trees in front of the house. Through the windows, Christy could see the glint of silver and crystal. At the door, a servant assited arriving guests.

It wasn't nearly as elegant as the parties that went on at the big estates among the truly wealthy class. But to Christy's eyes, used to the subtler beauties of Cutter Gap, it seemed unbelievably bright and colorful and wondrous.

Inside the house, they were swept along to the large parlor. Most of the furniture had been removed to clear a large area for people to wander about and talk while munching delicate morsels of food. Later, Christy knew, there would be dancing on the gleaming wooden floor. In one corner, a string quartet played music by Beethoven.

Mrs. Barclay swept toward them. She was a somewhat heavy woman, with iron-gray hair and eyes to match. "Good evening, good evening! I'm so glad you were able to come on such short notice."

"Mrs. Barclay," Christy said, taking the woman's hand, "allow me to introduce my friends, the Reverend David Grantland, Doctor Neil MacNeill, and one of my students, Ruby Mae Morrison."

"Charmed," Mrs. Barclay said.

"Thanks for having us." The doctor smiled stiffly.

"There's a Barclay family in Cutter Gap," David said. "Are you perhaps related?"

Mrs. Barclay's eyes narrowed. "I am quite certain that I would never be related to anyone from . . . where is it? Carter Gap?"

"Cutter Gap," Doctor MacNeill corrected.

"Yes, of course. That's the quaint little hamlet in the hills where Christy teaches the unfortunate illiterates. Christy, your mother tells me what you write in your letters. It moves me to tears to think of you up there among moonshiners with their blood feuds. No offense meant," she added. "The mountaineers don't know any better, I suppose."

Christy felt a stab of embarrassment. She

glanced at Ruby Mae, who just looked confused. Neil and David looked downright annoyed. The doctor started to say something rude in reply, but David cut him off smoothly.

"Yes," David said, "we are all very grateful to have Christy with us. She is an invaluable part of the mission. I don't know what we'd do without her."

"Probably wallow in ignorance while we drink corn liquor and shoot at each other." Doctor MacNeill's quick, dry humor was lost on their hostess.

"Exactly," Mrs. Barclay said. Christy, David, and Neil exchanged amused glances.

"Now if you three will excuse me, I simply must borrow Christy. There are so many of her friends waiting to see her!"

Before Christy could object, Mrs. Barclay had whisked her away. Suddenly there was a group of familiar faces all around her— Jeanette Grady, a childhood friend; Mabel and Melissa Bentley, sisters who were old school friends; and Elizabeth Deerfield, who had been in the church choir with Christy.

They crowded around Christy, chattering away at the same time.

"Christy, you have no *idea* what Terence Jones has been up to!"

"Christy, wait till I tell you what Martha Bates told me. You'll just *die*!"

"Christy, you simply *have* to come with me to this wonderful new dress shop in the square. They have all the latest fashions from Paris and New York!"

"Christy, it's so good to see you! Things just haven't been the same around here without you. And it's no secret that Lance Barclay has been missing you."

"Christy, have you heard the newest music? They call it ragtime. My father simply cannot *stand* it!"

It was like being caught up in a whirlwind. Christy was surrounded by silk and crystal, taffeta and silver, lace and polished mahogany. Everyone's hair was perfectly done up. Every face was clean and powdered. The air was filled with the scent of expensive perfume.

And then Christy happened to look down. She saw something that struck her as more noticeable than all the rest. Everyone was wearing shoes.

In the Cove, even many of the adults went around barefoot, whatever the weather.

Christy felt a pang of guilt. Suddenly, it seemed strange and wrong to be in a room filled with people wearing shoes.

She turned and looked for her friends. Her parents were nowhere in sight, but she soon located Neil and David and Ruby Mae. They were standing bunched together in a corner.

The three of them looked simple and rugged and weatherbeaten.

Christy felt as if she were being pulled in two directions. Part of her wanted to rush back to her friends from Cutter Gap. But these other people were her friends, too. It would be ridiculous to ignore them, simply because they came from the city, rather than the mountains.

"Christy," a new voice said.

She turned to see Lance Barclay, handsome as ever. "It really is you! And even more beautiful than I remembered."

"Lance," Christy said. She put out her hand to shake his. He took her hand, bowed, and gently kissed it.

"May I have the first dance?" he asked. "Unless, of course, you've already promised it to some other man."

Christy was caught off guard. She hadn't promised the first dance to anyone. "Um, no," she said. "I mean, yes. No, I haven't promised the first dance, and yes, I would be honored to save it for you."

As if on cue, the music brightened suddenly into a waltz. The shifting groups of people moved toward the edges of the room, opening a large dance area in the middle of the room.

"Shall we?" Lance asked, still holding Christy's hand.

Christy gave a little bow, then followed Lance out to the middle of the floor.

He truly was quite a handsome young man. His blond hair was perfectly combed. His smile was bright. His tuxedo was immaculately tailored.

Christy caught sight of David. He was standing to one side, looking severe and awkward in his dark suit. It was the same suit he wore on Sunday mornings when he preached. It *was* new, however. It had been a gift from his mother on her visit to Cutter Gap in May. David was watching Christy with an expression of shock.

Beside him, Neil seemed a trifle less awkward, but he looked even more out-of-place in his favorite tweed jacket. He was holding a glass and staring fixedly at the floor.

Christy felt a pang of regret. David had asked her to marry him. And even Neil had made his feelings for Christy known. It must look to the two men as if she had dumped them in a corner.

But following on the heels of her regret and guilt came a second feeling—resentment. Why should she have to worry about what David and Neil thought? Sometimes she felt as if she spent every minute of every day worrying about what people might think or say.

Every day in the Cove was a struggle to

hold the respect of the suspicious mountain folk. Every day she had to worry about the feelings of dozens of difficult students in her class. Every day there were worries over money for school supplies, and worries about the diseases that stalked the mountains, and worries over the ever-present threat of moonshine-fueled violence. Worry, worry, worry! It seemed like a thousand years since she'd spent a worry-free night.

She was sick of worry. Tired of it. Wasn't she entitled to some ease and comfort? Wasn't she entitled to put on her best dress and dance?

Lance put his left arm around her waist and began to move with the music. Round and round they swirled.

And when the first dance was done, Christy accepted another with Lance. Between dances, they chatted with their Asheville friends about art, and poetry, and the traveling theater troupe that would be arriving soon to perform Shakespeare's *Macbeth*. Lance asked her to go riding the next day, and she agreed.

It was late when the party began to break up. Christy found Ruby Mae in a corner, talking to a boy her own age.

"This here's Thomas Wolfe," Ruby Mae said. "Tom, this here's my teacher, Miz Christy. I been a-tellin' Tom all about folks in Cutter Gap," she added.

"I'd love to hear more," the boy said eagerly.

"But not tonight," Christy said. "I think it's rather late and we'd best all be getting home. Where are Reverend Grantland and Doctor MacNeill? Have you seen them?"

"Yes'm. They left some time back. Hours ago. I 'spect they were tuckered out. They both looked a might *down*."

"They left?" Christy asked in alarm. "They both left?"

"Yes, Miz Christy. They said they was a-goin' back to the house. They said I should remind you about Bessie having her operation tomorrow. If you was still interested."

"They said that? The part about 'if I was still interested'?"

"Yes," Ruby Mae said. "Although, factually speaking, it was the doctor what said it, and the preacher, he just nodded his head."

"As if I wouldn't care about Bessie," Christy said angrily. "Of course I'll be there."

Just then, Lance appeared at Christy's side. "You won't forget our date to go riding tomorrow, will you?"

"Of course not, Lance. I'll be there. Bessie's operation is at eight in the morning. I'll meet you at your stables at nine-thirty, just as we planned. That will leave plenty of time."

✺ Eight ✺

I'm scared, Miz Christy," Bessie Coburn said. "If it didn't hurt so bad I wouldn't let no one cut into me. No how, no way."

Bessie was in her hospital bed, propped on starched white pillows. Her face looked pale and drawn. Her eyes were wide with fear. Ruby Mae and David stood nearby. David seemed unusually withdrawn to Christy—almost as if he were pouting.

"Do you reckon it hurts much when the doctor cuts into you?" Ruby Mae asked.

"Bessie won't feel a thing, I'm sure," Christy said. "The doctor will give you ether, Bessie, and you'll simply fall asleep. When you wake up, you'll start mending, and soon you'll be your old self again."

"Let's hope we'll *all* be our old selves again soon," David muttered darkly.

"What did you say, Preacher?" Bessie asked.

David sent Christy a sidelong look. "I was just making a comment about people being their old selves, Bessie. As opposed to turning into someone different, just because they happen to find themselves in a different circumstance."

"I'm sure that would never happen to any of us," Christy said to David.

"Happens all the time," David said. "People change. Sometimes they change in the twinkling of an eye."

"No one has changed, David," Christy said with feeling. "Just because a person enjoys an evening relaxing and talking to old friends does not mean that person has changed."

"Ruby Mae?" Bessie whispered. "What are they goin' on about?"

"Miz Christy has herself a new beau," Ruby Mae said. "His name is Lance and he's about the handsomest—"

"Aha! See?" David said. "Do you hear what Ruby Mae is saying?"

Just then Doctor MacNeill came in. He was wearing a white cotton coat over his regular clothing. "So how's the patient?" he asked Bessie.

"Hush, Doctor," Bessie said, "we're listenin' to Miz Christy and the preacher fussing with each other."

"We are *not* fussing with each other, Bessie,"

Christy said. "Where did you ever get such an idea? We're here to see *you*, and to keep you company."

"And you should be glad of it, Bessie." The doctor grinned. "Miss Huddleston has *many* demands on her time. It's generous of her to be here at all."

Christy was stung by the accusations of David and Neil. True, she had spent most of the previous evening with Lance and her old friends. But that was only normal, wasn't it? She hadn't seen any of them in a long time.

"Are you ready to start your operation, Doctor?" she asked. "Or are you too busy making unfair remarks about me?"

"No, I'm not ready," the doctor said. "Doctor Mecklen, who'll be assisting me, isn't here yet. He had an emergency across town and will be delayed."

"Delayed? For how long?" Christy asked.

"We should be able to start the operation by eight-thirty." Doctor MacNeill narrowed his eyes suspiciously. "Why? Do you have a pressing engagement?"

Christy tried to look nonchalant. "I was supposed to go riding with . . . with a friend . . at nine-thirty."

"A friend!" David repeated. "A friend, indeed! I'll wager you mean that Lance fellow."

"The young man with the perfumed greasy hair?" Doctor MacNeill grinned again.

"That Miz Christy, she sure is something!" Ruby Mae said to Bessie. "Now she's done got herself *three* fellers."

"I have done no such thing!" Christy protested.

"It's all right, Miz Christy," Bessie said helpfully. "I'll be fine, if you have to go meet your new sweetheart."

"I do *not* have a new sweetheart," Christy said as forcefully as she could. "Lance Barclay is just an old friend."

"Is he kin to Granny Barclay?" Bessie asked.

"That hardly seems likely, Bessie," Christy said.

"On account of, see, Granny Barclay had a brother once what left Cutter Gap for the lowlands," Bessie explained.

"The Barclays are a very successful, very well-respected family in Asheville," Christy said. "I truly doubt they're related to—" She stopped suddenly. But it was too late. The snobbish, thoughtless words were out of her mouth.

"You were about to say, Christy?" David asked.

Doctor MacNeill's eyes had lost their twinkling amusement as he stared at Christy. "She was about to say that this powdered, pomaded, perfumed fellow Lance could hardly be related to a toothless old mountain woman who lives in a shack so tumbledown that Mr. Lance Barclay wouldn't stable a horse in it."

"That is not what I said, and it is certainly not what I meant," Christy said. "You're being unfair."

"Oh, are we?" the doctor muttered.

"You're embarrassed by us," David said. "Embarrassed by all of us."

"That is untrue!"

"Is it, Christy?" David asked. "Then answer this question. Back in the Cove, Fairlight Spencer is your closest friend. She's a fine-looking woman, but she owns no more than two dresses, and both of them are faded and frayed. She owns only one old pair of shoes, and when she speaks, it's the twang of the mountains you hear. And I very much doubt if she has an opinion on the Paris fashions. So, the question is, Christy, wouldn't you have been embarrassed to have Fairlight at that party last night?"

The question cut like a knife. How would Jeanette Grady and Elizabeth Deerfield and the Bentley sisters have treated Fairlight? Politely to her face, yes. But behind her back wouldn't they have tittered and smirked at her clothes and her hair and the way she spoke?

"Fairlight Spencer is my friend," Christy said, "wherever I am, and whomever I'm with. And so are all of you. I'm sorry you think so little of me."

"You'll have to choose, you know," the doctor said darkly. "Sooner or later, you'll come to it. Are you a part of Cutter Gap and the mountains? Do you *belong* there? Truly belong? Or are you just a decent young woman, trying to do good among people you'll always keep at arm's length?"

For a while, no one spoke. The silence was finally broken by Doctor Mecklen's arrival. Bessie had to be prepared for surgery and the two doctors had to go to the operating theater.

Christy waited in a small room with David and Ruby Mae.

They prayed silently for Bessie's well-being. When they were done, Ruby Mae occupied herself looking through copies of *Harper's Bazaar.* Occasionally she would mutter "Well, I never!" or "Land's sakes!" at something she saw in the magazine.

After a while, David joined Christy on the wooden bench where she was seated. "You know, Christy, the doctor and I rarely agree on anything. But I have to admit, he has wisdom. I wonder if perhaps he is right. And . . ." He hesitated, as if uncertain of how to say what was in his heart. "I wonder if this isn't why you said no to my proposal of marriage?"

"What do you mean?" Christy asked.

"Was it just *me* you were refusing? Or were you saying no to the whole idea of a life in Cutter Gap? I wonder." He smiled wistfully. "I suppose I can't help but wonder if your reply might have been different if I were the pastor of a church here in Asheville, rather than the minister for a tiny, struggling mission deep in the mountains."

"Of course that wasn't why I said no," Christy said. She looked into David's sad eyes. "David, I said no because I wasn't ready to make so large a decision. I have to be sure about marriage. Absolutely sure."

Doctor MacNeill appeared in the doorway. His white gown had smears of blood on it, but he was grinning. "Everything went perfectly. No problems at all. Bessie is fine. She'll be a bit sore for a few days, but she'll be good as new before you know it."

"Thank the Lord," David said.

"Yes, well, if I may say so, my technique had a little something to do with it," Doctor MacNeill said with a grin. "And Doctor Mecklen's as well."

"Can we go in and see her?" Christy asked.

"No, not yet. She won't wake up for another hour or so. Then I'm sure she'll want to see you."

Christy glanced at the clock. *Nine-fifteen. I should have left fifteen minutes ago*, she thought. *I gave my word to Lance, and he'll be waiting for me at the stables.* "I'm supposed to . . . I still have that appointment."

"Ah. The appointment," the doctor said teasingly.

"I gave my word that I would meet him at nine-thirty. It would be terribly rude of me to stand him up. You said Bessie wouldn't be awake for an hour or so. I'll be back by then."

It made sense, Christy told herself. Despite the looks that David, Neil, and Ruby Mae were giving her, it *did* make sense. And yet, as she turned and walked from the room, a feeling of guilt pursued her.

Neil's words echoed in her mind. *You'll have to choose, you know. Sooner or later, you'll come to it. Are you a part of Cutter Gap and the mountains? Do you belong there? Truly belong?*

❧ Nine ❧

Christy rushed back to her house to change into her riding clothes. By the time she got to the Barclays' stables, she was fifteen minutes late for her meeting with Lance, but he didn't seem to mind.

"I'd happily wait for you all day," he said. "How is the young lady doing?"

"Bessie? Oh, she came through the operation just fine," Christy assured him. "But I'm afraid I can't spend much time with you, Lance. I want to be there when she wakes up."

"I understand perfectly," he said. "I just wanted to ride a ways, and show you something I think will be of special interest to you."

The horse stable was behind the Barclay home. It housed four horses. Once, back when Christy was still a child, it had held twice that number. But that was before so many people began to own automobiles.

"I don't suppose you do much riding, up in the hills," Lance said as they saddled their horses.

"Actually, the mission owns a beautiful black stallion we call Prince. I ride him from time to time. Though many of the trails are so steep and narrow that they can only be traveled on foot."

"There are no roads, then?"

"Nothing that would be called a road here in Asheville," Christy admitted. "The cabins are spread so far and wide that connecting them all by roads would be hopelessly expensive. I'm afraid there are many more pressing concerns for the mountain people. Shoes, coats, medicine, school books."

She cinched the saddle tight. Lance came around to help her climb up. "I can manage, thank you," she said.

Lance smiled. "You've become very independent since moving away."

Christy swung easily up into the saddle. "I haven't had much choice about that, I'm afraid. I have a classroom of sixty-seven children, ranging from the smallest to some so large they almost frighten me. I have to manage them every day. David . . . Mr. Grantland . . . helps out, as does Miss Alice Henderson from time to time. But generally, I'm on my own."

Lance led the way out of the yard and down the road. "It worries me to think of you way back in those hills." He nodded in the direction of the Blue Ridge Mountains, a tall line that swept down and around Asheville. They were close enough to see, but with only their gentle foothills touching the city itself.

"Poverty. Violence. Sickness. Danger," Lance continued. "And no family and few friends for you to lean on in times of trouble."

Christy looked toward the skyline and frowned. Yes, she thought, there was violence and sickness and danger in those beautiful mountains. "I'm needed there," she said simply.

"I admire your feelings," Lance said. "But have you ever considered how your parents must feel? I know that they worry about you all the time."

Christy shifted uncomfortably. She had been expecting a simple, friendly ride. She'd imagined they would talk of old friends and good times. The conversation was taking a decidedly serious turn.

"I'm sorry if they worry," Christy said. "I try never to tell them anything in my letters that will upset them."

"Yes, but everyone knows what the mountain men are like," Lance said. "Just last week

324

there was a trial of a moonshiner who had killed a revenue agent. It was in all the newspapers. The crime took place very near to Cutter Gap, I understand."

Christy nodded. "I know about it. It was actually ten miles from Cutter Gap."

"But there are blood feuds in the hills."

Christy could not deny the truth. Sometimes the mountain men settled their differences with guns. The fights were often over long-ago insults between clans. Even in Cutter Gap, some families barely tolerated each other—families who had drawn blood in the past.

"The people are very poor," she said. "They've been forgotten by time and civilization, Lance. Faith and morality often weaken in the face of despair." She smiled wryly. "And evil is not entirely unknown here in Asheville."

"No, it isn't." Lance laughed. Then, more seriously, he said, "But still, *here* you would have your family, Christy."

"But *there* I have my mission."

"There are poor children here, too," Lance said. "Look around you."

Without noticing, Christy had followed Lance into one of the poorer sections of town. It was a neighborhood of tarpaper shacks and rickety lean-tos, in the shadow of one of the huge textile mills along the riverfront.

Ever since the railroad had come to Asheville in 1880, Asheville had grown rapidly. Mills and factories had been built. They had provided jobs to mountain people who came down from the hills. But often the jobs paid too little to allow a man to feed or house his family adequately.

"You see, there's poverty here, too," Lance said.

"Yes," Christy admitted. "And so near to our own homes." Here, too, she saw children without shoes, playing in the dirt. And here, too, defeated-looking men lounged in dark doorways, drinking from bottles of illegal whiskey.

"My father and I, and some of the other businessmen in town, are concerned for these folk," Lance said. "We pay our own workers a fair, living wage. But I'm sorry to say that many businesses do not. A lot of these folks are in terrible shape."

He reined in his horse and looked Christy in the eye. "Christy, these people need help just as much as the people in the mountains. You can see that."

"Of course I can," she said softly.

"There's a group of us," Lance said. "My father and the others. We've begun meeting at the church on Wednesday nights. As you know, Reverend Grantland will be speaking to us tomorrow night. Originally, we'd planned to help with your mission."

"We would gladly accept any help offered," Christy said.

Lance looked uncomfortable. "Well, the fact is, we've decided on something different." He pointed to a brand-new building. It was bare wood, not yet painted. "When that is done, it will be the start of our own mission. A mission to our own poor, right here in Asheville. That will be our school."

Christy was stunned—stunned and disappointed. If her church didn't help the Cutter Gap mission, there would be no new schoolbooks, no chalk, no pencils. Perhaps no more mission at all. But she knew she shouldn't be upset. If the church used its money to build this new mission, it would be wonderful for the needy people here.

Still, it was hard not to be heartsick at the possibility that her own mission might soon fail.

"Christy, we would like you to come with Reverend Grantland. We'd like you to tell us a little about your school."

"Me, give a speech?" Christy asked. The very thought made her throat clutch up. "What would I say?"

"Just tell us what you've done in Cutter Gap. Tell us what you've learned."

"I don't know what I've learned," Christy said helplessly. "Most days, I don't think I've learned anything. Except to watch out when frightened hogs are running loose," she added with a laugh.

"Then tell us about the pigs," Lance said. He leaned over and put his hand on Christy's arm. "Christy, there are important missions to be done everywhere. Sometimes far away. Sometimes very close to home. Close to those who . . . who *care* for you."

Christy met his gaze and she felt a familiar blush rising up her neck.

Then her eyes went wide. "Oh, no! Bessie! What time is it?"

~ ~ ~

They rode swiftly back to the stable, and Christy went straight to the hospital without taking time to change out of her riding clothes.

But when she arrived she saw Neil leaving the hospital alone.

"Too late," the doctor said flatly. "She woke up and asked for you. But now she's asleep again, and I won't have her disturbed. She needs her rest."

"I hurried back . . ." Christy began lamely.

"Yes, I can see that."

His sarcasm hurt. It hurt all the more because he was right. She had let Bessie down. The very reason she had come to Asheville was to take care of Bessie. Now she had failed.

"I'll apologize to her," Christy said. "I . . . I had other things on my mind. I became distracted."

"Yes, I know it can be very distracting, riding around town, nodding to all the fine gentlemen and ladies. Parading around in your fancy riding habit with that young squirt."

"Neil, I am desperately sorry that I wasn't there for Bessie when she opened her eyes. I feel terrible about it. But I wasn't parading anywhere. And I really think you would do us both a favor to keep your feelings of jealousy separate from your concern for Bessie."

"Jealousy?" the doctor said, a little too loudly. "Me, jealous of that . . . that . . . fop? Hah!"

"If it isn't jealousy, Doctor, then how else do you explain your contempt for a man you know nothing about? You're not usually so close-minded." She gave him a cold smile. "On the contrary, you're usually the very soul of tolerance."

The doctor sputtered, as though he might have something to say in reply, but in the end he merely grumbled, "Don't go disturbing my patient."

"Of course I won't disturb your patient. But I will go inside and wait quietly by her bed, so that when she does awaken again, I'll be there."

. The doctor had no reply. He slammed his hat on his head and stormed off, muttering, "Jealous! Of that over-moneyed puppy?"

Christy headed into the hospital. She found Bessie, still asleep, with Ruby Mae at her side.

Ruby Mae popped up out of her chair as soon as Christy appeared. "Miz Christy! How did your ride go with Mr. Lance?"

"It went fine, Ruby Mae," Christy said. "How is Bessie?"

"Oh, she's doin' good. What happened with you and Mr. Lance? Did he up and propose to you?"

"Ruby Mae, where on earth did you ever get such an idea?" Christy demanded.

Ruby Mae nodded wisely. "Oh, I seen the way he looked at you at the jollification last night."

"Did he try and kiss you?" a weak voice asked.

Both Christy and Ruby Mae spun around in surprise. It was Bessie, wide awake.

"Bessie! You're supposed to be asleep," Christy cried.

"I had to wake up to hear about you and this Lance feller, Miz Christy. Ruby Mae says he ain't quite as pretty as the preacher, and ain't quite as smart as the doctor, but he's more like a mixin' of both of them."

Christy had to laugh. She shook her finger

at her two students. "You girls need to learn to stay out of other people's business. What a pair of old gossips you are! You could give Granny O'Teale lessons in gossiping."

"Are you going to marry Mr. Lance if'n you stay here in Asheville?" Bessie asked.

Christy frowned. "What do you mean, 'if I stay here in Asheville'? Where did you get that notion?"

Bessie and Ruby Mae exchanged a long glance. "I kinda happened to overhear the preacher and Doctor MacNeill talkin'," Ruby Mae said. "They was sayin' as how you'd probably never go back to Cutter Gap, on account of how much easier life is here in Asheville."

"They said that?" Christy demanded. "They have no right to say those kinds of things!"

The two girls were staring at her solemnly. "Is it true, though, Miz Christy?" Ruby Mae asked softly.

No, Christy wanted to say. No, it's a ridiculous idea. Of course I'm going back to the Cove. But something held her back. She hesitated. And she was shocked by her own hesitation.

Was she really considering *not* going back to Cutter Gap? She hadn't even formed the idea in her head, at least not consciously. But now that Ruby Mae had posed the question, the answer was not so easy.

"I have every intention of returning to Cutter Gap," Christy said evasively.

From their worried expressions, it was easy to see that neither Ruby Mae nor Bessie was convinced.

✺ Ten ✺

The next day, Ruby Mae woke early. She usually woke with the sun. Back home at the mission, she had morning chores to do. But here in Miz Christy's house, there were no chores. Leastways, no one had asked her to do anything.

Miz Christy had promised to take her shopping after they went to visit Bessie. And of course they would get something for Bessie as well.

But when Ruby Mae climbed out of bed and went out into the hallway, she found her teacher's door still shut. The doctor and the preacher were both still asleep, too.

She headed downstairs. The feel of the carpeted stairs on her bare feet was amazing. It must be a mighty fine thing to wake up on a cold morning and be able to walk on rugs. She'd never even heard of the like before.

She followed a delicious smell toward the kitchen. There she found Miz Christy's mama, pulling a pan of fresh biscuits from the oven.

"Ah, Ruby Mae, good morning," Mrs. Huddleston said cheerfully. "I see you're an early riser, like me."

"Yes, ma'am," Ruby Mae said. "Mostly, that is. Sometimes I lay abed till the sun is almost up over the ridge."

"Would you care for a biscuit? And perhaps some tea or coffee?"

"I wouldn't want to impose on you, ma'am," Ruby Mae said. But the biscuits did look awfully good. And she had a powerful hunger.

"Nonsense. I was just making coffee. And I baked these biscuits to be eaten. Come, have a seat. I've been meaning to have a talk with you."

Ruby Mae took a chair and watched with wide eyes as Mrs. Huddleston piled the biscuits high on a plate. Then she brought out sweet cream and fresh butter and two kinds of fruit preserves, orange and boysenberry.

It was a regular feast, and Ruby Mae dug right in. "This biscuit is a pure taste of heaven, Mrs. Huddleston, it truly is."

"That's very kind of you." Mrs. Huddleston grinned. "Ever since we lost Mathilda, I've been doing all the cooking. I'm afraid biscuits are the only thing I cook really well."

"Was Mathilda kin of yours?"

"Oh, no, she was our servant. She did a lot of the housework and some of the cooking as well. She finally got married and now takes care of her own family."

"A servant?"

"Yes. You know, she helped out and lived with us. She was almost a part of the family. I wish I could find someone to replace her."

Mrs. Huddleston was looking straight at Ruby Mae, like maybe she was thinking on something. Nervously, Ruby Mae checked the front of her dress, to see if she'd spilled some jam or crumbs.

"So, tell me about your life in Cutter Gap," Mrs. Huddleston said. "I know that you live at the mission house with Christy. Do you enjoy living there?"

"Oh, yes, ma'am. We get plenty to eat, and on cold nights there's a small fire and all. Of course, it's nothing near so fine as this house."

Mrs. Huddleston nodded. "And how do you like having Christy as a teacher?"

"Miz Christy is purely the best teacher in the whole world. Most everyone loves her. Except for some folks that don't like outsiders. And the moonshiners, they don't like her much, since she and the preacher spoke against them. There's some folks say she and the preacher and even Miz Alice should go back to where they come from and leave well enough alone."

"And how does Doctor MacNeill feel about the mission? And Christy?"

Ruby Mae hid a smile. Now they were getting around to what Mrs. Huddleston *really* wanted to talk about. "The doctor? He says he doesn't really approve of the mission, but that's just what he *says*. If you know what I mean, ma'am. It ain't the mission he doesn't want around, it's mostly the preacher."

"I see. So Reverend Grantland and Doctor MacNeill don't get along?"

Ruby Mae wondered if she should say anything more. But like Miss Ida was always saying, Ruby Mae *did* like to talk. "I reckon you already heard me say that the preacher and the doctor is both sweet on Miz Christy," she said.

"Yes, and I'd already guessed as much," Mrs. Huddleston said with a smile.

"I wonder, though . . . surely Doctor MacNeill could establish a practice somewhere else. Say, in a city. Right here in Asheville, even. And Reverend Grantland could no doubt find a church in need of an eager young preacher."

Ruby Mae swallowed the last crumbs of biscuit. Then she looked up at Mrs. Huddleston. "I reckon they could. If'n they wanted to."

Mrs. Huddleston sighed. "To be honest with

you, Ruby Mae, I miss my daughter. I wish I could find a way to convince her to come home. But I fear that Reverend Grantland and Doctor MacNeill are giving her powerful reasons to stay in the mountains."

"I don't think the doctor would ever leave the mountains," Ruby Mae said. "He's born and raised in those mountains, even though he did go away to learn his medicine in some faraway place. He come back to the mountains, and I 'spect he'll stay."

"I see."

"But I calculate as how the preacher will leave someday. He's not from the mountains at all. I figure there will come a day when he says, 'I done my work here, it's time to move on.'"

"So if my daughter chooses Reverend Grantland, I may be able to see her move back to Asheville, and raise her family here where I can see them grow up. But if she chooses Doctor MacNeill, I'll see her only rarely." Mrs. Huddleston leaned across the table and said in a low voice, "You're a bright girl, Ruby Mae. Whom do you think she will choose?"

Ruby Mae smiled. She had a pretty good idea which man Miz Christy liked better—even if Miz Christy wasn't sure herself. At least she *had* been sure, before she came with Miz Christy to Asheville. Now she wasn't sure of anything.

"If it was a straight-up choice betwixt the preacher and the doctor," Ruby Mae began, "I'd have to say Miz Christy would —"

"Good morning," Christy said loudly as she entered the room.

Ruby Mae and Mrs. Huddleston both jumped at the sound of her voice.

Christy looked from one to the other. "I believe my ears are burning. If I didn't know better, I'd swear there'd been some gossiping going on here."

"Gossiping?" Mrs. Huddleston said. "What a thought! No, I was just talking to Ruby Mae. You see, I was just about to make her an offer."

"An offer?" Christy repeated.

"Yes. I was about to ask Ruby Mae whether she would like to come and live here permanently. She could take over some of Mathilda's work. I could really use the help."

Ruby Mae's mouth dropped open. And so did Christy's.

— — —

June 11, 1912

I have just come from the hospital. Bessie is fine and in good spirits.

I wish I could say the same for David and Neil. Especially David. I told him about our church's plans to start their own mission. He knows now that they will not be able to help him with the mission at Cutter Gap. Naturally, he said he wished them all the best. But I know he is disappointed. It was not what he had hoped for. But nothing is turning out quite the way we all had hoped.

Here I am, home again in Asheville. Among people I've known for many years. It's good to be with my family and to sleep in my old bed. But somehow I don't feel the way I thought I would.

Nothing seems quite right. I feel as if all that should be most familiar has become strange. Neil and David both seem to be angry at me. Perhaps they are jealous that I have spent some time with Lance. But Lance is just an old, dear friend. There is no reason for David or Neil to be jealous.

Or is there? There was a time, back when Lance and I were little children playing together, that we said we would be married when we grew up. That's just the prattle of little children, and doesn't mean anything. But still, I believe Lance does have some feeling for me.

Ruby Mae, too, is acting differently toward me. Or is it that I am behaving differently toward her?

And even though everything here in Asheville should seem familiar and welcoming to me, it seems changed somehow. Perhaps it is I who have changed. Perhaps once you've left, you can never really go home again.

I only know that I am confused. I no longer feel certain of where I belong. I care deeply for my students and Fairlight Spencer and Miss Alice back at Cutter Gap. But my family is here in Asheville.

Too many questions are swimming around in my head. What are my true feelings for Neil and David and Lance? What are my true feelings about Cutter Gap and Asheville?

I suppose it all comes down to one question: Where do I belong? I was certain that God had led me to the mission in Cutter Gap. But now that I am back here, I wonder if He has not shown me a new way—a way that brings me back to my family.

Tonight I am to speak to the meeting of businessmen organized by Lance and his father at our church. I think I know what they are going to ask of me. And I don't know what answer to give.

All I ever wanted was to help people, to make a difference in people's lives. How am I to do that? Where am I to do that?

My church here will give no help to the Cutter Gap mission because they are building their own mission. Without that help, the mission that Miss Alice founded may fail.

Against that, there may be the chance to do wonderful work, right here in Asheville. Thanks to mother's offer, I could even keep Ruby Mae with me. But what about David? And Neil?

David and Neil think I will be influenced by the comforts of home. And I must admit, if I am honest, that I do enjoy those comforts. But I hope I can set aside such unworthy considerations and find the way to do God's will.

I feel as if I am caught up in a tornado, being spun wildly around with David and Neil and Lance; with the poor children of Cutter Gap, and the poor children of Asheville; with my parents, and Miss Alice and Fairlight; and, yes, with my warm, comfortable room.

It's all too much. I pray that God will show me the way, because I am unable to find it alone.

❧ Eleven ❧

It may interest you to know, Reverend, that the bells in our steeple were cast by the same foundry that fashioned the Liberty Bell." Mr. Barclay, Lance's father, had David by the arm and was showing him around the church. They were waiting for all the members of the businessmen's association to assemble in a meeting room off the church.

Lance was with them, too. Christy was careful to avoid seeming friendly to either David or Lance. The last thing she needed was to have either man feeling jealous.

"We have almost fifteen hundred in our congregation now," Mr. Barclay said. "Many of the most prominent citizens of Asheville. You'll meet some wealthy and influential men here tonight."

Christy felt a little sorry for David. Mr.

Barclay was justly proud of the church, but she worried that David might be feeling a little overwhelmed.

"That must be an awesome burden for your pastor," David said. "Our congregation is quite a bit smaller. In fact, I believe we could fit most of them in the first two pews of this church and have room left over."

"Don't you find it frustrating sometimes, having so small a flock, when you are obviously such a bright and energetic young man?" Mr. Barclay asked. "There's always a place for a smart fellow like yourself here."

"I feel that God led me to do His work at the Cutter Gap mission, Mr. Barclay." David laughed easily. "Perhaps the Lord has a less complimentary opinion of my abilities than you have."

"In any event," Lance said smoothly, "no congregation could ever seem poor that had Miss Huddleston as a member." He gave a little bow in Christy's direction.

"Indeed," David agreed, a little frostily.

Christy pretended not to have heard either man.

Besides, her thoughts were on more serious matters. She was troubled by David's easy confidence that he was doing the right thing by staying at the mission. How could David be so sure of his calling? She wished she could be that confident.

Christy looked around at the church. She had been baptized in this church. She had first taken Holy Communion in this church.

She thought of the church in the mountains. It was easy to recall every detail, since it was also her schoolroom. The altar was her desk. The pews were supplemented with her student's desks. And the hogs snorted in the mud beneath the building on Sundays, the same as every other day.

"I believe we are about ready, Christy," Lance said, breaking into her thoughts.

"Oh. I'm sorry, I guess I was daydreaming."

"Now, don't be nervous," Mr. Barclay counseled. "These men all want to hear what you and Reverend Grantland have to say. You know that we hope to reach out to our own poor, right here in Asheville. You two are the experts, so we'll listen very carefully."

The meeting consisted of almost a hundred men, all wearing conservative business suits and looking rather intimidating. After David spoke for a few minutes, explaining the purpose of the mission and its importance to the mountain folk, it was Christy's turn. She said a quick, silent prayer, then walked shakily to the podium.

She faced a sea of whiskers and waistcoats and skeptical looks. Then she saw Lance's face. He smiled encouragingly. And David gave her a little wink.

"Gentlemen, my name is Christy Huddleston. I suppose some of you know my family. We—"

"Speak up!" someone yelled out. "I can't hear her."

In a louder voice, Christy went on. "My name is Christy Huddleston. I am the teacher at the mission school of Cutter Gap. We have sixty-seven students, all in one classroom. I teach all the subjects except math and Bible studies, which Reverend Grantland takes care of. The students range across all ages. Some are almost as old as I am. A few had some schooling before the mission opened. Others had very little or none at all."

For ten minutes Christy told them all she could think of about the school and the students. But soon she began to wonder whether she was simply rambling on. She faltered.

"I . . . I don't know what else I can tell you," she said.

An old gentleman raised his voice. "Do you think that similar schools, combining all sorts of different students, could be made to work in other places?"

Christy shrugged. "I'm sure they could. I believe that most children want to learn, given the chance. It's not just a matter of having new books and desks and fine buildings . . . although we could certainly use those," she added with a self-conscious laugh.

"But the truly important thing is simply to give the children the *chance* to learn. They will seldom disappoint you."

Mr. Barclay stood and joined her on the podium. "As you know, Miss Huddleston, we've been discussing the possibility of establishing a sort of mission to the many poor and uneducated families that have come to Asheville to work in the mills. Many have come down from the mountains in search of work. Others are from foreign countries and speak very little English. They need medical care and a school for their children."

"Yes, I think it sounds like a wonderful idea," Christy said enthusiastically.

"We have already put up a school building. But a school needs more than a building and desks. More, even, than students, be they ever so willing to learn. A school needs a teacher."

Christy tried to keep a smile plastered on her face. She knew what was coming next. She caught David's eye and could tell that he was filled with concern.

"A school needs a teacher," Mr. Barclay repeated. "One with experience in doing a great deal with very little. A teacher accustomed to working almost alone. A teacher with experience in large classrooms full of diverse children. In short, Miss Huddleston, what our school needs is you."

After the meeting was over, David and Christy walked back to her parents' home.

For a while, they were silent. Christy tried not to think, but simply enjoy the evening, as lights came on in the windows of the houses they passed and street lights glowed yellow. A mix of automobiles and horse-drawn wagons passed, dodging around the careening street-cars. Other couples were out walking as well. They would smile politely, the gentlemen tipping their hats. The moon was just appearing in a violet sky.

"I suppose I'll have to consider how the mission will replace you," David said at last. He sounded tense and clipped.

"What?" Christy said in surprise.

"I need to consider finding a teacher to replace you," David said. "I assume you will accept their offer."

"Well, *I* don't assume any such thing," Christy said.

"Nonsense," David said with surprising force. "The offer has everything in its favor. You would have a beautiful new classroom. Those gentlemen will see that you have all the school books and supplies you could ever want. No more sharing battered books with half the pages gone. No more worrying that you'll run out of everything. No more hostile, suspicious community. No more dealing with superstition and foolishness. No more hogs under the classroom."

"Do you honestly believe I would be swayed by new books?"

David smiled crookedly. "No," he admitted. "I don't think you could be swayed by a promise of new books. But I think you could be swayed by the chance to do important work, while being close to your family and friends."

"David, I don't know *what* to do," Christy admitted.

"You would be rid of me, if you stayed here."

Christy stopped walking. She put her hand on David's arm. "David, whatever I do, you have to know one thing—I have no desire to be rid of you."

"Really?" he asked. "You turned down my offer of marriage, after all."

"That was for other reasons," Christy said. "And I never said no. I just said I wasn't ready."

"And now you *are* ready to return to Asheville," he said bitterly.

"David, I just don't know. I . . . I felt that God led me to Cutter Gap. Might He not be leading me back here now?"

David hung his head. "I've wondered that same thing," he admitted. "Is this your true mission? To be here and help the community where you grew up? To do God's work and still have your family around you?" He shook his head. "There's no doubt that this school for the mill workers is a wonderful idea. And there's no doubt that you would be the best possible teacher they could ever hope to have. Am I just putting my own selfish interests ahead of God's will?"

"How can I know what is right?" Christy pleaded with him. "Tell me, David, and I will do whatever you decide."

David laughed gently. "No, Christy. It's not my decision to make, much as I would like to have you return with me to Cutter Gap. It is your decision. God will guide you."

Christy looked off toward the west. The sun had set behind the Blue Ridge Mountains, turning them into a dark silhouette. They seemed so far away, so alien.

It would be cold at the mission right now. If she were there, she would be grading papers, squinting in the dim light of the tiny lamp she allowed herself. There would be no big roaring fire, just a small one on the coldest nights. The shadows in the trees would be close about, isolating the mission. She would go to her lumpy, cold, bed and listen to the wind and the howls of distant wolves. And she would never be sure that she was safe from the dangerous moonshiners who plied their trade in the night.

Here there was light. Light, everywhere she looked. Her mother would have a late supper of roast beef and fresh-baked bread and sharp cheese waiting for her when she got home. Afterward, they would sit by a cheery fire and read or talk. And then she would go up to a feather bed, secure and peaceful.

Was it necessary to suffer in order to do good? No, that was vanity. The children of the mill workers needed a teacher just as much as the children of the mountains.

David had said that God would give her guidance. She hoped he was right. Tomorrow morning they were all to take the train back to El Pano, and then it would be on to Cutter Gap.

Whatever she decided to do, she would be on that train. The school year was not over yet. And she would at least have to say goodbye.

Christy was awake long before dawn. In fact, she had been lying awake in bed for hours by the time she heard a distant rooster crow, signaling the rise of the sun.

She had prayed many times for an answer to her dilemma. But she still felt uncertain and unsettled. One way or the other, she knew she would be getting on the train to El Pano with the others. Whatever her decision was, she had to return to Cutter Gap, even if it was only to get her things and say goodbye.

While she waited for the rest of the household to awaken, she packed her bags. When she smelled the familiar aromas of coffee and biscuits coming up the stairs, she went down.

She found her mother and Ruby Mae in the kitchen. Ruby Mae was assisting in the preparation of a new batch of biscuits.

"Good morning, sweetheart," Christy's mother said.

"Ruby Mae, are you learning your new duties? Does this mean you've decided to stay here?" Christy wondered aloud. Maybe Ruby Mae's decision would help with her own.

"Oh, no, Miz Christy," Ruby Mae said. "I was just a-learnin' your mama's recipe so I can fetch up a batch of these biscuits when I get back home. Won't Miss Ida be surprised?"

"Yes, I suppose she will," Christy said.

"I am very disappointed that Ruby Mae won't be staying here," Mrs. Huddleston said. "The house will seem so empty with *both* of you gone again."

"Miz Christy will be back soon, though," Ruby Mae said.

"Is that true, dear?" Mrs. Huddleston asked eagerly.

Christy was flustered. "Ruby Mae, I haven't decided whether that's true or not." She looked helplessly at her mother. "I'm sorry, Mother. But I'm still not sure. I just don't know."

"Whatever you decide, your father and I will support you," she said. "But of course you know how we feel. It would mean everything to us to have you back home."

"Yes, Mother, I know."

Just then, Christy's father entered, followed

by David and Neil. The three of them stood stock still and stared expectantly at Christy.

"I don't know!" she said, exploding in frustration.

"Now, everyone leave Christy alone," Mrs. Huddleston said. "There are hot biscuits and coffee. Eggs and ham will be along in a moment or two."

"I'll have to make do with just a biscuit, I'm afraid," Doctor MacNeill said. "I've got to get over to the hospital to make sure Bessie's ready."

"I'll come with you," Christy said quickly.

"No need," the doctor said. "She's no longer to be your concern, is she?"

Christy felt anger rising in her. Everyone seemed so sure that she'd already made her decision. She followed the doctor out into the parlor, out of hearing of the others. "I have not decided yet, Neil. And as of this moment, Bessie Coburn is still my responsibility as much as yours."

"Responsibility? That's rich, coming from you. A responsibility is something you can't just walk away from."

Christy tried to rein in her anger. The doctor always seemed to bring out the worst in her. "Neil, you're a doctor, and so you have certain responsibilities. If you were faced with a choice between helping a patient you knew for certain could be saved, or helping a patient who might be beyond help, what would you do?"

The doctor fidgeted and looked away. "Are you telling me you think the Cutter Gap mission may really have to shut down?"

"I don't know," Christy said. "Miss Alice never seems to worry. David is concerned, I think. I had hoped to get some contributions from my church here in Asheville. But now it seems they have their own mission to support."

The doctor was silent for a moment. At last he said, "The answer to your question, Christy, is that if I had to choose between helping those who *can* be helped and those who *can't*, I'd have to help those who can be helped. But," he added, "I'd first make very certain that someone was beyond help, before I would walk away."

"Even if the Cutter Gap mission survives, why choose to do my work there, rather than here? I am needed just as much here. What if it turned out, Doctor, that *both* your patients could be helped, but you only had the time and ability to help one?" Christy searched his face, as if he might really have the answer.

The doctor smiled. "I guess sometimes you just do the best you can and pray."

He'd said it as a sort of joke. Christy knew that the doctor did not pray. Or at least, if he did, he denied doing so. And yet his answer was perfect.

"Do the best you can and pray," Christy repeated softly.

— — —

Christy wiped tears from her eyes as the train pulled away from the Asheville station. She waved through the window to her parents, who stood on the platform.

Bessie Coburn was sitting across the aisle with Ruby Mae. Ruby Mae was busily telling Bessie all about Asheville and automobiles and the Huddlestons' fine house.

"I missed out on everything," Bessie complained. "Although I reckon just being rid of that terrible pain is enough for me. I feel so good I could *run* all the way back to Cutter Gap!"

"No running, Bessie," Doctor MacNeill said sternly. "Not for at least a month. If I find out you've been doing any running, jumping, skipping, or heavy chores, and you ruin my beautiful stitches, I warn you, I will not be happy."

Bessie grinned. "I would never do nothing to ruin your stitchwork, Doctor. Why, it's almost as fine as my mama's quilting."

"What?" David said in mock horror. "Only 'almost'? Doctor MacNeill, running second place to Lety Coburn's quilting stitches?"

Christy smiled, despite herself. The train

picked up speed, and soon she could feel the drag of gravity as they began to climb back up the mountains. Soon they were high on the mountain's side, crawling along the narrow ledge above a precipice.

"We'll be home soon," Ruby Mae said to Bessie.

"Home," Bessie agreed. "Traveling is good, but home is best. Isn't that right, Miz Christy?"

"Yes, it is," Christy said. She sent Bessie a smile. But then her face darkened again. Yes, home was best, she thought. But she wasn't *going* home, she was *leaving* home. Again. Her home was behind her. Her friends, her family, all back in Asheville.

What was she to do?

Do the best you can and pray. The doctor's words came back to her.

Christy closed her eyes. She tried to shut out the sounds of conversation all around her. She tried to quiet the voices of her own will, her own demands. *What am I to do? How am I to choose between home and Cutter Gap?*

She opened her eyes. She looked across the aisle at Bessie and Ruby Mae gossiping. Ruby Mae was dressed once again in her own simple, homespun hand-me-downs.

Christy looked at David. He was deep in thought. His handsome face was clouded with concern, and she knew all the reasons for his worry. Would the mission survive? Would Christy stay or go?

Then she looked at the doctor. He was reading a medical journal and trying to look nonchalant. But his eyes weren't on the pages. He was staring blankly out at the sheer drop below.

I wish Miss Alice were here, Christy thought. *When I get home, I must ask her advice.*

When I get *home?*

Christy smiled.

Screeeeeech!

It was a sound like a saw going through metal. Christy could feel a shuddering vibration rattle the entire train.

Screeeeech!

Out the window, Christy saw sparks being thrown up from the brakes.

A man walking in the aisle was suddenly tossed forward, knocked to the floor at Christy's feet. Christy was thrown hard against the seat in front of her. Handbags and luggage flew over her head. The air was filled with a thousand grinding, ripping, tearing sounds, all at once.

Screams! People all around were screaming! The train car tilted far over to the left, then lurched heavily back to the right.

Boom! The car turned over. Up was down and down was up. Christy fell to the ceiling. Then the floor jumped back up and hit her.

Bodies were being tossed everywhere, like straws in a tornado.

The car slammed against a tree. One entire side of the car was peeled away, like the skin of a banana. Cold wind blasted in.

Christy felt herself flying through the air.

❧ Thirteen ❧

Christy flew, weightless, through the air. She fell, down, down, down. But when she hit, her landing was soft. Thick bushes had cushioned her fall.

She took a deep breath—a gasp, really. She was still alive! Alive and surrounded by flowers. It seemed ridiculous somehow.

She struggled to her feet. All her limbs were still working, and she breathed a sigh of relief.

But as she looked around, her relief was short-lived.

The entire train was off the tracks. Fortunately, none of the cars had gone over the edge of the cliff.

But half the car she had been riding in dangled precariously over the side of the cliff. Most of one entire side had been peeled back to reveal the interior.

Christy gasped.

"Are you all right, Christy?" It was David. He came hobbling over to her. His ankle had been badly twisted. He took her in his arms and held her close.

"Yes, I'm fine," Christy said. She raised her voice to a shout. "Ruby Mae? Bessie? Neil?"

"Miz Christy? Help!"

"That's Ruby Mae's voice," Christy said.

David pointed. "It came from over there."

Christy rushed over, followed more slowly by David. They found Ruby Mae wedged between two big rocks. She was unhurt, but stuck.

"I cain't get loose, Miz Christy!" Ruby Mae wailed.

"Here, let me help you," Christy said. She tugged and pushed at the rocks. They were too big to move much, but it only took an inch to allow Ruby Mae to wiggle free.

"Christy!" Doctor MacNeill came rushing over. His left arm appeared to have been hurt. It dangled limply at his side.

"Neil!" Christy cried in relief.

"Doctor," David said. "Thank God you're alive. Is your arm hurt?"

"A simple fracture," the doctor said. "Painful, but not dangerous."

"Bessie," Christy said. "Where is Bessie?"

They scanned the faces of the others who had climbed or crawled from the train car.

Up and down the tracks, people were walking around aimlessly, looking stunned. Some were bleeding. Some were crying out in pain and fear.

"We have to find Bessie," Christy said.

Just then, they heard a pitiable cry. "Help me. Someone please, help me!"

Christy froze. It was Bessie's voice. It had come from inside the train car—the train car, which even now dangled over the precipice.

"Bessie! Hold on!" Ruby Mae cried.

"I'll go in and get her," David said.

"I doubt you can, not with that ankle," the doctor said.

"Better than you, with that arm," David said. "Besides, Neil, you're probably the only doctor here, and there are people who need medical help. If something happens . . ." David managed a brave smile. "Better I go over the edge of that cliff than you, Doctor."

"Someone help me!" Bessie wailed again.

David turned away quickly and hobbled toward the car. A strong gust of wind blew up the valley. Christy saw the rail car tilt, as if it would plunge off the edge. She held her breath. The car came back to rest. But it was balanced as precariously as a teeter-totter.

David reached the car and rested against the jagged, torn opening. He started to hoist himself up, but then his grip failed and he fell back. He landed hard on his already strained foot.

"Ahhh," he moaned in pain.

Suddenly, without even thinking about it, Christy found herself running forward. She ran to David's side and helped him into a sitting position on a rock.

"You can't do this," she said. "Not with that leg. I'll go."

"Absolutely not!" David said.

"Christy! Get back here," the doctor yelled. "That car could slip over the side at any moment."

"Yes, I know. That's why we don't need any more weight in there than absolutely necessary. And I *am* smaller than either of you."

"I absolutely forbid it!" David said.

"So do I!" the doctor said.

"Wonders never cease!" Christy said. "That's the second time this week the two of you have agreed on something." Then ignoring them, she called out, "I'm coming, Bessie!"

Christy clambered up through the torn hole. The floor was tilted at a crazy angle. And as she stood up inside, she could feel the unsteadiness of the entire car.

Christy looked around and her heart sank. Bessie was at the far end of the car—the far end of a teeter totter that might need only the weight of one young woman to send it crashing over to certain death.

"Bessie? I'm here," Christy said. "I'm right here."

"Miz Christy? Is that you?" Bessie moaned.

"Yes, Bessie. Can you move?"

"No, ma'am. The seat has got me pinned down. It's all twisted around so's I can't move an inch."

"Are you hurt?"

"No, I don't think so," Bessie said. "I just ain't got the strength to get free. Help me, Miz Christy."

Christy took two small steps forward. The floor tilted forward. Christy froze.

What should she do? Bessie was crying for help. But if she moved forward, she might be making a fatal mistake.

It might be that Bessie *couldn't* be helped.

Forward or backward? What was the right thing to do?

"Do the best you can and pray," Christy whispered.

"What did you say, Miz Christy?" Bessie asked.

"I said . . . I said I'm coming, Bessie. I'm coming."

Christy took a deep breath. *Please, God, let this be the right choice*. She walked forward, as slowly as she could. Halfway to Bessie, Christy felt the floor tilt further down.

But Christy kept going. One step after another. Inch by careful inch. At last, after what seemed like hours, she reached Bessie's side.

"I'm here, Bessie," she said.

"I'm sorry to put you to the trouble, Miz Christy."

Christy almost laughed. Almost. She put her hands around the twisted metal bar that held Bessie down. She pulled with all her might. Slowly, slowly, the bar moved. Then, suddenly, it pulled away.

Bessie was free!

"I reckon we best get out of here," Bessie said.

"I quite agree," Christy said. She helped Bessie to her feet. Together, they hobbled up the slanted aisle toward fresh air and safety.

David and Neil and Ruby Mae were all anxiously waiting for them. They helped Bessie down to the firm ground. Christy climbed down, too, and breathed a huge sigh of relief.

The instant her feet touched the ground, she heard a scrunching, crushing sound. The near end of the rail car tilted wildly up in the air.

"There it goes!" David cried.

The rail car went over the side of the cliff and disappeared. For a long moment, the world was still. Then there was a tremendous *boom* as the car hit bottom.

"You was almost kilt!" Ruby Mae cried.

The doctor was squinting skeptically. "That

makes no sense at all. It *should* have fallen over when your combined weight was on the far end. When you went to get Bessie, it should have overbalanced."

Christy nodded. "Yes, that would make sense, Neil. And yet . . . that's not what happened. I wasn't sure if I should walk the length of that car to Bessie or not. I thought I might kill us both, and that would have made no sense at all. And yet my heart told me the right thing was to go to her. So I did."

"How on earth did you know it was the right thing?" the doctor demanded. "I'm telling you it makes no logical sense."

"Maybe sometimes right is just right, even if it doesn't make any logical sense," Christy said thoughtfully. She sent the doctor an impish grin. "Or maybe, Neil, we humble human beings don't always know what makes real sense. And then we can only listen for another voice. A voice that speaks to our hearts and guides us in the right direction. In other words, I did the best I could and prayed."

For the next two hours, Christy and David helped Doctor MacNeill see to the injured. Miraculously, no one had been seriously hurt. There were broken legs and bruises and strains, but nothing more serious.

It took two hours for help to reach them. When it finally arrived, it came from both directions. A small steam engine came uphill from Asheville. It carried volunteers, sent to help. In addition, riders on horses came downhill from the direction of El Pano.

"Is that Miss Alice?" David wondered.

Christy squinted. "It is! Although I shouldn't be surprised. Wherever there's trouble and folks need help, that's where you'll find her."

"Not unlike another woman I know," David said, smiling at Christy.

"Good heavens," Doctor MacNeill said, looking in the other direction. "It's that young pup, Lance Barclay. And his father."

The two Barclay men were among the dozen volunteer rescuers who had come up from Asheville on a spare locomotive. They came rushing over as soon as their train had stopped.

Just moments later Miss Alice arrived and was glad to see her friends were all well. "I was in El Pano when we learned that the train was late and possibly wrecked. I came to help treat the injured. But I see the three of you have taken care of everything."

"Yes, a most amazing little field hospital," Mr. Barclay agreed. "We received a call from El Pano that something must have happened to the train."

"We were terribly worried about you,

Christy," Lance said. "About *all* of you, I should say."

"Yes, I'm sure," David said dryly.

"Well, we didn't want to lose our new teacher," Lance said.

Miss Alice's eyebrows shot up. "New teacher?" She looked searchingly at Christy.

"Yes, Christy is considering taking a position at the new mission school in Asheville," David explained.

"Indeed?" Miss Alice asked.

"Actually," Christy said. "I haven't made a decision. Or rather I should say that I had not made a decision. But now I have."

Neil shook his head. "Yes, I suppose the train derailing must look very much like a message from above that you are not to return to Cutter Gap."

"What nonsense, Neil," Miss Alice said. "As though God goes around derailing trains. I rather suspect we'll find there was a small rock slide. Really!"

"Don't keep us in suspense," David said.

"I have decided to follow my heart and return to Cutter Gap," Christy said.

The doctor and David both brightened amazingly. Lance looked crestfallen.

"But what about the chance to be with your family again?" Lance asked. "What about your home?"

"Just before the wreck, I was thinking of

Cutter Gap," Christy said. "And I realized, to my surprise, that when I thought of it, I thought of it *as* home. Cutter Gap is my home now, as much as Asheville. And David and Neil and Ruby Mae and Miss Alice and all my students, they're also my family now, along with my parents and friends in Asheville. I guess what's happened is that I have *two* homes. And a larger family than I'd realized."

"Well, what will we ever do for a teacher?" Mr. Barclay asked. "Who else can we find with your unique experience?"

"You do realize, Christy, that the Cutter Gap mission may not even survive without funds," David pointed out.

"I've been thinking about that," Christy said. "I wonder, Mr. Barclay . . . I have very little to teach anyone about teaching itself—"

"Nonsense," Mr. Barclay protested.

"But between myself and Miss Alice and David, I dare say we could manage to train some bright, willing teacher. Perhaps if the teacher you find could spend a couple of months with us . . ."

"You would do that?" Mr. Barclay cried. "You would train our teacher for us?"

"Yes, she would," the doctor said suddenly. "And in exchange, you could help support the Cutter Gap mission."

"Doctor!" Miss Alice protested. "We give our help freely. We do not charge for our services."

Mr. Barclay laughed. "The doctor is a very direct man, Miss Alice. And he's right. I think we can help each other out. Two successful missions are surely better than one. And the people of the mountains need a mission as much as those in the city."

"Yes," Lance agreed. "After all, many of our poor and ignorant *are* mountain men, only recently come to the city."

Mr. Barclay nodded. "And so are some of our richer and more successful people. In fact, Lance, since we are so near to Cutter Gap, I believe it may be time for you to meet someone very important in our family."

"A member of *our* family? Here?" Lance looked around skeptically at the mountains.

"My great aunt, *your* great-grand-aunt," Mr. Barclay told his son. "Her name is Isabelle. Although I believe people just call her Granny. Granny Barclay."

"Aha! Then you *are* related to Granny!" the doctor cried. "I believe I distinctly heard your wife deny any such thing."

"Well, Mrs. Barclay is very concerned about what society might think. But as for me, I'll always be the grandson of a mountain man. And I'm proud of it."

"Well, then," Christy said, "we'd better be

going. I have lesson plans to prepare, and I miss my home."

"Even the hogs?" Neil and David and Miss Alice asked at exactly the same moment.

Christy grinned. "Well, maybe *not* the hogs."

About the Author

Catherine Marshall

With *Christy*, Catherine Marshall LeSourd (1914–1983) created one of the world's most widely read and best-loved classics. Published in 1967, the book spent 39 weeks on the New York Times bestseller list. With an estimated 30 million Americans having read it, *Christy* is now approaching its 90th printing and has sold over eight million copies. Although a novel, *Christy* is in fact a thinly-veiled biography of Catherine's mother, Leonora Wood.

Catherine Marshall LeSourd also authored *A Man Called Peter*, which has sold over four million copies. It is an American bestseller, portraying the love between a dynamic man and his God, and the tender, romantic love between a man and the girl he married. *Julie* is a powerful, sweeping novel of love and adventure, courage and commitment, tragedy and triumph, in a Pennsylvania town during the Great Depression. Catherine also authored many other devotional books of encouragement.

THE CHRISTY® JUVENILE FICTION SERIES

You'll want to read them all!

Based upon Catherine Marshall's international bestseller *Christy®*, this new series contains expanded adventures filled with romance, intrigue, and excitement.

VOLUME ONE
(ISBN 1-4003-0772-4)

#1—The Bridge to Cutter Gap

Nineteen-year-old Christy leaves her family to teach at a mission school in the Great Smoky Mountains. On the other side of an icy bridge lie excitement, adventure, and maybe even the man of her dreams . . . but can she survive a life-and-death struggle when she falls into the rushing waters below?

#2—Silent Superstitions

Christy's students are suddenly afraid to come to school. Is what Granny O'Teale says true? Is their teacher cursed? Will the children's fears and the adults' superstitions force Christy to abandon her dreams and return to North Carolina?

#3—The Angry Intruder

Someone wants Christy to leave Cutter Gap, and they'll stop at nothing. Mysterious pranks soon turn dangerous. Could a student be the culprit? When Christy confronts the late-night intruder, will it be a face she knows?

VOLUME TWO
(ISBN 1-4003-0773-2)

#4—Midnight Rescue
The mission's black stallion, Prince, has vanished, and so has Christy's student Ruby Mae. Christy must brave the guns of angry moonshiners to bring them home. Will her faith in God see her through her darkest night?

#5—The Proposal
Christy should be thrilled when David Grantland, the handsome minister, proposes marriage, but her feelings of excitement are mixed with confusion and uncertainty. Several untimely interruptions delay her answer to David's proposal. Then a terrible riding accident and blindness threaten all of Christy's dreams for the future.

#6—Christy's Choice
When Christy is offered a chance to teach in her hometown, she faces a difficult decision. Will her train ride back to Cutter Gap be a journey home or a last farewell? In a moment of terror and danger, Christy must decide where her future lies.

VOLUME THREE
(ISBN 1-4003-0774-0)

#7—The Princess Club
When Ruby Mae, Bessie, and Clara discover gold at Cutter Gap, they form an exclusive organization, "The Princess Club." Christy watches in dismay as her classroom—and her community—are torn apart by greed, envy, and an understanding of what true wealth really means.

#8—Family Secrets

Bob Allen and many of the residents of Cutter Gap are upset when a black family, the Washingtons, moves in near the Allens' property. When a series of threatening incidents befall the Washingtons, Christy steps in to help. But it's a clue in the Washingtons' family Bible that may hold the real key to peace and acceptance.

#9—Mountain Madness

When Christy travels alone to a nearby mountain, she vows to discover the truth behind the terrifying legend of a strange mountain creature. But what she finds, at first seems worse than she ever imagined!

VOLUME FOUR
(ISBN 1-4003-0775-9)

#10—Stage Fright

As Christy's students are preparing for a school play, she reveals her dream to act on stage herself. Little does she know that Doctor MacNeill's aunt is the artistic director of the Knoxville theater. Before long, just as Christy is about to debut on stage, several mysterious incidents threaten both her dreams and her pride!

#11—Goodbye, Sweet Prince

Prince, the mission's stallion, is sold to a cruel owner, then disappears. Christy Huddleston and her students are heartsick. Is there any way to reclaim the magnificent horse?

#12—Brotherly Love

Everyone is delighted when Christy's younger brother, George Huddleston, visits Christy at the Cutter Gap

Mission. But the delight ends when George reveals that he has been expelled from school for stealing. Can Christy summon the love and faith to help her brother do the right thing?